LOCKED AWAY

THE LOCK AND KEY SOCIETY BOOK 1

LORI MATTHEWS

ABOUT THE BOOK

Kat Rollings' brother mysteriously vanishes while searching for pirate treasure. Unfortunately the treasure is rumored to be on a Caribbean island owned by the secretive Lock and Key Society. To save her brother, Kat must gain membership to the Society, but the price she pays might be more than she bargained for.

Rushton Fletcher, one of the Society's elite enforcement team, is tasked with handling a new member who might have murdered one of the Society's more popular women. When he reports to the island to enforce the Society's darker edicts and mete out justice, he is entranced by the sexy and beguiling Kat. Despite evidence suggesting her guilt, Rush finds himself drawn to her, unable to believe she could be the killer he seeks.

In a race to rescue her brother, and with a hurricane bearing down on the tropical paradise, Kat walks a treacherously thin line between bending the Society's rules and succumbing to her growing feelings for Rush. Preserving the Society's well-guarded secrets may force Rush to make an unthinkable choice – to eliminate Kat.

The dangerous game of cat and mouse to find the coveted bounty and her brother leaves their lives hanging in the balance.

Locked Away
Copyright © 2023 Lori Matthews
eBook License Notes:

You may not use, reproduce or transmit in any manner, any part of this book without written permission, except in the case of brief quotations used in critical articles and reviews, or in accordance with federal Fair Use laws. All rights are reserved.

This eBook is licensed for your personal enjoyment only; it may not be resold or given away to other people. If you would like to share this book with another person, please purchase an additional copy for each recipient. If you're reading this book and did not purchase it, or it was not purchased for your use only, please return to your eBook retailer and purchase your own copy. Thank you for respecting the hard work of this author.

Disclaimer: This is a work of fiction. Names, characters, places, and incidents are products of the author's imagination, or the author has used them fictitiously.

This one is for Sara. Thanks for being such a fabulous right-hand woman. (Let Tom try and steal the credit for this one!)

ACKNOWLEDGMENTS

Once again thank you doesn't seem enough when it comes to my editors, Corinne DeMaadg and Heidi Senesac. They truly are miracle workers. Another amazing individual is my assistant, Sara Mallion. She makes everything so much easier and I would be lost without her. Amanda Robinson and Jenn Herman are also part of my outstanding team and I owe them both a big thanks. My fellow writers, Janna MacGregor, Stacey Wilk, Kimberley Ash, and Tiara Inserto, are all truly amazing authors but even more, they're the friends that talk me down on a regular basis. Thank you, ladies, for always being there. My super supportive family also deserves a big thanks. They keep me laughing and make every day better. And last but not least, to you, the reader. Your emails and posts mean everything to me. The fact that you read my books is what keeps me doing what I enjoy most, writing stories of intrigue and love. Thank you so much.

PROLOGUE

Lord Hugh, the new Earl of Somersby, also known as BlackEye because his eyes were so dark it was like gazing into an obsidian pool, stood on the deck of his ship staring at the scenery. The island was lush, green, and uninhabited, or so he'd been told. He had no reason not to believe the sailor who'd made the claim that it was deserted. No one wanted to lie to BlackEye. His reputation for inflicting death and destruction had been spreading of late. None dared annoy him lest he run them through. Of course, the assertions were nothing more than rumor, but that was the best weapon on the high seas. The whispers had helped make him become a very rich man.

With a jerk of his head, he flicked hair out of his eyes and ran his gaze over the island one more time. It would have to do. There was little choice now. Getting back to England as quickly as possible was a necessity. His wretched cousins would no doubt be already fighting over how to carve up his father's estate. A tight smile tugged at the corners of his mouth. The shock on their faces when they found out he was still alive, well that would make the long difficult trip home worth it.

Home.

He hadn't thought of England that way in a long, long time. Still, no help for it now.

"Captain." William his first mate interrupted his musing. "The boys are ready to go. Are you sure you want to do this?"

"No choice. I'm not giving the King any more of the spoils of my hard labor than strictly necessary."

William's watery eyes were wary. "I still think it would be better to take our chances. What if we don't make it back?"

"We'll come back. I must get things sorted with my father's estate and then we can come back for it. If we bring all the treasure now, King George will claim it and leave us with little or nothing. In a couple of years, he will be busy and will have forgotten all about us. We'll come and get the treasure. Then we'll slowly cash it in. This takes patience, William, but we'll get our money. All of it, rather than some paltry sum King George thinks we should have."

"If he doesn't have us killed as pirates."

Hugh grinned and clapped his friend on the back. "We are pirates."

William grimaced. "Yes, and that's why we should stay here in the Caribbean. Why go back to England where it's bloody cold?"

Hugh sighed. "Because I promised my father. If nothing else, I'm a man of my word. I know, a strange sentiment for a pirate, but in my case, it's true. I do not lie. I gave my father my word I would return home upon his death"—*and not a moment before*—"so I will do so. We do not have to stay long, a few years and then we'll be back on the high seas again." He nudged his friend. "It won't be so bad. We have money now. That means better food and warmer beds. Winter won't be so cold in England as it used to be." He sighed at William's sour expression.

"Don't worry. King George is greedy. He'll want the prizes we will offer him. He'll sign the papers and we'll go from being pirates to privateers. A letter of marque from the King is worth its weight in gold." He grinned. "We'll divide the rest of the treasure up before we hit the docks back home. The boys can jump ship far enough out that they can get away. I have my solicitor already working out a deal with the king. I'll reach out to him before we dock just to make sure."

William nodded but rubbed his bum leg absently, which meant he wasn't sure. William could never play poker. That rubbing of his leg, his tell, always gave him away.

Hugh threw a sack containing the tools he'd need over his shoulder, walked over to the waiting boats, and climbed into the first one. Five chests were divided among the other three boats. Five large chests containing gold coins, gold dust, silver ingots, solid gold religious statues, jewels, swords, thousands of diamonds, and solid gold crowns. The recent years had been good to him. He'd worked hard and built the right crew. They were savage but good. Spanish gold was the target, and most ships were no match against the *Dagger's Revenge*.

He gave the order and the men started rowing. Twenty minutes later they pulled up on shore. Night was falling which was good. He needed to hide the treasure and be back on the ship by daybreak. Burying treasure was a risk. William had not been wrong to be concerned. They might not get back to claim it, but the worst-case scenario would be if someone else found it. He would be taking steps to make sure that did not happen.

"Leave the trunks on the beach and head back to the ship. William, go with them. McCreary and Jones, you two stay. Daniels and Miller, stay as well." He nodded to William, "Come back and get us before dawn."

William's eyes narrowed. "I should stay here with you."

Hugh moved closer so he towered over the shorter man. "You should stay with the ship to make sure she's still there when I return." He dropped his voice. "If everyone knows where the treasure is buried then we have to kill them all. You can stay if you want to carry a trunk." Despite his reputation, he had no interest in killing. It was unavoidable that his men knew what island the treasure would be buried on, but they weren't to know where on the island if he could help it.

William glanced down at his bum leg. Then back at his captain. "You heard the man, back to the ship," he barked at the sailors assembled.

Hugh waited until the boats were back aboard before turning to the remaining men. "Each one of you, pick a trunk and follow me." He bent down and picked up one end of a large trunk and started dragging it into the trees. His men did as they were told.

An hour later they were at the edge of the clearing, and it was just like the sailor had described it. Miller finally reached the edge and dropped his trunk. "Jesus," he muttered. His eyes were huge.

Sailors were a superstitious lot and something like this was every sailor's idea of hell and that's why it was the perfect spot to hide the treasure.

"I knew it," Miller exclaimed. "I heard whistling this morning and the sky was red. Both bad omens. But this…" He shook his head. "The water is glowin'." He made the sign of the cross and backed up. The rest of the men followed suit.

Hugh smiled. This was going to work perfectly. He turned to the men. "You must never tell anyone of this. This place is cursed. Anyone who speaks of it…dies. Go back to shore and wait for the boats. I will handle the rest." They didn't need to be told twice. They all moved swiftly back the way they'd come.

Hugh waited until all sounds of the men had dissipated. Then he waited a bit longer in case they'd changed their minds. Finally, he took the bag off his shoulder and pulled out the rope. He looped it around the first chest and then threw it over a thick tree branch. This had better work, he thought as he moved forward. He wasn't superstitious but he wasn't putting his body in the glowing water. Who knew why the hell it was glowing? But no one would be happy about going in so it was the perfect place to hide his treasure.

Three hours later, he was back on the beach. His body hurt and despite the tropical climate, he was frozen. But his secret task was done. William had returned with the boats. He climbed on board, and they rowed back to the *Dagger's Revenge*. He would miss this. The high seas had been his way of life for a long time. He'd always been up for adventure, his attitude happily devil-may-care. Free to sail the seas, and live without the restrictions of polite society, and the responsibilities that came with a peerage. For the most part, his life had been a true adventure. He sighed. Now, with his father's passing, it was time to act like the man he was and go home.

He climbed aboard his ship. "Set a course for England," he instructed William as he sauntered across the deck. He took one last look at the island as the sun rose and vowed silently he would return.

The pledge had no sooner formed in his mind than a shiver coursed down his spine, as if someone had walked over his grave.

CHAPTER ONE

THREE MONTHS AGO

"You don't understand what you're getting involved with," the woman said as she backed away from the man with the knife.

"I need your token," he spoke just above a whisper so she wouldn't recognize his voice.

She shook her head. "You're making a huge mistake. They won't let you get away with it." Her hand closed around the railing; her knuckles bone-white in the gloom.

He inched closer. His hand, holding a nine-millimeter with a suppressor, was steady. His plan was unfolding as he'd planned. It was much easier than he thought it would be. She was staring at him, studying him. Trying to memorize every detail, he was sure. It didn't matter. The black hoodie he was wearing masked his features. He knew he seemed familiar to her, but she wouldn't be able to place him. Already he could tell there was no recognition in her eyes. The wind blew her dress around her legs, and she stumbled a bit as she tried to back up.

"Give me your token, or you die," he rasped.

She licked her lips. "You really have no idea what kind of

trouble you're asking for. This is way more than anything you can imagine."

She was trying to stall, to figure a way out. He admired her fortitude in the face of danger. "I know exactly what I'm getting into." He moved yet another step forward. "Your token. Now."

"Archer won't let this go. He'll come after you." Her voice shook.

He smiled. "Archer Gray has to live by the rules of the Society. When someone shows up with your token, he has to be let in. You will be on the outside. Archer can't help you."

Her eyes got big. It was sinking in that Archer's hands would be tied by the Society rules. "You're already a member."

He chuckled. "Of a sort." Oh, the irony of it all.

"You're getting this for someone else."

"You talk too much, Angel," he ground out. "Token. Now."

"I-I don't—"

"Don't even try it. Everyone knows you never leave home without it. It's the reason I chose you. I don't have to go looking for the token." He waved the gun in front of her nose and her eyes widened. A burst of triumph flitted through him. "Last chance."

Her reaction told him she'd read the situation correctly. He was serious. Her hands shook as she pulled her token out of her bra. "Archer has extra tokens, and he can choose who to give them to. When I get back in, I'm coming for you. I'll tell everyone what you've done."

He reached out and snatched the token out of her hand. Damn. She was right. He'd forgotten the loophole that allowed Archer to add members whenever it suited him. He paused for a second. He'd always planned on killing her. No point in leaving any witness alive but now he really didn't have a choice. Pulling the trigger, he put two bullets into her heart.

He glanced around quickly as if even with the suppressor there might have been someone to hear. Still no one in sight. Adrenaline was his friend at the moment so he managed to heave her body over the railing into the river below. He watched her corpse plunge under the surface, bob back up, face down, and then smiled grimly as she was swept downstream by the current. He regretted having to take this step so soon, but witnesses to what he was up to would bring about drastic consequences that could cost him his life. And he wasn't willing to give that up. Not just yet.

CHAPTER TWO

Katherine Rollings leaned on the boat's railing and stared into the water. It was the first time she'd ever seen the turquoise water of the Caribbean. Under normal circumstances, she'd be thrilled, excited to be on a trip like this. But these weren't normal circumstances.

Nothing about her life had been normal since her brother disappeared.

She looked up as they approached the island rising out of the water, a green jewel in the sea of blue. A small building stood sentry at the end of the pier. Beyond that were cabins painted in what she considered Caribbean colors, blues, yellows, and corals, but they all had white shutters and white verandas. The scene was perfect enough to be featured on a postcard. But was it too perfect? *Stepford Wives* perfect?

A small jolt of adrenaline electrified her blood when the sound of the boat's engine changed. This was it. If she got off the boat, she'd never be able to turn back. The worst part of all of this was she wasn't sure exactly what she was getting into. Who the hell was the Lock and Key Society? Why were they so secret? And seriously, a secret society in this day and age? Ridiculous.

The realization of how crazy this all was didn't stop her hands from shaking.

"We're here, ladies and gentlemen," the boat driver said as he folded out a set of steps onto the dock. She'd been accompanied by two couples on the boat, and they were laughing, as if excited to be there. Obviously, these four were members and knew what to expect. Kat bit her lip. They looked happy, so maybe it wouldn't be that bad.

The other couples had gone ahead and it was now Kat's turn to leave the boat. The boat driver offered his hand to her.

"Thank you." She put her hand in his.

He squeezed it. "Are you sure you want to do this?"

She blinked. "W-what?" How did he know? She looked into his deep brown eyes.

"You look very nervous. I just asked if you're sure."

Kat swallowed. "I'm fine. Boats make me nervous," she improvised.

He hesitated but nodded. "My name is DeShawn. If you want to get off the island, call me." He pressed a card into her palm as he helped her onto the dock and then placed her roller suitcase beside her.

"Thank you," she said as she clutched the card.

She faced the building at the end of the dock. It was small, like a grass hut with a thatch roof but the doors were glass so the grass hut part was obviously just an illusion. Illusion that pretty much summed up treasure hunting. It was all just an illusion and had no basis in reality at least none that she'd ever seen.

The walk to the hut wasn't long but with every step her heart rate accelerated, and queasiness fluttered in her belly. A fine sheen of sweat broke out on her back. *You can do this.* Danny was counting on her. That's what she'd been telling herself since her brother disappeared six weeks ago.

When he'd last contacted her, he'd spewed a story about a secret society and buried treasure that had made her roll her eyes. But the manic edge in his voice had frightened her. And the utter lack of communication since that rushed phone call. The mantra had kept her going. Doing as much research as she could on the Lock and Key Society kept her focused when she hit dead-end after dead-end on the secretive organization.

She'd repeated the charge to herself as she'd read about BlackEye's treasure. *You can do this.*

Treasure. She hated treasure. To her very marrow. Swallowing hard, she walked into the building at the end of the pier, pulling her bag behind her. The room was empty save for a tall man with an impressive head of white hair and a bit of a paunch. His cold blue gaze assessed her from behind a rather plain desk.

"May I help you?" He had a soft accent she couldn't place.

"Yes. I've come to…have an extended stay on the island."

The man's eyes narrowed. "This is a private island. I'm afraid you can't stay here unless you're a member."

"I would like to become a member," she asserted. How the hell was she supposed to do this? There were no "how-tos" on joining a secret society at least none that she'd found.

He arched a brow. "It's not that simple."

She frowned and bit her lip. What was she supposed to do now? "What do I have to do?"

The man stood. "I'm afraid I can't tell you that."

He moved around the desk and came towards her. Looking over her shoulder, he gave a small nod. She turned to see a man who was obviously some sort of security standing there. He was average height but the size of two men with bulging muscles everywhere. The scariest thing however was his eyes. They were black holes in his face. Zero emotion. Dead.

Kat swallowed and turned back to the first man. He was going to give her to security. *Shit.* This wasn't going as she'd imagined it might.

The behemoth behind her stepped forward, and she shied away. Now what should she do?

The token! Chastising herself for not leading with the significant little trinket, she dug in her purse and withdrew a tiny white porcelain teapot decorated with messy purple flowers. It was the size that would fit in a dollhouse or one of those miniature houses. "I have this token," she said, opening her hand and showing him the teapot.

A look flitted across the man's face. Surprise? Anger? She couldn't tell. But then, he unleashed a smile.

"Ah! You are a new member. Please have a seat." He nodded at the scary guy who left and then went back around the desk. He indicated the seat across the desk from him.

"I'm Peter. My wife, Daisy, and I run the island for the Lock and Key Society." He offered his hand and Kat shook it.

"Kat Sanders."

"Well, Ms. Sanders, since you've never been to a Society property before, you're going to need to fill out some forms. Just a way for you to tell us a bit about yourself."

She kept her smile fixed but her knees went weak. Damn good thing she was already sitting. Creating a false identity had been the one thing she'd been most terrified about. Would her cover hold up? In the end, she'd gone to someone her dad used on occasion when he wanted to do something that wasn't one hundred percent above board, which happened quite frequently in the treasure hunting game.

"May I see your passport? I have to take a picture of it and your token."

She pulled out her passport and the token, then handed them over. The passport was a fake but a good fake, or so she'd been told. It wouldn't pass customs. She'd used her real passport when she'd landed in the Bahamas. But if she was going to use this passport for ID, then Merlin, the man who made it, assured her it would be fine. Sitting here now, she suddenly regretted believing those assurances.

Peter smiled. "May I get you a beverage of some kind?"

"No, I'm fine thank you." She just wanted this over with. Glancing around her, she noted that the grass hut illusion stopped on the outside. The inside was all office space. The floor was a highly polished wood. The two desks were plain but made of an expensive wood as well. Behind the desks, were pictures of the Caribbean hanging on the cream-colored walls. Bright blues and turquoise made the office seem inviting but the steel door in the corner was a stark contrast. It didn't fit in at all but then again, she had the distinct impression it wasn't supposed to. She swallowed. Hard.

Peter handed her a tablet. "If you'll fill out the online form, we'll get you processed and on your way. While you're doing that, I'll call housekeeping and get a cabin set up for you. Do you know how long you'll be staying?"

"I— Is there a time limit?" That had never occurred to her. What if they didn't have a room? She found the panic clawing at her throat.

"You may stay as long as you like, dear," said a voice behind her.

Peter smiled. "This is my wife, Daisy."

"I-it's nice to meet you, Daisy," Kat turned and extended her hand. She was shocked to see it wasn't shaking as her voice had been. Her insides were quaking at a ten on the Richter scale.

The small, bird-like woman with the long white braid and warm hazel eyes smiled. "Nice to meet you too Kat." Even her hand was warm, welcoming.

Daisy was even smaller than Kat's own five feet two inches. The older woman's presence immediately calmed her down. Kat liked her instantly in spite of herself.

"May I get you anything?" Daisy offered. "A juice or a cocktail? How about a cup of tea?"

Peter touched his wife's arm. "I just asked but she said no."

"I'm good for the moment," Kat said and added, "but thank you."

"Okay, you get started on the forms and I'll get your cabin sorted." He picked up a cell phone from a holder on his desk. Daisy sat down beside him and started organizing some papers.

Kat glanced down at the tablet and touched the screen. The first thing they wanted was her name and a phone number. That was simple enough. Then they asked about some of her likes and dislikes. Yes, she liked fine dining. No she didn't like basketball or football. Then they moved on to health questions. Did she have any ongoing health issues? The form had a long list of ailments she could select. Any dietary restrictions? Did she drink alcohol? Did she do drugs? And, if so, what kinds?

She didn't get the sense that they were admonishing her for her lifestyle choices, more just trying to find them out. It was kind of creepy the level of detailed information they were gathering. She almost shrugged but forced herself to remain still as she worked through the form. Initially, she'd been inclined to lie, but her father's voice resonated in her head…*stick as close to the truth as possible when lying*. It's easier to remember. Merlin had seconded that thought. So, Kat was truthful with her answers. She also told the truth about her reason for being on the island. She put that she was in desperate need of a vacation. And she was. That wasn't the whole truth, but it was at least part of it.

Finally, a few minutes later, she was finished. She handed the tablet back to Peter. "Lots of questions," she murmured.

"Yes, but it helps us get to know you so we can provide what you want and need during your time on the island and beyond." He checked a few things on the tablet and then put it in the desk drawer. "Now, there's the small matter of your fee."

Kat tried to maintain her sense of calm but her heart took off at a gallop. She had no idea how much they were going to ask for, but she knew it would be steep. Bracing herself she asked, "How much will it cost and where should I send the money?"

Peter grabbed a piece of paper and a pen from the top of his desk. "The initiation fee is one hundred thousand dollars. After that, you will deposit quarterly another one hundred thousand dollars into the account I'm about to give you."

One hundred thousand dollars was all the money she had. It was the proceeds of the life insurance policy she'd inherited from her parents when they died, mixed with her own savings over the last five years and some investments that had done well. She'd put everything into one account before she'd left but had never dreamed they'd want it all. Her palms started to sweat.

"Is there a problem?"

"Er, no. Not at all." She swallowed again.

Peter smiled. "Here is the Swift number and the bank's identifying number. And this is the account number." He tapped the last number on the paper. "If you could just transfer the money, then we can get you settled in."

She nodded but didn't trust herself to speak. Instead, she

went into her bank and filled out all the necessary information to do a wire transfer. It suddenly hit her. "This might take a few days to hit your account."

Peter nodded. "To be expected. No problem. Just show me the screen where you sent it and we'll be fine."

Kat did as she was told, careful to keep her fingers covering her name on the screen. Then she cleared the screen and locked her phone.

He smiled. "Excellent. We have a few rules to go over. The island is isolated so it's really a great way to ease into being a Society member. You should have no problem following the rules. When you stay at our other locations, sometimes it's harder. Too many temptations to break the rules."

What the hell did that mean? What set of rules was he talking about? She worked to keep her breathing even.

"By the way, where did you get your token?"

Peter asked the question casually, but Kat's breath caught in her throat. His smile didn't reach his eyes. He was watching her intensely.

She cleared her throat. "I'd rather not say," she replied. How was she supposed to say her brother had given it to her but refused to tell her anything about it other than it was the way to join the Lock and Key Society and if things didn't go well she might need it?

Daisy removed a thick manilla folder from a drawer and set it down on the surface of the desk in front of Kat. "These are the rules."

"Wow. That's a lot of rules," she blurted. She shouldn't have been surprised but she was. The contract had to be almost an inch thick. "Are you going to go through it rule by rule?" They'd be here for days.

Daisy chuckled, "Good heavens, no. Peter will go over

the gist of it and then you can read it at your leisure. I'm afraid you are required to sign it today, but you are bound by the rules regardless of if you sign. Everything in here," she put her hand on top of the contract, "stems from what Peter is going to tell you."

Kat stared at the paper. The queasiness was back. How was she supposed to get through this without losing her nerve? Damn Danny and his treasure obsession.

"Don't worry, dear. It's not as bad as it looks." Daisy offered another sweet smile and then sat back and waited for her husband to start.

Peter leaned forward. "The rules, or at least the major ones, are as follows. You are not allowed to discuss the Society with anyone. Ever. At all. If you tell someone about it who is not your immediate heir and you aren't ill, on your deathbed, or under significant threat to your life, your membership will be revoked and depending on who you tell, you could be…eliminated."

She started to laugh. He couldn't be serious. Death for talking about this place? No way. But the laugh died in her throat at the blank look on his face. His eyes drilled holes into her. He was deathly serious. She stifled the hysterical laughter bubbling up her throat. This was insane. *Who were these people?* He had to be kidding. She gave him a nod since there was no way she could make her vocal cords work at this moment.

"Two: You may not tell anyone who the other members of the Society are. People come here specifically because we guard their privacy fiercely as we will guard yours. If you reveal that someone else is a member, it carries serious consequences that may include, but are not limited to, death."

Jesus. This just couldn't be real. Was it too late to leave? She wanted to turn tail and run, far, far away. Sadly, her knees wouldn't hold her at this moment so she wasn't going anywhere.

"Three: You cannot lie to us. If someone who works for the Society asks you a question you must tell the truth. Deception will not be tolerated in any form. If we find out you've lied to us, depending on the lie, it can bring about dire consequences. We will not tolerate being lied to."

All the oxygen got sucked out of the room. She'd already lied to him. A few times. A bead of sweat slithered between her shoulder blades. But at least he hadn't said death this time. Dire wasn't as bad as death. She wanted to go home but it was already too late for that. She had no choice. Her brother Danny was here somewhere and she had to find him, even if it meant risking her life.

"Four: Kat, I cannot stress this one enough. You will see people, happenings, and events that do not align with your moral code. You *must* not interfere. You may join if you are invited or you may choose to avoid certain areas at certain times. Whatever your choices are, you may not harass, bother, draw attention to, or bully any other member. If you do not like what you see, just ignore it. We firmly believe in live and let live in the Society. If you create any kind of disturbance or cause any kind of problems for fellow members then you will be asked to leave the Society.

"This brings us to five: No member may leave the Society. Ever. Unless they are removed for one of the above reasons or for failure to pay dues. If that happens all the same rules still apply. Speak about the Society and nothing good will come of it. Do you understand these rules?"

Kat just stared at the man. She'd stopped being able to breathe ages ago. What the hell had her brother gotten involved in? She gulped a lungful of air. "Yes," she finally uttered. "I understand."

"Good. You are now a member of the Lock and Key

Society. For life." He handed her a piece of paper and a pen. Her hand shook slightly as she signed her name. Her fake name. According to the rules she'd just committed a deadly sin.

Peter stood.

Kat tried to get to her feet but stumbled a little.

"Peter, you've scared the poor woman. Don't worry about all that death talk, dear. Hardly ever happens. You'll be fine."

Hardly ever? Somehow that didn't make Kat feel any better. Another bubble of laughter rose in her throat and she bit the inside of her cheek to stop it from erupting. This was all so ludicrous, so outlandish, it just couldn't be true.

Peter frowned. "Don't worry, my dear. It all seems scary now but you will see how wonderful everything is at the Society and it will make going back to reality seem so disappointing. We are all family here, aren't we, Daisy?"

She nodded. "For better or for worse but we take care of one another. You will find your place and then it will all be worth it."

Kat straightened and offered him a small smile. The only thing she wanted to find was her brother and then she wanted to get the hell away from these people.

"Now, allow me to escort you to your cabin." He walked over to the steel door in the corner of the room. "Please put your hand on this panel." He pointed to a flat screen that stuck out from the wall at about a thirty-degree angle. He touched the screen a few times and then moved out of the way so she could put her hand on it.

She placed her right hand on the device and a bar of light traveled down the screen and back up again. Kind of like a photocopier. The screen beeped.

"There now. Your handprint is in our system."

She pulled her hand back and resisted the urge to turn it

over and look at it. She knew it was fine but she still wanted to check.

Peter used the screen again, touching it in various places and then moved back again. "See that round eyepiece on the wall? I need you to put your right eye up to it."

She hesitated.

"Don't worry, it won't hurt."

After clearing her throat again, she said, "I'm too short."

Peter chuckled and moved the sensor downward until it was at the right height for her. She leaned forward and placed her face directly in front of the optical scanner. A light went over her eye and then the screen below beeped again.

"Excellent. Your retinal scan is in the system. Now when you go to any Lock and Key Society location, you just put your hand on the screen by the entrance and then do the same with your eye and the door will open. Give it a try."

She did as instructed and the door popped open. "Um, neat."

"Let me just grab your bag and we'll go. So you know, the only way on or off the island is through this building to the dock unless you want to swim for it. The nearest island is about ten miles away, through open water."

He held the door, and she walked out into the sunshine. Peter closed the door behind them. "You can't get to the dock unless you go through this door using your biometrics. The foliage around the building is thick and you can't get through it without a machete and there are a few surprises in it anyway that the machete won't fix. So, my dear, please let us know when you wish to leave, and we'll arrange it." He smiled and started down a manicured stone path. "By the way, I can give you a tour anytime. Would you like me to show you around now?"

The idea of spending more time with anyone who worked here made her break out in a sweat. She needed to keep a low profile. "I'm rather tired, so I think I'll pass for now." Her voice came out barely above a whisper.

"Okay." He glanced over his shoulder. "I'm always around."

A shiver went across her skin. What the hell had Danny gotten them into?

CHAPTER THREE

Rushton Fletcher sat across the desk from the devil. That's what many called him. Certainly, a lot of the members of the Lock and Key Society thought of him that way. He was the man who oftentimes had to pass judgment. God might have been a better nickname but Rush understood why they called him the devil. Archer Gray had the coldest eyes and, as far as Rush was concerned, an even darker heart.

But for Rush, it was a case of the devil he knew. Archer had a difficult job and he made tough decisions. Some of those decisions concerned whether people lived or died. And as horrific as that sounded, the reality was those types of decisions are made every day, all around the world by all kinds of people for all kinds of reasons. Archer's role was to protect the Society and enforce the rules. The Society would fall apart if that didn't happen and no one, no general member or board member wanted the Society to disappear. The loss of support should something happen to the Society could be fatal to certain members. The organization equaled freedom for some who were so rarely allowed to be free. It also kept the true monsters in line. That was Rush's job, monster wrangling.

Archer handed him a photo of a woman. It was a candid shot. She had no idea her picture was being taken. Her auburn hair waved loosely around her shoulders and a few stray strands danced in the wind. Her eyes were covered by large sunglasses, but her cheeks were lightly dusted with freckles and her full lips were a becoming shade of pink.

"That was taken from the arrival dock at the island. She gave her name as Kat Sanders and handed her token to Peter to be examined. Said she was a new member but declined to say how she'd received the token." He handed Rush another picture. This time it was of her passport. "The passport is a fake. Not the worst fake ever but not the best either."

He silently handed Rush a third picture. It was of the token. A small white porcelain teapot with purple flowers. Rush's fingers tightened on the photo. As part of the security team for the Society, he knew what everyone's token looked like. Most did not share what token they had with other members, although doing so wasn't forbidden. Here was the real reason Archer had called him. This token belonged to a beloved member of the society. Angel Wheaton was everyone's favorite aunt; funny, kind, and capable of making the most curmudgeonly person crack a smile. She also made the best chocolate chunk cookies ever.

"Angel," he said softly.

Archer nodded. "I still miss her. Some days it was only her smile that made this job worth it."

Angel wasn't her real name and she wasn't actually anyone's aunt. She was a permanent resident of the Lock and Key Society. She bounced from location to location, meeting people and making them smile. She enjoyed her days and made sure everyone else enjoy theirs.

Archer took the pictures back from Rush and handed

them to Ryker Sterling. "To catch you up, Ryker, Angel turned up dead seven weeks ago. Her body was found floating in the Hudson River. The police said she appeared to be the victim of a mugging gone bad. There'd been a lot of muggings in the area recently. But Angel would have had no reason to be in Riverside Park. You know how she was… rarely leaving a Society safe site. She was attacked in the park, shot twice in the heart, then tossed in the water."

Rush barely suppressed a feral growl at the callous treatment one of his favorite people had received.

"Does anyone believe that story?" Ryker asked.

"Other than the police?" Archer asked. "No."

Rush added, "And since Angel was an elderly woman with no family and no one to come forward, they are unlikely to bother looking for anyone other than the mugger."

Archer sighed. "There hasn't been much to go on until now. The teapot token was Angel's. I want to know how this woman got it. I want to know what she knows."

"Rush, will you take this one?" Ryker had just been overseas and by the look of him, needed a break. He explained, "Calder and Cash are involved in something in Greece and Lincoln is currently in Canada." All the other monster wranglers were busy.

"I'll take it." Rush took the picture of the woman back from Ryker and studied it. Was she involved in Angel's death? If so, she was about to experience a world of hurt. "She's still on the island?"

"Yes. Go down there and get to the bottom of this. Find out who she really is because Kat Sanders is an alias. Get all the details you can and then kill her. We don't tolerate fake identities." Archer leaned forward in his chair. "I want Angel's killer to pay."

Rush nodded grimly and stood. "I'll be on the next plane."

Archer tapped his finger on the desk. "Keep me informed."

Five minutes later he'd left the bookstore and was walking down the street on the Upper West Side. He needed to pack some clothes and grab his guns. He'd be taking a Lock and Key jet to the private island in the Bahamas. The Bahamians were very friendly with the Society. They wouldn't bother to search him so he didn't have to worry about customs or passport control.

The image of the woman floated up in his mind. She was beautiful. He idly wondered what color her eyes were. Not that it mattered. She'd be dead in a matter of days, but he was curious. Whoever she was, she'd gotten involved in things way beyond herself and she was about to find out what it was like to deal with the devil and his crew.

CHAPTER FOUR

Kat stood in her cabin's kitchen and stared out at the Caribbean Sea. It was beautiful. If only she had come for vacation. It would be perfect. Sighing, she swallowed the last of her coffee. She needed to get out and meet people, ask questions. So far, in the two days she'd been on the island, she hadn't managed to do more than exchange a few polite words with other members. No one seemed eager to talk to her. She needed to change that. Danny's life depended on her finding out about the island. He had to be here. She refused to let herself consider that he might already be dead.

Walking through the bedroom, she entered the bath. The luxurious shower and tub were all done in white marble tile with beachy accents everywhere. She'd started towards it when the outdoor shower caught her eye. Dark green foliage and bright blooms draped the tiled walls. It looked so appealing, she decided to use it. She wasn't one to use an outdoor shower, but this seemed different. She dropped the robe and gathered her toiletries and then slid the door open. She set everything on the teakwood shelf and reached for the tap when she remembered she'd need a towel. Two minutes later she stepped back outside and hung up her towel.

"I don't know," a female voice said from the other side of the wall. "It sounds risky."

Kat froze, not wanting to draw the woman's attention.

"Everything is risky these days," a male growled back. "But we have to do something, I'm telling you, we're broke."

The woman sighed. "It can't be that bad."

"It can and it is," the man responded.

"Who's fault is that?" It sounded like the woman was speaking through clenched teeth.

The man snarled, "Don't start with me. You were happy enough to spend the money as well." There was a silence. "Look, we have to gamble on this. I'm not sure I can come up with the rest of the money in time without it. I've got an ace in the hole so I think we've got a good chance."

Kat held her breath. The last thing she needed was for them to discover her eavesdropping.

"But what if it doesn't work? It's not exactly an easy fix. What if you don't find it?" the woman whined.

"Just pray that we do, otherwise we're screwed. Life as we know it is over. So, if you can use your feminine charms to find out anything, now would be the time, wife of mine. You'd better work at it."

Asshole. Kat was pretty sure that's what the woman said before the sound of rustling fabric and receding footsteps reached her ears.

A chill traveled down her spine. The man had sounded desperate. She recognized the tone from all those years with her father. Desperation only ever resulted in bad things happening. Putting her hand on the tile wall to steady herself, she took a few deep breaths. Her stomach, already tied in knots, clenched tighter. Suddenly the idea of an outdoor shower had lost its appeal. She took everything including the towel back inside and turned on the marble shower.

She needed to stop flailing around in the dark. Since arriving two days ago, she'd accomplished exactly nothing. While she shampooed her hair, she worked out a game plan in her head. First, she needed to talk to either Peter or Daisy and ask for a tour. She'd been anxious to avoid scrutiny in the beginning, but she really needed an overview of the place. Then she would create some sort of grid and start her search for her brother methodically. Maybe she'd get lucky and find him fast. If he was still alive. She cursed and let the water run over her face. She would not cry. Positive thinking was the key. She needed Danny to be alive. He had to be. *I can do this.*

She rinsed out her hair and added conditioner. With an abundance of possible buildings on the island, searching them all would take a month of Sundays. There was no way she wouldn't be noticed at some point. What she needed was more information. A grid search yes, but only of the areas that were most likely to house her brother. To figure out that, she needed to know if her brother was hurt, or if he was being held captive.

"I've got it all under control this time, Kat. I really do." Danny's voice floated back to her. *"I've done my research and I know what I'm doing. This could open all kinds of doors for me."*

She had stared at her brother. "When has treasure ever brought us anything but misery? And what's this secret society? Why are you involved with that?

"Don't worry about that. The token…it's just a sort of insurance policy."

"Insurance against what?" When had he gotten so caught up in this stuff? She'd been working long hours at the hospital and not paying enough attention to him. It was her fault that he had too much time on his hands. He was her twin, so he was thirty-

five just like her, but he was more like a sixteen-year-old. He'd never fully matured after their parents died. Their unexpected demise had stunted him somehow.

"Danny, you're a damn good plumber. You make good money. What do you need with treasure and a secret society? What does that give you?"

"Somewhere to belong. Don't you see? I don't belong anywhere. I don't fit in with the other guys at work. They all watch sports and drink beer. I like books on archeology. I hate beer. I don't want to go to the bar on Friday night. I don't want to bowl. I want to see the world and meet people like me. People interested in all kinds of things. Things like archaeology and history and—"

"Treasure hunting. That's what this is about, isn't it? You want to go treasure hunting. Just like Dad."

Her brother had shut up then. He knew what she thought of their father. He'd gone all around the world looking for treasure and dragged them with him. Then when they were old enough to say no, he and their mom went without them. In the end, treasure hunting had killed their parents. She wanted no part of it.

She rinsed her hair and then toweled off. Her brother hadn't listened to her. He'd gotten involved in treasure hunting that had something to do with this damn secret society that made him disappear. He'd given her the token as an insurance policy, and she still had no idea what that meant but she'd cashed it in. Now she just had to figure out what was going on and find Danny.

She brushed out her hair and let it hang down over her shoulders. Studying herself in the mirror she tried not to notice the dark smudges under her eyes or the fine lines that radiated from the corners. Both were new phenomena, appearing just as Danny disappeared. She also decided to ignore the deepening creases on her forehead. Danny's disappearance was aging her. No point on dwelling on that fact.

She pulled out a green summer dress from the closet. The color accentuated her eyes. If she was going to chat up Peter she was going to need all the help she could muster. One false move and they'd kick her off the island just like on those reality TV shows. Who was she kidding? They'd kill her. Then what would happen to Danny?

Kat pulled on the dress and added a pair of low mules. They were too big, a size six to her size five feet but they were cute and matched the dress perfectly. She left the cabin, locking the door behind her.

She squared her shoulders and moved slowly along the path trying not to trip. The uneven stones on the pathway, and the too-large shoes, made walking difficult and required all her concentration to stay upright on the treacherous surface.

"Damn shoes," she muttered.

"You know you can take them off," a voice said.

She turned to look behind her and immediately tripped over the stones on the path. The man who had spoken reached out and caught her, pulling her to his chest to keep her from falling. She looked up into his ice-blue eyes. "Oh dear! I'm not usually so clumsy."

He was gorgeous with a capital G.

A lock of his dark unruly hair curled over his forehead as his lips curved into a smile. "Sure."

She found herself smiling in return. "No really, I'm not. My shoes are too big." She continued to stare at him. Kat suddenly realized she was still in the man's arms when a nurse went by and mumbled an 'Excuse me.'

"I'm so sorry." She started to back up and stumbled again. He grinned and steadied her. Heat flew up her cheeks. This was ridiculous. She was going to hurt herself or someone else. "Fine," she grumbled. She steadied herself on his arm as she pulled the offending shoes off her feet. "Thanks again for saving me."

"Not a problem. Enjoy this beautiful day." He stepped around her and continued down the path. She watched him go before she started walking. He was tall, had to be over six feet because her five feet two inches put her in the middle of his chest. He'd rolled the sleeves of his white button-down shirt to his elbows. The soft jeans he wore had to be hot in the Caribbean heat but man, did they fit his ass well. All in all, he was a twelve on a scale of one to ten. Even the men were better looking at the Lock and Key. She was starting to understand her brother's fascination. If only everything didn't lead to death. She shivered.

The path skirted the beach and the Caribbean sun danced brightly on the turquoise water as the waves lapped on the white sand. She made her way down the stone path which was lined with tropical flowers that smelled divine and were a riot of colors. If she wasn't so desperately worried about her brother, this would be heaven. Maybe once she made sure he was safe, she'd make an effort to come back. Or maybe not. She bit her lip.

She turned off the main path and headed for the grass hut. Hopefully Peter would be there. Coming to a stop in front of the steel door, she took a deep breath. "Here goes nothin'." She put her hand on the screen and then put her eye on the reader.

The door popped open and she found Peter behind his desk.

"Hey there," she said in a friendly manner. She was hoping her informal approach might set the mood for an affable encounter. At least it might keep him from mentioning the rules again.

"Kat," he said as he rose to his feet. Peter was probably in his seventies. Today he wore a pale blue button-down and a pair of beige shorts. He didn't seem nearly as intimidating as he had the other day. She decided immediately that stress must have colored her perception of this man. His bright smile hid the pain that his dark eyes did not. If she had to guess she'd say he was having some serious health issues. He moved like he was in pain and the color in his cheeks was blotchy. She'd seen enough cancer patients to recognize the signs. She worked in the business side of the hospital but she saw sick people every day.

She waved him off. "Oh, please don't bother standing."

"How are you today?" He smiled, warming the deep brown of his eyes,

"I'm well, Peter. How are you?"

"Good. Good. What can I do for you?"

She licked her lips. "You'd mentioned a guided tour of the island when I checked in. I was wondering if I could possibly take you up on it whenever you have time. I thought it might be nice to understand…" her voice faltered. She'd inadvertently arrived at a pool yesterday where various people had been having sex and she'd turned tail and run almost immediately. She'd like to avoid that happening again.

He grinned. "The areas you might want to avoid?"

She nodded.

"I would love to show you around. Have a seat and I'll give you a map of the island. It's easier if I explain a few things first."

As soon as Kat sat, he offered her something to drink but she declined. "So, tell me all about the island."

"The island is only about sixty-five acres, so not that big. No airport, which is why you arrived by boat. Everything comes by boat. All our supplies. The Society bought the island about one hundred years ago, and we've been here ever since. It started out with just a fishing shack and then over time, buildings were added until it became what you see today, a fully functioning luxury resort."

"How many buildings are on the island?"

Peter leaned back in his seat. "There are twenty that accommodate everything from food preparation to a small hospital."

Her stomach plummeted. *Twenty?* There was no way she was going to be able to search every one of those.

"Then," Peter continued, "we also have the guest facilities. Forty-five cabins and about twenty rooms are scattered around the island in various buildings."

It only got worse. How the hell was she going to find Danny?

Peter unfolded the map. "Most of the buildings are clustered here in the south part of the island. This is us here." He pointed to a building with a pier in front of it. It was about midway up the east side of the island. There weren't many buildings beyond this one.

She studied the map for a second. "Why aren't there any buildings on the north side of the island?"

Because up here," he tapped a finger on the map, "is a bit unsafe."

"Unsafe?" her voice cracked.

Peter chuckled. "Don't worry there aren't any monsters, or anything, okay maybe some alligators but mostly there are sinkholes. We've done what we can to shore it up and reroute the water when it rains heavily but mother nature has her own rules. That's why we don't build up there. The trees and mangroves help keep the ground stable. That said, there is a lagoon up there. It's stunning. You should definitely go see it. There is a reinforced boardwalk to take you up that way. Just don't go at night without the flashlight supplied with your cabin, and stay on the path. If you venture off the path, it becomes a bit trickier."

Just what she needed—sinkholes. "I think I'll check it out during the day." *If at all.*

"Wise choice. Now if you want, we can start the tour." He got to his feet again and came around the desk.

Kat stood. "You don't have to take me. You seem like you're in a bit of pain."

"Oh no. I'm right as rain."

She touched his arm. "Peter, I work in a hospital. I've seen enough patients to know the signs. Stay here and save your energy. I'll take the map and look around. If I have any questions, I'll come back."

Peter opened his mouth, probably to protest but closed it again. "Thank you for your kindness. I appreciate it."

She hesitated. Not that she wanted to push her luck but finding out more about Peter might not be a bad idea. Maybe if she offered him some kind of assistance, he would be more inclined to…to what? Not kill her? He seemed like a sick old man today. Not so threatening. But still. "Not that it's any of my business, but do you get treated here on the island? I know there's a hospital."

He nodded. "I get chemo here but I had to do the bulk of my treatment in New York. I must say, I enjoy New York but it just doesn't compare to the Caribbean."

"I totally agree." She gave him another smile and then grabbed the map off the desk. "I'll find my way but if I don't make it back by dinner, send a search party."

"Deal," he said and then went back and sat down again behind his desk.

Kat gave him a small wave and then went through the whole James Bond-style process again with the door and left the office. Her heart went out to Peter and Daisy. Dealing with illness was difficult for all involved. She let out a sigh and then started down the path. Opening the map, she was trying to decide which building to search first when she walked straight into someone.

"Oh, I'm so sorry," she said as she righted herself. Glancing upwards, she gave a small cry. "Oh. it's you."

The man with the beautiful blue eyes chuckled. "Yes, it's me." He glanced down at the map. "Are you lost?"

"What?" She blinked. "Oh, no. I didn't do the tour when I arrived, and I just thought I would take a quick peek around but there are a lot of paths so Peter gave me a map."

"If there's something specific you're looking for maybe I can help."

"No," she blurted out. That's the last thing she wanted, someone else to know she was looking for her brother. She backpedaled and put on a smile. "Just trying to find my way around. Sorry again for bumping into you."

"Rush."

"Excuse me?" Kat asked.

The man took the map out of her hands and said, "My name is Rush. I work here. Let me give you a guided tour."

Kat's first instinct was to refuse again. She might get to search one of the gazillion buildings if she were alone, not to mention anyone who worked here completely freaked her out. But maybe she could pick Rush's brain a bit. "Um, well sure. Why not? I'd love a tour."

Rush folded her map back up. "We've discussed developing an app for this but honestly it's sort of quaint to hand out maps." He jutted out his arm, crooked at the elbow, and looked at her expectantly. Did men still do this type of thing? Did he mean for her to take it?

Kat gingerly wrapped her hand around his bicep. "Sure."

"First," he said looking down, "why don't you take off the shoes? It will be safer for both of us."

Heat filled her cheeks. She'd put the shoes back on when she'd gone in to talk to Peter. She glanced down and decided he was right. After pulling off the shoes, she straightened. "Ready."

He extended his arm. "Shall we start? How long have you been here?" he asked.

"Just a couple of days." They came to a fork in the path. She'd always stuck to the one on the left so far because it skirted everything and stayed close to the beach. The only time she'd taken the path on the right, she'd bumped into the group orgy by the pool.

Rush took the one on the right. "And how long are you staying for?"

"Not sure really. Just needed a break." She tried to think of something to ask him. Anything to steer the conversation away from herself. "So, what do you do here?"

"Honestly, I don't work here normally, I mean not on the island. My work for the Society takes me all over the world."

That was a vague answer. "Doing what?" she pressed.

"I'm sort of a fixer. If there's an issue with something, then I come and try and solve it. Sometimes it's better to have someone from outside give a different perspective."

"I see." Her heart gave a thump. Was the problem her brother and his treasure hunt? Did they know about it and Rush was brought in to 'fix' the situation? "S-so what thing are you fixing this time?"

"This visit is actually just routine. I consult on security as well and it's just time to review our security measures, make sure everything still works the way it should."

He was here checking security. Routine, he'd said but was he telling the truth? She risked a glance at his face but there was nothing in his look to say either way. She surreptitiously wiped her sweaty palm on her dress. She needed to calm down or he'd notice her sweaty hand on his bicep. They'd come to a pool that she hadn't seen before. It was empty. "Is this a hot tub?"

He nodded. "It's one of five. This is kept at one hundred and two degrees. There are others that are hotter but this one is the most secluded."

He was right. There was jungle all around it. Very romantic. This would be a great place to be with a boyfriend. Not that she had one of those. She met Rush's gaze and immediately regretted it. Heat crept up her neck into her cheeks. His soft chuckle met her ears.

He linked her arm through his and moved her along the path. "The next thing is the fitness center." Within a minute they came up to a one-story long building with a thatched roof.

"Yuck. I hate exercise."

Rush grinned. "We'll skip the tour of the building then. But there are two weight rooms and all kinds of treadmills and ellipticals not to mention Pilates reformers and other equipment."

"I'll pass on all of it."

Rush kept them moving. "You don't ever exercise?"

"I walk. Sometimes for miles. I find it relaxing but I'm not big into organized fitness."

He glanced over at her and let his gaze roam her body. "You don't appear to need it."

She chose to ignore the comment and keep going. Was he flirting with her on purpose? He worked there. Was he allowed to flirt with her? On the other hand, maybe she should flirt back. Maybe she could pump him for information. She shot him a sidelong glance. Somehow, she didn't think Rush ever said anything he didn't want to say.

"So, we've come across the island. After the gym building, we have the main dining area. You must have eaten here."

She nodded as they rounded the curve in the path and a

long low building came into view. "The food was amazing. Is it Michelin starred?"

"Yes. We pride ourselves on providing the best fine dining possible."

Several guests were having cocktails on the veranda that ran around the perimeter of the restaurant. On the far side of the building was the beach where she'd taken a table the previous evening. It was later than she thought. Already gone noon. She was hungry after not eating much for breakfast but she was going to stick with Rush and see if he might let something useful slip, not that she had a clue what would be useful short of *we have your brother. He's in the cleaning supply closet.*

"You seem to be lost in thought."

She glanced over at him. "Sorry. Just a lot on my mind I guess."

"The best way to cure that is to sit with a cocktail and watch the ocean."

"Is that an invitation?" she blurted out. Not the smoothest of comebacks but it would have to do. She needed him to talk to her. Any information she could get about the island would be helpful.

Rush smiled easily at her. "It can be. Would you like to have a cocktail?"

"That would be nice. Let's grab a table on the beach." They strolled up the stairs, through the dining hall, and out onto the terrace. Rush's hand hovered over the small of her back, not quite touching, as he escorted her to a table in the far corner. The spot was very secluded, with the building behind them, a wall of green foliage on their right, and the ocean in front of them. There was only one other table within earshot. Kat didn't know whether to be flattered that a man as gorgeous as Rush wanted her to himself or to be terrified because a man who worked for the Society wanted her all alone. Her heart lurched and she clenched her fists reflexively.

As they got settled, he asked her what she would like to drink and signaled the waiter. "John, this is Kat. She's a new member."

"Hi, Kat," the young waiter greeted her. "What can I get for you?"

His smile was welcoming and warm. She couldn't help but wonder did he really know what was going on here? "Um…" Her mind went completely blank. What could she drink that wouldn't get her tipsy? Nothing. She wasn't a big drinker and she hadn't had anything since her brother disappeared. Too easy to end up drinking every night and she didn't want to go down that road. Life was hard enough.

"She'll have a rum punch," Rush said. "It's the bartender's specialty. He adds a few unusual ingredients."

"Sounds great." Rum punch was not the way to stay sober.

"I'll have one as well."

John nodded. "Very good, sir." He left the table and went up to the bar.

Kat took the moment to admire the beach. It was stunning. The sky was a gorgeous shade of blue, not unlike Rush's eyes. The waves lapped the shore of the immaculate white sand beach. She'd never imagined Hell would look so incredible.

"Gorgeous, isn't it?"

"The view? Yes," she agreed. "It's almost perfect." She glanced at Rush.

He cocked an eyebrow. "Almost? What's missing? What would make it perfect for you?"

Her mouth went dry under his steady gaze. This man seemed to be able to turn her on with just a look. She wanted to fan herself. He made her warm in all the right places.

What was wrong with her? It was crazy to be thinking about sex at a time like this.

"Er, I'm not entirely sure." Great. She was definitely winning him over with her witty repartee. "What about you? What would make this perfect for you?" The question spilled out, and she found she really wanted to know his answer to the question.

Rush let out a small sigh and for an instant, the shield dropped. For an instant, he looked sad, but then his face went blank again. "I think it's perfect the way it is." His blue eyes twinkled at her. "So why did you pick the island? Why here?"

John returning with the drinks saved her from replying. The question was loaded and she wasn't prepared to answer. Yet. If ever.

After the waiter left, Rush raised his glass. "To you, Kat. Welcome to the Society and to the island." They clinked glasses and she took a sip of her drink. Sweet pineapple juice, potent spicy rum, and the limey aftertaste danced on her tastebuds, and she almost hummed with appreciation. She took another hasty sip. This cocktail would disappear all too easily.

Rush's cell phone went off and he glanced at the screen. "Sorry, I have to take this." He rose and wandered across the dining area.

She took another sip of her drink. It really was yummy, and the resort was stunning. It almost made up for Danny being missing and the fact she'd already broken the rules which could result in her being as dead as she hoped Danny wasn't.

But besides that, it was all good. She let out a long sigh. *Fuuuuck.*

"I told you… Yes," a voice hissed behind her.

She looked over her shoulder at the lush hedges, but couldn't see anything.

The voice continued. "I've checked. It's not there. I've checked all over the damn island. It's not anywhere." The speaker was a man, she thought but she couldn't be sure because the voice was a half-whisper. The smell of cigar smoke wafted in her direction. A cigar smoker? "Short of getting a shovel and digging, I'm not sure what you want me to do."

It was a different voice than earlier. Was this person looking for the treasure too? Maybe he knew where her brother was.

Rush suddenly appeared at her elbow and she jumped. "Are you alright," he asked as he sat down.

"Just daydreaming, I guess."

He caught her gaze. "Good things, I hope."

"Of course." She gulped her drink. Getting away from Rush seemed like the smartest plan. There was no way he was going to tell her anything he didn't want her to know. She just wasn't that accomplished at getting people to talk.

It didn't help that he was overwhelming her senses with his sexy voice and gorgeous blue eyes, not to mention he smelled fantastic. Some sort of citrusy male scent. Yeah, she needed to get the hell away from Rush. As attractive as she found him, he was too damn dangerous to her. "Um, I think I might head back to my cabin. I'm a bit tired. Not sleeping well. Having a hard time relaxing." All so friggin' true it hurt. She was exhausted.

He smiled at her. "The island is a great place to relax. Have you seen the lagoon yet?"

"No. Peter told me about it although he made that end of the island sound kind of dangerous."

Rush leaned in. "He's not wrong. You shouldn't go alone. The ground is unstable in spots. You must stick to the boardwalk. It can be very dangerous. I'd be happy to take you if you'd like." His voice rumbled through her, as if a string pulled taut inside her was vibrating with his timber.

Butterflies took flight in her stomach. *Say no. Say no. Say no.* "That would be nice." What the hell was she getting herself into? She took a large sip of her drink.

He brushed a stray hair out of her face. "I'll pick you up at eleven tomorrow."

"S-sure. That would be good."

Rush nodded. "Here's your map." He laid it on the table in front of her. "I'll see you tomorrow morning." He leaned over and rubbed his thumb across her lips and then kissed her cheek.

"Yes," she managed to croak but he was already sauntering across the dining room.

She stared after him. What the hell had that been about? Her breath shortened as if her lungs were signaling just how over her head she was with Rush. A shiver danced across her skin. It hadn't really occurred to her before now, but no one knew she was here. No one knew where to find her. She was totally and utterly alone.

CHAPTER FIVE

"Got anything yet?" Archer demanded.

Rush ground his molars together. "I just spoke with her. She seems tense and possibly scared."

"As well she should be. Any idea why she's there?"

"None at all. I'm meeting her tomorrow. I'll find out what's what and we'll go from there."

Archer sighed. "Make sure you do." And then he ended the call.

Rush's chair squeaked as he leaned back and scrubbed his knuckles down his jaw. He'd always liked coming to the island. It was relaxing and the food was outstanding but even more, he liked the ocean. The azure color was mesmerizing, and the sound of the waves calmed every nerve in his body.

Too bad he was here to work.

Kat Sanders. Or whatever her real name was. She was a bit of a mystery. Genuine on one level and yet hiding something on another. Her big green eyes were very expressive. If she knew just how much, she'd have worn sunglasses all the time they were together. He'd had no problem reading her thoughts back at the hot tub. He smiled. He'd been having the same ones. He'd love to see Kat wearing nothing but sunscreen in that tub for an afternoon. He hissed out a long sigh and fought that particular craving. She was the enemy. As fun as she might be, he never mixed business with pleasure. Not ever. His ex-wife had taught him that lesson the hard way.

He shoved away from the desk and headed into the control room. High tech stations lined the walls and members of the security team sat in front of stations monitoring the happenings across the island. "What's going on, guys?"

There were a few mumbled responses but mostly the men in the room kept their heads down. They knew he was a monster wrangler and were all likely just a bit afraid of him. Rightfully so. He only got the call when something went wrong because the Society knew he got shit done. When they couldn't handle something, they called Archer and Archer called Rush or Ryker or one of the others. They were the last line of defense or the tip of the spear, depending on the situation. No one on staff, or even in the Society, wanted to get too friendly.

Rush walked over to one screen. "Hey, Danton. Can you pull up this woman?" He pointed to Kat on screen. She was sitting at the bar, not speaking to anyone, just eating a late lunch.

Danton's fingers flew across the keyboard. "She's only been on property for about forty-eight hours. Arrived Wednesday. Looks like she's spent quite a bit of time by her cabin on the beach so there's not much data on her."

Rush just nodded. "Put it up anyway. I'll fast forward through it."

Danton brought it up on a screen and got up. "Sit here and do it. I'm due for a break anyway."

"Thanks." Rush didn't take offense that the man beat feet to get away from him. Happened all the time.

He sat down and started the playback. Twenty minutes later, he'd come to the same conclusion Danton had. There wasn't much there. Kat hadn't done anything suspicious since she arrived on the island. She hadn't even really spoken to anyone. The shock on her face when she came around the corner to the alfresco pool was priceless but other than that, her stay had been boring so far.

So, why the hell was she here and why lie about who she was? How the hell did she get Angel's token? Finding out was his motivation. Angel had been a Lock and Key member but more than that, she had been family. No one messed with family. If Kat was responsible for Angel's death, he'd follow orders and make sure she paid with her life.

Danton returned and Rush rose, stretching his back. "Thanks, man. All yours."

He strolled out of the control room. More research was needed on Kat Sanders, but he decided he could do it in his room. He left the operations building, nicknamed the Hub, and walked back to his room. His cabin overlooked the ocean and was about five down from Kat. He picked it on purpose. The island rounded to a point where the cabins had been built, so the back of his unit had a line of sight through the trees to the back of hers. Better to keep an eye on her.

He mounted the steps to the veranda and paused. "What do you want, Ronnie?" he demanded as he glanced over his shoulder towards the far side of the veranda.

His ex-wife, Veronica, unfolded from the hammock she'd been lying in. "I wanted to see you, Rush." She strode across the plank porch to join him.

"Save the bullshit, Ronnie." He wasn't in the mood to go another round with her.

"It's Veronica. No one calls me Ronnie and lives." She

said it with a smile but the humor never reached her dark eyes.

If she thought she could kill him, she would. Rush had known that the moment he'd served her with divorce papers. Ronnie wasn't big on forgive and forget. Neither was he and their mutual stubbornness was the problem.

She leaned against the door frame. "Are you going to open the door?" She brushed his chest with her fingertips. "You've been working out."

The familiar tug Ronnie always had on his libido pulled his nerves taut. That urge is what had gotten him in trouble in the first place. Veronica Woodly was five feet, ten inches of sexy. Her raven hair curled about her shoulders. She was long and lithe, spending a lot of time at the gym to keep her figure and her flexibility. Her dark eyes didn't miss that he still found her attractive, no matter how hard he tried to ignore her.

She leaned into him. "I'd love to check out your… muscles. I'll show you mine if you'll show me yours."

He grimaced. "Not interested."

"That's not what your body says." She looked pointedly at his crotch.

But he was determined to keep his distance. "What do you want?" he demanded again. He hadn't been this close to her in a while. She had lines forming around her eyes and across her forehead. Her once flawless skin was showing signs of age like everyone else. Sadly, she was starting to look… hard. Too much ambition could do that to a person.

"I heard you were here and I thought I would come say hello. You know, for old times' sake." She was still leaning into him.

He took a step back. "We're divorced. Have been for five years. There are no old times that I want to remember. Don't come see me again."

Yes, he was still attracted to her, but he knew he'd never, ever touch her again. Five and a half years ago, he'd found her screwing a guest in one of the private daybeds on the beach at one of the Society's Greek locations. He'd seen the curve of her ass and known instantly it was her. It didn't matter that he couldn't see the rest of her because she was being taken from behind. He'd known. And it was over instantly. Rush didn't share, and he didn't tolerate liars. Lie to him and it was over for sure. His version of fuck around and find out. Ronnie had found out pretty damn fast.

"Rush," she cooed, and took a step closer but he immediately backed away. She put on a fake pout. "I only wanted to say hello."

God, how had he ever... "You have never just wanted to say 'hello' in your entire life. What do you want?"

Her eyes narrowed "Fine," she said as she straightened and folded her arms across her chest. "What are you doing here?"

"It's none of your business." He could've bit his tongue. The instant the words were out of his mouth, he knew they were a mistake. Now she wouldn't leave him alone. Honestly, it hadn't taken him long to regret the decision to let her remain in the Society.

"I *knew* you were working. Why are you here? I need to know. I run this place and if there's a problem, I need to know about it."

Rush shook his head. "Peter and Daisy run this place. You run the fitness center and the sports activities. You don't need to know jack shit from me. I'm here to work on things that don't concern either of those areas. Don't think you're more important than you are, Ronnie. It won't go well for you."

She glared at him. "Fine," she said through gritted teeth

and rushed down the steps. She disappeared around the bend in the path.

"Fuck." He scrubbed both hands down his face.

His ex had always brought out the worst in him. It had just taken a while before he realized it. If he were being honest, the affair was the excuse he needed to get out of the marriage. Ronnie was like a drug. The drama, the fighting, the make-up sex, it all wore him down but he'd struggled to get away. The affair let him cut her off instantly. It took him a while to realize the feeling in the pit of his stomach had been relief, not grief at failing at his commitment.

Now he wanted nothing to do with her.

He entered his cabin, soaking in the cool air. It was good to be inside out of the heat and away from Ronnie. After he settle on the chair, he booted up his laptop. He gladly put Ronnie out of his mind so he could concentrate on Kat.

He needed more information. What the hell was she up to? What was her goal? Why did she become a member of the Society? He didn't think it was voluntary. She didn't want to be here. If he had to guess, she was terrified, and no one chooses terror unless they have to.

He started with the Society's database and did a search. Archer had created the database of members and prospective members, their circle of friends and anyone of interest. Rush often used it to gather background information. If there was nothing in the database then, he'd move on to others he had access to.

Three hours later he closed the top of his computer and rubbed his eyes. He was hungry. He'd missed lunch and his head throbbed with the lack of food and from staring at a computer screen for so long. Mostly he was annoyed because even after all the effort, he still had no clue why Kat was there.

The only high point of his research was at least he had her real name and some details about her life.

Katherine Rollings was a hospital administrator. She'd stayed close to the truth on her application but there were some differences. The hospital she worked at was in NYC not upstate New York. She'd failed to disclose the existence of a brother on her application. And she changed her last name. The lies by themselves were enough to invoke retaliation from the Society.

However, none of what he'd uncovered told him *why*. She was just an average person, with an average life. None of this made any sense.

He stood and stretched. A slight breeze and the rush of waves on the shore came through his open window. He loved being by the water. It always made him sleep better but he knew it wasn't going to work its usual magic tonight.

Rush's cell buzzed and he answered it. "Archer, I've still got nothing. Not making much sense."

"I got a call from Veronica. She wants to know why you're on the island."

Shit. "Sorry she involved you. I should've just said I was on vacation when she asked. She's always been overly ambitious and she thinks being in the loop about what's going on will help her move up the ladder."

There was a pause. "The only reason she is still employed by the Society is because you requested that I not terminate her. If she becomes a problem, she'll be gone. You're far more valuable to me than she could ever be. Get her under control."

"Understood." *Shit. How could she still be making his life difficult?*

"And I shouldn't have to say this but in case you get any ideas, you can't kill her on Society property either. I don't care what you do on your own time but rein yourself in when you're on mine."

Rush let out a bark of laughter. "As much as I dislike my ex-wife, I have no intention of killing her."

Archer sighed. "I thought I'd better remind you, just in case. Your ex-wife is annoying as fuck, but I won't tolerate any adverse attention brought to the Society. And against all odds, Veronica is very popular with certain members."

"I just bet she is." Rush worked to keep the bitterness out of his voice. He didn't really care anymore but old habits die hard.

"Just don't do anything stupid or I'll have to kill you and that would annoy *me*." Archer disconnected the call.

Rush tossed aside the phone with a chuckle. That was about as warm and fuzzy as Archer got. Still, he appreciated the sentiment. Archer looked out for him in his own limited way. Ronnie was becoming a problem and not just for him. Reading between the lines, it was clear her time with the Society was running out. Her ambition to move up, to be seen as important was going to land her in hot water. She was popular now with some of the men, but that wouldn't last, and then things would go downhill fast. Archer would be left with no choice but to deal with Ronnie in some manner or another. One of the other wranglers would have to handle it. Archer would tell Rush when the situation was taken care of. If Rush didn't get out in front of this, it would be too late. Just another damn thing to worry about.

His cell rang and Rush glanced at the clock. Six a.m. Something was wrong. "Archer."

"We have a problem."

"Only one?" Rush sighed. He hadn't slept much and his mood bordered on black.

"Funny. Eli Fisher."

Rush's gut tightened. "Is he here on the island?"

"Yes. And he's up to his old tricks."

"He has underage girls here? How the fuck did he manage that?"

"He didn't, at least not on the island, but he was keeping them on a nearby island," Archer growled. "You're onsite, so instead of sending one of the others, I want you to keep a close eye on him. Find out why he's there. He should be in the Hamptons this summer."

"I'll see what I can find out on this end." He clicked off the call.

It had taken everything in his power not to crush Fisher like the cockroach he was after the last incident. Archer had stopped him. Said even they had to obey the rules of the Society whether they liked them or not.

Rush rolled out of bed and hurried through a cold shower. Twenty minutes later, he walked into the Hub. Danton was leaning against his table, with his back to his screen, eating a muffin and sipping coffee. He was chatting with one of the other techs, DeRhonda. She was smiling and eating as well.

"Morning," Rush greeted them.

They looked up and Danton instantly straightened, setting his breakfast aside on his desk. "What's up?"

Rush glanced at DeRhonda, and she immediately murmured, "I'm going to get more coffee, can I grab one for you?"

"No need. Danton, with me." He turned and left the room, heading to the office he'd been working in the previous day. Danton followed him in and closed the door behind them.

"What can I do for you?" Danton asked.

"Someone might be smuggling people onto the island." He didn't think it was likely. Fisher wasn't that stupid. He wouldn't take that kind of risk. Probably. Better to be sure than just guess.

Danton paled. He fisted his hands and then opened them again. "I— That is— I mean— Are you sure?" His voice was an octave higher than it should've been.

Rush narrowed his eyes. What the hell was going on? He'd been taking a stab in the dark but Danton's reaction was too over the top. "Cut the shit. What the fuck is going on, Danton?"

The man seemed to collapse in on himself. "Aw, fuck." He rubbed his face with his hands. "I might as well tell you."

"Tell me what?" Rush's jaw clenched painfully.

"There have been a few incidents. Weird shit that's happened."

Rush had to cross his arms over his chest to stop himself from choking the man in front of him. "Define 'weird shit'."

"Cameras being moved, unexplained noises, some of the members are convinced the place is haunted. They've heard cries for help and shit but when we investigate, no one is there. We can't find anyone on the cameras, or the cameras have been repositioned so whoever it was didn't show on the video feeds."

"How long has this been going on?" he demanded.

"A few weeks, a month, maybe a little more," Danton mumbled.

Dammit. "Which is it?" he demanded.

"About a month."

Rush knew the answer, but he still had to ask the question. "And why didn't you share this earlier?"

"You know why. No one wants to disappoint Archer

Gray. Shit. We're all terrified he's going to kill us because of the breach in security."

Rush shook his head. "He won't kill you, but I might. I want everything. All the dates and times of the incidents. I want to know locations where the cameras were altered and I want comprehensive lists of who was on the island at the time. Members and employees. Everyone and all of it. And I want it now. Understand?"

"Yes, sir." Danton turned and started for the door.

"And," Rush continued, "I want to know who you think is involved."

Danton froze. Then he turned slowly. "I—I—"

"To hide the activity, you know someone has to be on the inside. I want to know who you suspect. Protecting anyone would be a colossal mistake. It's your ass or theirs."

The other man nodded and then left the room.

Rush stared through the open door. This was unacceptable on all kinds of levels. The Society had rules in place so this type of shit couldn't happen. That was the problem with using fear to control things. It often stopped the flow of information. Everyone's fear got in the way of their common sense.

He glanced at his phone. This was going to take all day. He was going to have to cancel his plans with Kat. A pang hit him in the chest. He'd been looking forward to spending time with her. *Not good.* It didn't matter how drawn to her he might be, he had to keep reminding himself that she was also work.

He ran a hand through his hair. Eli Fisher couldn't be this stupid, could he? It would be nice if he was. Then Rush would be happy to take care of him for breaking the rules. And it wouldn't be painless.

Danton came back into the room with a flash drive in his hand. "Here it is."

"Get a chair. We're going over this together." Rush took the flash drive and Danton nodded, then left the room again.

His reaction to being questioned told Rush he wasn't involved. Danton was not a fool. He knew the score. He didn't want to volunteer things were falling apart on his watch, but he wasn't stupid enough to break the rules. Still, he would pay close attention to the other man while they went over everything. He'd run a deep background on him later, just in case.

He shook his head. This was not turning out to be the trip he'd expected. Kat was too sexy for words. Ronnie was more than just a pain in his ass, and now someone was screwing with the security on the island. Somehow, as bad as this seemed, his gut told him this was only the beginning.

CHAPTER SIX

Since Rush had canceled their plans, Kat had spent the morning studying a map of the island and then searching online for any information she could about the island and the buildings on it. The Society must have had to register plans with a government somewhere. This island had originally belonged to the Bahamas so theoretically something should be on file, but so far, she hadn't found it. Short of leaving the island and going to Nassau, there wasn't much else she could do.

She'd put the trip to Nassau on the back burner and tried instead to search for information on Rush. Who in this day and age didn't leave some sort of digital footprint? But the man didn't exist online. No social media that she could find. She'd tried all the people she'd met on the island but they didn't pop up on any of the popular sites either. Must be one of the rules.

Sighing, she switched her thoughts to Daisy and Peter. She'd tried googling them but couldn't find a thing about either one. Of course, not having last names made it almost impossible. Still, she thought she might at least find a shot of a grandkid or something, that was a dead end as well.

The fact that Rush had canceled their plans for the day made her edgy. Was it because he'd discovered who she was? What she was after? Kat glanced at the note card he'd sent. She should feel relief. Spending time with Rush might turn out to be very dangerous but the hollow feeling in her belly wasn't from relief.

She let out a sigh. What the hell was she doing acting like an amateur sleuth? She was not fucking Veronica Mars. Mooning over Rush wasn't helpful in finding her brother. Jesus, how pathetic had her life become that she wanted to spend time with a man simply because he showed interest in her? She should be questioning him about Danny, or at the very least, about the island and buried treasure. As an employee, he must know something.

She glanced at the clock over the fridge and swore. The massage she'd booked herself was due to start in twenty minutes. Grabbing her key, she headed out the door, wearing flip-flops this time. Minutes later, she arrived at the spa huffing slightly. *God, she was pathetically out of shape.*

"Ms. Sanders." The woman behind the desk smiled "No need to rush. I'll show you into the locker room and then you can get changed. My name is Sunitha, in case you need anything."

Kat murmured her thanks and followed the woman down the hallway. Sunitha was about Kat's height but dropdead gorgeous with amazing skin and deep brown eyes. She oozed warmth. Why couldn't everyone on the island be like Sunitha? Kat would be a hell of a lot more relaxed if they were.

She gasped as they entered the locker room. It was right out of a magazine. The teak-wood lockers, the stone floors, and off-white walls. Everything done with a goal to soothe. It even smelled divine. Some sort of earthy scent that made her whole body relax.

The spa was far better than anything Kat had ever been in before. Calm music played in the background. The perfect backdrop relaxed Kat's shoulders immediately. Drawing even breaths became easier as well.

"Here are the steam rooms and the saunas, in case you'd like to indulge after your massage." Sunitha walked a bit further down the hallway to where it opened into a room with a vast skylight but no windows. "This is the ice plunge pool in case you would like to try it. Use the sauna, the steam room, and then plunge into the icy water. Quite rejuvenating."

My ass. There was no way she was plunging anything in that cold water. Who in their right mind would do that on purpose? This was for those polar bear club people. *No thanks.*

Sunitha led her through another door back into the locker room. "Choose any locker with a key in it. It will have a robe and slippers. Just slip the key into your robe pocket once you've changed, and then take a seat around the corner in our waiting area. There is a variety of water and teas to choose from, as well as fruit and cucumber slices to add to your water. Please enjoy." With a final smile, Sunitha left Kat on her own.

She quickly stripped out of her clothes and put on the plush cream-colored robe and slippers provided by the spa. A lemon-lavender scent wafted off the robe, enhancing her sense of bliss. She was enjoying a cup of jasmine tea while sitting on a lounge chair when someone called her name.

"Kat Sanders?" the slight woman said.

Kat stood up. "Yes, that's me." It had taken her a second to respond since Sanders wasn't her real last name. It was a damn good thing she hadn't changed her whole name; she was having problems enough with just the different last name. *Friggin' Danny.*

"I'm Mya. Please come right this way." The uniformed woman led her down the dim hallway. "Have you been here before?"

"No." Kat had to concentrate on her walking. The mood lighting which she'd admired when she was wearing flip flops, made it hard to see and the uneven stone floor combined with the one-size-fits-all slippers, except her foot; the slippers were many sizes too large for her, making it hard as hell to walk.

"Welcome to the Orchid Spa. It's our pleasure to have you here. Is this your first time on the island as well?"

"Yes." Kat didn't want to answer any questions. She had a backstory all made up and had rehearsed it a few million times, but reality was so much different than she thought it would be. The stakes were higher than she imagined. If she screwed this up, any hope of finding her brother would be gone.

The small woman pointed to the open door. "Please take off your robe, get under the sheet and lie face down on the massage table. I'll be back in a minute."

Kat went in and closed the door. She'd been hoping for more of a chance to look around back here before the woman came back but she didn't think she had more than a minute or so before the masseuse returned. With any luck, she might be able to poke around after the massage.

The spa was connected to the hospital section of the building. Kat really wanted to get a chance to look around in there but she couldn't think of a way to get in. If her brother was hurt, he'd be in there. It was also a great place to hide someone which she knew from personal experience. Part of her job was making sure the A-list celebs who came to her hospital for plastic surgery, or whatever, were hidden from the rest of the world.

She hung her robe on the back of the door and climbed under the blanket on the table. She adjusted her face on the ring. Nothing to do now but enjoy the massage. The heated bed shouldn't have felt so great in the Caribbean climate, but dang, the gentle warmth radiating under her belly was exquisite.

Mya re-entered and the door clicked softly shut. She murmured a few things about essential oils and suddenly the room smelled divine. Lavender and citrus? She'd have to remember to ask. Mya folded the blanket down low on Kat's back, drizzled some warmed oil on her skin, and started the massage.

"You are very tight. You have many knots in your muscles."

No shit. Any wrong move and she would die. She'd lied to them so she was already on borrowed time. Hard to relax under that kind of pressure.

Ninety minutes later, Mya finished. "I will go get you some herbal tea. Take your time getting up. There's no rush." Kat waited until the door closed and then sat up. She'd damn near cried when Mya used her elbow to dig into the knots in her back. For such a little woman, she was brutally strong. Kat was going to be sore, no doubt about it.

She got off the bed and quickly pulled on her robe and slippers. Opening the door to the hallway a crack she listened. No sound. She opened it fully and moved into the empty hallway, heading away from the locker room. She moved as quickly as she could in the damn slippers, coming to the door that she thought separated the spa from the hospital wing. She took a deep breath and pulled the door open.

The hospital wing was a total contrast to the spa. It was

light and bright. Where the spa was meant to be relaxing, soothing for frayed nerves, the hospital was cheery. The cream-color walls were adorned with bright artwork. The marble tile floor gave the illusion of an upscale luxury clinic. The type of thing Kat had always imagined she'd find in Switzerland where all the celebrities get work done or go on some kind of weird diet while being hovered over by a gazillion doctors. Kat was amazed they had a hospital at all for the size of the island, but she was beginning to understand that the Society had the best of everything at all times, including the best health care.

Two women were seated at the nurses' station, so she turned right and instantly came face to face with a couple more nurses. At least she assumed they were nurses. They were wearing what looked to be pink, tailored scrubs. Instead of being baggy or boxy, the scrubs fit them to a tee. *Must be nice*. They each had a small name tag pinned on their chests and stethoscopes hanging around their necks.

Kat smiled automatically as adrenaline rushed through her veins. They were chattering away to one another and just smiled back as they passed. Kat's slipper-clad feet made less noise than her ragged breath as she continued down the hallway. She passed two more nurses who were serving a man a meal.

The rooms were well beyond anything they had in her hospital. Even the VIP section wasn't as nice as this. Extreme luxury in a hospital setting. It was so far outside of her norm, she almost couldn't comprehend it. Would be so much fun to show this to the gals in the office at the hospital. They'd never believe it.

Most rooms were empty. There were a few patients that seem to be recovering in style. The rooms all had sofas and flat-screen TVs, as well as beds with luxury duvets instead of blankets. It was hard to tell, but she was pretty sure each room had its own bathroom and outdoor space. These hospital rooms were more like high-end hotel rooms to lounge in while recovering from some elective procedure. *Must be nice.*

At the end of the hallway she turned right. The double doors ahead of her were closed. She pushed but they wouldn't open. She tried a bit harder. Nothing. Locked. The narrow windows in the doors had been covered, which make it impossible to see into the hallway.

Her heart rate ticked up over the evident attempt to obscure what lay beyond. Could this be where they were holding her brother? It would make sense. Lock him away in the hospital wing that no one is allowed to enter. She'd brought her lock picks to the island but not to the spa, so she was going to have to come back, preferably at night when there were fewer people around.

"Excuse me, what are you doing?" said a voice behind her.

Turning, her stomach dropped. This had to be a doctor. The tall blond man had cold blue eyes. He was wearing a button-down shirt with the sleeves rolled up, a pair of khakis and leather loafers.

She tried to smile. "I'm so sorry. I was at the spa and I seemed to have walked through the wrong door and then I got all turned around." She did her best to seem innocent.

The doctor's shoulders dropped, and his lips curved into a small smile. "Don't worry. Happens all the time. I'll escort you back."

She reached out and touched his arm. "I am so sorry to disturb you. This is my first time on the island, and it's all so wonderful but somewhat confusing."

The doctor grinned as he offered her his arm. "It can be." He escorted her around the corner and back down the hallway to the nurse's station.

"Bear," someone called from behind them.

The doctor turned. "Yes, Kyla?"

A woman wearing high-end yoga gear hurried toward them. She had a stethoscope but there was no mistaking she was a doctor. She wore her confidence like a lab coat. Several nurses at the station glanced up and immediately looked down again. *Not so popular*, Kat noted.

"What's she doing here? She's not a patient."

The nurses' reaction made sense now. Kyla was not the friendliest sort. Her demeanor made Kat's belly roll.

"She got lost coming from the spa." He turned back to Kat. "Diane"—he said gesturing to one of the nurses behind the desk—"will get you back where you belong."

"Oh, thank you, doctor." Kat forced a smile.

Diane came out from behind the desk and gestured for her to move toward the door she'd entered through. "This way."

"I'm so sorry," Kat murmured. "I just got turned around."

Diane offered her a quick smile. "It happens. It's so damn dark in the spa it's a wonder anyone can find their way out."

"Right?" Kat asked with a laugh as her shoulders sagged. Diane didn't seem in the least alarmed by her presence. They paused by the door while Diane retrieved some sort of key fob from her pocket.

"I don't care, Kyla. I'm not doing it. I won't force a patient to do what he doesn't want to do." Bear's voice carried down the hallway.

Kat glanced over her shoulder toward the nurses' station.

Kyla stood in front of the desk, fists propped on her hips. "You have to. Do you want to be the one to tell Archer you killed the man?"

"I'm not killing him. He's choosing to stop treatment. And I won't be telling Archer anything. It's none of his business." He leaned forward. "You won't be telling him either or I will report you for violating HIPPA regulations." He turned and strode out of sight. Kyla followed at his heels.

A loud buzz sounded, and Diane pulled open the door. "Here you go."

Kat said in a quiet voice, "She doesn't seem like the nicest person."

"You don't know the half of it," Diane murmured with an eye-roll.

"Thanks for helping me," Kat offered before walking back through the door.

"Ms. Sanders, there you are!" Mya had appeared at her elbow. "We thought we lost you there for a few minutes."

"Oh," Kat said with a start. "I'm so sorry. I got turned around."

Mya handed her the tea. "It's not a problem. Happens all the time." She walked with Kat all the way back to the locker room. "You are welcome to stay and use the pools and the showers or head to your room in the robe and slippers. Whatever makes you happy."

Kat murmured her thanks and silently cursed. There was no way she'd be able to do any more snooping now.

She entered the locker room and took a sip of the tea. It was tasty. This place had everything. The showers had luxury brand body gel, shampoo, and conditioner. There were brushes of all sorts on the counters by the mirrors. Hair, tooth, eyebrow, blush…everything a woman needed to look her best but the thought of getting in the shower over here when she could use the one in her room was just not appealing. Too exposed. She glanced around the empty locker room to see if anyone was watching her. *What a ninny.* She was alone, but her heightened senses told her the impression was false.

She gathered her clothing and put it in the little tote bag

that was in the locker. Then she left the mug on the counter by the hairdryers and headed out into the sunshine.

The island was stunning and of course, everything was immaculately groomed. The Lock and Key Society didn't screw around. For the price of admission, they'd better not. The full one hundred thousand she'd saved to just walk onto the island and become a member. She blinked back tears. *Danny, you better be alive. I'll kill you if you've deserted me forever.*

The inside of the cabin was cool. She went through the small kitchen on her right to the far wall and adjusted the temperature on the AC. Kat let out a breath. Every time she ventured out of the cabin, her blood pressure went up. She leaned on the island with a granite countertop and tried to guess at the price of the stainless-steel appliances. She should be so lucky in her apartment back in New York.

She grabbed a bottle of water out of the fridge and admired the scene of the ocean from the window by the door. This window also had a view of the building next to hers. She left the bottle on the kitchen island and was moving around the sofa to go to the bedroom when something caught her eye. When she looked through the sliding glass doors, she started. A large colorful bird sat on the railing. She could have sworn it was staring in at her. It should have been beautiful but somehow Kat thought it was more of a warning. *We're watching you.* She shook her head. Now she was really losing it.

CHAPTER SEVEN

After a quick shower, Kat decided it was high time she met some people. She'd have to figure out a way back into the hospital, but until then, maybe she could find someone who knew about the treasure. Approach the problem from that direction. That would give her a place to start. And no better place than the bar at the main pool.

Checking her look in the mirror, she decided the deep green bikini that matched her eyes was a good choice. She threw a long white linen cover-up over it and donned a sun hat. Then she slid her feet into flip-flops and headed to the pool. It was time to soak up some late afternoon sun and possibly some island gossip. Anything that might help.

"What can I get you?" the bartender asked as Kat came to a stop in front of the bar.

She glanced at her watch. It was just approaching five p.m. "Might be a bit early for a drink," she murmured.

The light-haired woman seated on the stool next to her snorted. "Oh honey, it's never too early for a cocktail. She'll have a mimosa," she told the bartender. Then, she turned back to Kat. "Start small. Champagne and orange juice."

Kat laughed. "Okay, why not?" She nodded at the bartender.

The woman offered her hand. "I'm Tatum Wellington."

"Kat Sanders."

"Nice to meet you, Kat." She turned back to the bartender. "I'll have a margarita. I have no qualms about drinking early."

Tatum was about average height with blond hair and hazel eyes and looked to be somewhere north of thirty-five, but it was hard to place an age on her. She was attractive and seemed friendly. The bartender put the mimosa and a margarita down in front of the women.

Kat picked up her drink. "Cheers."

Tatum smiled. "Cheers." The two clicked glasses and then took a sip.

"Have you been on the island long?" Kat asked as she set her drink down.

Tatum sighed. "Too long."

"Oh, are you not enjoying it?"

The other woman shook her head. "I was enjoying it. Very much." She glanced around and dropped her voice. "But the last couple of nights, I've heard some strange sounds. It's kind of freaking me out."

Kat's curiosity got the better of her. "What kind of sounds?"

Tatum glanced around again but the bartender was at the other end of the bar and no one else was around. "I thought I heard a scream."

Kat's stomach tightened. "Really?"

Tatum nodded. "Look, I'm all for live and let live but that did not sound like someone having fun. I told the front office and they said they'd call security but"—she shrugged—"it's a crapshoot if they did anything. I heard the same thing the night before last, too." She shivered.

Kat sipped her drink. This conversation was cementing her dread over just being on this island. If Danny turned up alive, she'd kill him herself. "Was the scream from a man or a woman?"

Tatum stared at her for a moment. "You know? I just immediately said woman in my head but when I think about it, there's no real way to know. It was just a scream. I tend to equate screaming with women but to be honest, one of the guys I work with is a screamer and it could've easily been a sound he'd make."

Kat was glad she was sitting because her knees had gone weak. Were they torturing her brother? "Where is your cabin?" she asked. Her voice had risen at least an octave so she cleared her throat and gulped her drink.

Tatum swallowed and set her glass down. "On the other side of the island. Not far from the spa building."

"You don't think it was someone in the hospital, do you? You know someone in pain because they had some procedure, or…"

"Jesus, that's a scary thought. I don't think so but what do I know." The other woman shivered.

"Are you here by yourself?"

Tatum nodded. "My family has been a member for about twenty years. My dad became a member on his own, so my grandfather left me his membership. Keep it in the family. I also work for the family law firm so it makes sense, I guess. I don't usually spend much time in the Society locations." She took a large gulp of her drink and swallowed. "They kind of make me nervous but I just finished a big deal at work and I wanted a couple of weeks to relax. Corporate law is very dog eat dog and I am tired of pushing to be the top dog. I knew I could come here and still get work done but be able to relax too. Or that was the plan. Now I'm thinking of heading back to New York."

"Hey, Tatum," another woman called as she approached the bar. "What are you drinking?"

Tatum smiled. "Margarita."

"Sounds good," the dark-haired woman agreed. She signaled the bartender and placed her order. Then glancing over at Kat, she offered her hand. "I'm Remy Tanger."

"Kat Ro - ah, Sanders," she stammered. "Nice to meet you."

Remy turned to Tatum and said in a quiet voice, "I heard the screams last night too, so it's not just you."

Tatum's shoulders seemed to relax a bit. "Thank God. I was starting to doubt myself. I was just telling Kat about it."

"I called to complain as well. The scream made my hair stand on end." Remy smiled her thanks as the bartender placed her drink in front of her. "Completely freaked me out. Couldn't sleep for the rest of the night. Peter tried to tell me it was some kind of animal." She snorted. "If that was an animal, it was the two-legged kind."

Tatum turned to Kat. "Remy is here by herself too. We know each other from a Society gathering in New York. She's fairly new to the Society as well."

Remy nodded. "Tatum has been a godsend, helping me adjust to the Society lifestyle. Hawk, my husband is coming down in the next couple of days though, and I will be super happy to see him."

"I thought I read in the rule book that with married couples, the spouse didn't get membership," Kat said and then immediately apologized. "Sorry. No questions. None of my business."

Remy chuckled. "No, you're right and I don't mind answering. I'm on the board. We get a bit more leeway with things."

"Oh, that explains it. Thanks."

Remy leaned towards Tatum and Kat. "Just be careful, Kat. There are some not so nice people here."

Tatum snorted. "You can say that again." The sound of loud male voices interrupted their conversation. "Speak of the devil," she murmured. "Here comes one of those now."

"I hear what you're saying, Valentine, but I respectfully disagree. I think the market is headed for an even larger fall which is problematic for a lot of reasons. I'm not investing at this time." The man in question was a little shorter than average with a large belly and a balding head. He headed to a table just behind them and sat down. The man named Valentine sat with him and a couple of others joined them.

"What do you think, Fisher? Will the market stabilize?" one of the others asked. He was taller and thin. He was probably in his mid-forties but looked much older. His brown hair was graying at the temples, and he held a glass filled with amber liquid.

Kat stared at the table. She recognized the voice of the man who had asked the question. It was the guy she'd overheard in her outdoor shower. The one who was broke.

The portly man shook his head. "I was just saying that I think it's headed downward. Now is not the time to buy. We haven't hit bottom yet."

Tatum leaned over to Kat. "Do you know Fisher?"

Kat glanced at the aging overweight bald man and shook her head.

"Good. Keep it that way. You don't want to have anything to do with him." She shuddered. "As a matter of fact, stay away from everyone at that table. Rumor has it that they're into some not so good things."

"How do you know?" Kat asked.

"As I said, my family has held a membership for years. You start to hear certain things. But also, these guys are all from New York. My family law firm is there. We move in the same circles so trust me when I say they are not the kind of men you want to be around."

"I think the tall skinny guy is broke," Kat blurted out. Then silently cursed. It was the alcohol. She hadn't really eaten much and now she was drinking.

Tatum's eyes lit up. "Oh, I love it. Let's spill the tea." She dropped her voice and both Kat and Remy leaned in to hear her better. "His name is Frank Humber. He's married to Donna Lundquist. They are both members because Humber is on the board. He hit it in the stock market years ago, and his wife came from money. They are part of the high society social scene; you know… Met Gala invitees and all that but there's been rumors back in New York that they are sinking fast. The money is supposedly gone and we're talking millions here. My parents hobnob with that crowd a lot and my mom shares all the dirt." She turned to Kat. "How do you know they're broke?"

Kat swallowed. "I was about to use my outdoor shower when I heard his voice and a woman talking. He was telling her the money was gone. He sounded quite desperate."

"I shouldn't wonder. Being broke is the kiss of death for that set. No one will speak to them again if it becomes common knowledge that they don't have money." Tatum shrugged.

"Valentine, what are you into these days?" Humber asked.

The other man shrugged. "I'm diversified. Some in the market. Some in real estate. Doing some stuff in Africa and South America at the moment. Mostly just holding tight until the market evens out."

"Nothing too interesting? No hot tip?" Humber pressed.

Valentine shook his head. "Nothing hot to speak of. The only way to make money right now is to wait the turmoil out."

Humber took a large swallow of his drink. "Well, I guess we'll have to find the pirate treasure buried here on the island then." He let out a loud bark of laughter and the others just sort of smirked.

Kat risked a glance at him. Was he the one behind the treasure search? The member who had brought her brother here?

"Tell me about Valentine," Remy prompted.

Tatum signaled to the bartender to bring another round but told him to make Kat's a margarita as well.

Kat bit her lip. She was going to have to be very careful with the drinks. She needed to be able to focus and stay on top of things. The people around her needed to talk and answer her questions but she had to be sober enough to ask the right ones and remember the answers. The drinks arrived and the women clinked glasses again before taking a sip. The tart drink was rather tasty.

Tatum started, "Jed Valentine is first-generation money, I think. That's the thing. No one knows. He's always vague about things. No one can pin him down. Rumor has it, he made his money in blood diamonds, but again, no confirmation on that. They also say he works for someone or an organization."

"What do you mean?" Kat asked. She had no clue what Tatum was referring to.

"I mean he either works for the mob or some other crime organization, or he works directly for the head of something like that. No one knows but there's a lot of speculation. "Actually, Archer Gray must know." She turned to Kat. "He runs the Society, so he knows everything. No one keeps secrets from Archer."

Kat's lungs froze. Dear God, was that true? No, it couldn't be. If this Archer Gray knew her secret then she'd already be out on her ear. Or worse.

"Do you know the story of the pirate treasure on this island?" Valentine asked Humber. "I'd love to hear it. Treasure hunting sounds like fun."

"Well, I only know what I heard," Humber backtracked. "Just that some pirate was supposed to have left his treasure somewhere around here. I don't even know if it's a real story. You know people make this stuff up all the time." He shook his head. "I would think that if it was buried here, it would've been found by now," he blustered.

Valentine shrugged. "Maybe."

Fisher snorted. "Treasure. That's a fool's errand. There are much better ways to make money and a lot better ways to spend it." He chuckled at his own joke.

Kat's skin crawled. There was something off about Fisher. He set alarm bells ringing. "What's Fisher's story? He seems… for want of a better word, creepy."

Tatum nodded. "He's a big-time slime ball. He goes through assistants like water. Hires some young pretty thing and she's gone in less than a year but with some kind of payout because he's allegedly assaulted her." She put air quotes around the words. "He's just bad news. The other thing I've heard is he likes his women as young as he can get them. Disgusting. And mean as shit. Like snakebite mean." She dropped her voice even further. "And he holds a grudge.

"There was a guy, Kyle Baker, who apparently went up against Fisher somehow. Fisher spread rumors and shorted the shares of the company so the value dropped. Baker almost went under. Honestly, I've heard he is still struggling to rebuild."

The hair on the back of Kat's neck stood at attention. She turned and suddenly Fisher was beside her.

"I don't believe we've met." He leered at her as he offered his hand. "I'm Eli Fisher."

"Um, Kat, Katherine Sanders." She gave his hand a quick shake and tried to let it go but Fisher held on tight.

Fisher studied her for a second. "You're new here. I would remember if we'd met before. I have an excellent memory for faces." He scanned her body with a leer, as if he had a good memory for other things as well.

Kat was suddenly grateful for the white coverup she'd decided to wear. "Um, well, …y-yes."

"I thought so. Welcome to the island. It's lovely to have you here," he said and then finally released her hand. "I hope we can get to know each other. Life on the island is always better when you share it with others."

She made a non-committal noise and discreetly swiped her palm on her dress. Fisher looked over her head to take in the other two women. "Tatum, how nice to see you."

Tatum's smile was frosty. "Fisher," she murmured.

"And who is this?" Fisher asked shifting his lecherous gaze towards Remy.

"Remy Tanger. Granddaughter of Remington Tanger. Former board member," answered a deep southern voice.

Kat turned to see Senator Austin Davis approaching the bar. *Oh boy.* She was not a fan of the Senator from Texas. He was a little bit too into conspiracy theories for her.

Fisher and Davis exchanged hearty greetings and a big handshake before Fisher turned back and offered his hand to Remy. "Nice to meet you and congratulations on being on the board."

Remy shook hands with the man and murmured her thanks before Davis asked, "What are you doin' here, Remy? Not the best time to be in the Caribbean. What brings you down?"

"I was invited to see some friends in the Caymans next week and I thought I might as well stop here on the way. What brings you here, Austin?"

Her tone was chilly and Kat was sure the overall temperature around the pool had just plummeted. No love lost between these two.

"I wanted a chance to catch up with Fisher and a few other folks. Always nice to get away for the weekend. But I hear there's a storm comin'. Be careful you ladies don't stay too long. I wouldn't want you to get swept away."

Kat thought that Davis's warning sounded more like a threat than anything else. The urge to get away from these people warred with her need to pump them for more information. The screams and the hospital were terrifying but she had to find out if it was where her brother was.

The bartender delivered drinks to the men although Kat was sure they hadn't ordered any. *Regulars*.

"Davis," Valentine called. "What do you know about the treasure supposedly buried here?"

Davis turned and smiled. "Well now, that's a story and a half." He turned to Kat. "Are you interested in treasure, Ms…"

She swallowed. "Sanders. Kat Sanders."

"Would you like to hear about treasure, Ms. Sanders?"

She drew in a deep breath. This might be her opportunity to learn something that would help locate and rescue her brother. "Sure, who doesn't like a good story about treasure?" she offered him a smile.

"Well then." He offered her his arm. "Why don't you ladies sit a spell with us and I'll tell you all about the legend of BlackEye's treasure?"

"Um, okay." That wasn't what she had in mind but it wasn't like she had other options. She slid off the stool and took the arm Davis offered. She glanced over at Tatum and Remi, shooting them what she hoped was a pleading expression. *Please don't leave me*. They both gamely slid off their stools and followed her and Davis to the table. After a minute or two of getting seated and having the bartender deliver their drinks, Davis commanded everyone's attention once again.

"Well now, it was back in—"

"Davis," Rush said as he approached the table. "Nice to see you."

Davis turned and his mouth tightened slightly. "Fletcher." He nodded and accepted Rush's proffered hand.

Davis might not be happy to see Rush but she sure as hell was. She ended up being sandwiched between Fisher and Davis. Not somewhere she wanted to be. She looked up and met Rush's gaze. *Please.*

Rush's eyes narrowed slightly but he said nothing. Instead, he got another chair and brought it over. Everyone made room and Rush ended up at the head of the table opposite Davis. "I'd like to hear the pirate tale." Rush's deep voice soothed Kat's frayed nerves.

At least now she knew nothing bad would happen while they were sitting there. Rush wouldn't let it. A weird thought, considering she'd just met the man. But the thought eased the crows beating their wings in her stomach. She drew a deep breath of ocean-scented air. She wasn't sure why she trusted him so profoundly, but she did. Somehow, she knew he would protect her… well, until he found out she was lying and then he'd have to tell someone in security and they would have to kill her. The instinct to laugh bubbled up and she had to bite down on her cheek to stop it from erupting. She pushed those thoughts away and concentrated on the story. This was all about finding her brother. Nothing else.

"As I was sayin', Hugh Bainton was also known as the pirate, BlackEye. He was supposedly fierce and had a lot of success attackin' a lot of Spanish ships, grabbin' their gold and treasures and then sinkin' them. His daddy died back in England, and he inherited the title, Earl of Somersby.

BlackEye was smart. He knew he couldn't go home as a pirate. He would never be accepted into genteel society. But he could go if he got a letter of marque from King George that said he was a privateer goin' after Spanish gold for the realm.

"The story goes that BlackEye buried the bulk of his treasure on this island save for a chest or two to bring back for the king. He didn't want to give up too much of his gold. He'd earned it fair and square and had no intention of givin' it up."

Fair and square? Who the hell was Davis kidding? Did he not understand piracy? There was no fair about it. BlackEye, like all pirates, targeted Spanish ships laden with gold and they took it for their own after murdering the crews. Davis was on a roll now, though. It was obvious he enjoyed being the center of attention. The smug look on his face was a dead giveaway.

"Bainton arrived back in England with the gifts and King George gave him a letter of marque, so all was forgiven. He claimed his estate and became a part of high society again. He even got married to some society lady from a good family." He paused and took a sip of his drink then swallowed. "And here's where it gets interestin'. After a few years, BlackEye decided to come back and get his treasure."

Kat's ears perked up. Nothing she'd ever read mentioned this part. No one said Bainton came back. Where the hell was Davis getting this information? Was he making it up? She desperately wanted to ask but there was no way she wanted to draw any more attention to herself, nor did she want to bring attention to the fact she was so interested in the treasure.

"Bainton left his wife and children and gathered the men of his crew who were still around. He commissioned a new ship and sailed across the ocean to right here"—Davis rapped his knuckles on the table—"this island. The story says he and four more men went ashore and stayed overnight. When they weren't on the beach by mornin', his first mate, William took more men and went lookin' for him. They found him and the others in the middle of the island, sick as dogs, covered in rashes and barely able to breathe. Bainton died a short time later. As did the men who'd gone with him. According to legend, his first mate, fearin' that whatever killed Bainton was contagious, lit the bodies on fire and then buried the bones in the sand."

"And the treasure?" Humber demanded. "Did the first mate give any clue as to where it was or what happened to it?"

Exactly what Kat was wondering. She wanted to read this account of what happened herself. She'd read all the research Danny had left behind at his apartment and even found some more documents at the New York Public Library but there had never been a mention of Bainton coming back. Maybe she could glean a detail or two from this new account that might help her find Danny or at least figure out where he was looking for the treasure.

Davis shrugged. "The first mate and the crew figured the place was cursed and never went searchin' for it. They were all too afraid. So theoretically, it's still here somewhere."

"I've never heard that Bainton came back," Rush commented. "Are you sure that's true?"

Davis frowned slightly. "Yes. The first mate kept a journal. A very good friend of mine in New York is a collector and he showed it to me."

Valentine paused from lighting a cigar, "So, the treasure could still be out there, just waiting to be found."

Davis's smile grew. "Yes sir. But beware of the curse. No one who went to retrieve the treasure lived to tell the tale."

Kat glanced at Valentine. The cigar. It smelled like the

one from the man in the bushes. She wanted to scream and run. She wasn't a big believer in curses but the fact that the hair on the back of her neck was standing up and her heart was slamming against her ribcage lent some credence to Davis's words, never mind the fact that her brother had disappeared.

Goddamn treasure. It would be the death of her.

CHAPTER EIGHT

Rush's jaw ached from clenching it as Davis answered questions about the pirate story. Davis loved being at the center of attention, but Rush wouldn't put it past him to have made up the whole bit about Bainton coming back. He didn't trust Davis at all. It was odd that he was on the island right now, too. Something was not right about his sudden visit.

Actually, he glanced around the table, all of these men usually spent their summers in the Hamptons. Why were they on the island now? Most of them were what he'd call chickenshits, and hurricane season was impending. Yet another mystery and maybe their visits were connected to the recent breaches in security. One could only hope. Nothing would give him greater pleasure than to get rid of Davis and Fisher.

"Valentine, are you into lookin' for treasure?" Davis asked. "We could make a game of it."

Valentine smiled. "I'm into making money. If searching for treasure is the way to make that happen, then I'm happy to play."

Davis turned to Humber. "What about you?"

He grinned. "Oh, I'm definitely in."

"Ladies? Would any of you like to join us in this game? That would make it infinitely more interestin'."

"I think I'll pass," Tatum offered. "Not really my cup of tea."

Remy nodded. "I think I'll sit it out as well."

"Kat? You look like a woman up for adventure." Fisher leaned towards her and put a hand on her knee. "Would you like to join us in the game? I can guarantee it will be fun."

Rush fisted his hands on his thigh. Damn Fisher for just saying Kat's name let alone touching her. "Gentlemen, perhaps I should remind you that if the treasure does exist, which is a big if, after all it's been locked away for hundreds of years, but if you find it, it belongs to the Society. You don't get to keep it."

"Of course," Davis agreed with a smile that didn't reach his eyes.

Rush knew if they, by some miracle, found the treasure, they would keep it for themselves.

"Well," Rush said as he pushed back his chair, "we must get moving." He looked at Kat and she hopped up as well. "The ladies and I are having dinner. I would invite you gents to join us but it's really just an information session about the island and some of the rules of the society. I'm sure you all have better things to do. Good luck with your treasure hunt."

Remy, Tatum, and Kat immediately rose, murmured their goodbyes, and followed Rush across the pool area toward a stone path.

"Rush, darling, I cannot thank you enough for bailing us out," Tatum said. "Being with that crowd is like swimming with sharks. You know it's just a matter of time before you get bitten."

"Not a problem, Tatum. Glad to be of service. I would

suggest to all of you that those gentlemen should be avoided. They are not..."

"The nicest of people?" Remy asked.

Rush hesitated and then nodded. "Yes. I was going to say something stronger but yes. I don't know what game they want to play regarding the treasure, but consider yourselves warned that Archer Gray is deadly serious about enforcing the rules around that. If one of you discovered it, it would all go to the Society and any attempt to take some of it for yourselves would put you in a very dangerous situation."

"Dealing with *that* group would put us in a dangerous situation, whether we found the treasure or not." Tatum linked her arm through Remy's. "Remy and I have some catching up to do so I think we'll pass on your dinner invitation, Rush." He nodded and she turned to Kat. "I would love to hang out tomorrow. My cabin is number 42. Call me when you get up and we'll plan something. Remy, if you're free, join us."

Remy agreed, "Sounds good."

"Thanks. I'd love to hang out. It was nice to meet you both," Kat added.

The two ladies headed off down the path.

Rush turned to Kat. "How about it? Are you free for dinner?"

Her eyes widened. "Um…sure. I just need to change."

She'd been surprised by his offer. A small warning bell went off in his head. What was she up to? He ran his gaze over her body. She looked damned fine to him. Changing wasn't necessary unless it was to get out of those clothes and stay naked. "I think you look amazing." He wanted to say sexy as hell and follow it up with an invitation to go to his cabin, but she was work. He had to earn her trust but she was still the enemy.

"Um," she mumbled as color rushed to her cheeks. "I feel a little underdressed for dinner."

"Fair enough. Why don't you go home to change and meet me on the beach out in front of the main dining building? We'll have dinner and watch the sunset."

She smiled up at him. "That sounds…wonderful. See you in about thirty minutes?"

He touched her cheek with his knuckles. "Thirty minutes." He leaned in. "Don't keep me waiting," he whispered in her ear and pressed a kiss to her cheek.

She nodded and then turned on her heel and strode off down the path. Yeah, he did admire the view as he watched her retreat.

"I don't blame you one bit," Fisher said as he came to a stop beside Rush.

Rush had to resist the urge to walk away without acknowledging the man. Calling Fisher scummy was accurate. And maybe not fair to pond scum. "I wasn't joking about the whole treasure thing, Fisher. You do not want to mess around with that."

He smirked. "Now Rush, it's just a little game. What's the harm in that? It will keep the boys happy. You're welcome to join us for dinner as we discuss the rules."

"I'm good, thanks. Just be warned, Fisher. I'm keeping a close eye. Be very careful."

The other man started walking down the path. "Always am, Rush. I always am."

Rush went in the other direction, as much to get well away from Fisher as anything else. He really needed to go back to the Hub and check in with Danton. The data he was pulling was more than a little alarming. Way too many cameras had been repositioned. The pattern, though, was confusing. Cameras in the south part of the island were off kilter as were others around the hospital in the center of the island. He had to figure it out and fast. Whatever the hell was going on, it wasn't good.

As he walked in the direction of the Hub, the memory of a previous op rose in his mind. The smell of honeysuckle in the air. The sound of the crickets. It was a warm night in New Orleans. When he, Sterling, and Archer entered the upscale mansion in the Garden District, they'd had no idea what they were walking into. Or at least he hadn't. Archer probably had an inkling, which is why they were there.

Fisher had used his Society membership and contacts to get some items delivered to that address several times, according to Archer, but he didn't elaborate on what those things were. It wasn't necessarily against regulations, but it could be considered being on the razor's edge. If the delivery raised eyebrows, questions would be asked and then the Society could be mentioned. Usually, people only took delivery of things from the Society to known addresses for that reason. This address was an unknown, and Archer hadn't liked it.

It had turned out that the mansion was rented in a bogus company name and the items in question were sex toys and torture devices. Had he known that going in, Rush wouldn't have hesitated to kill Fisher on sight. Probably why Archer kept him in the dark.

They'd entered the house in stealth mode. Making no sound, alerting no one. Rush's stomach churned at the memory. He'd quietly opened the door to what should have been a parlor and froze. There were three girls inside, chained to the ceiling. They couldn't have been more than twelve or thirteen although it was hard to tell. One girl looked to be of Korean descent and the other two were white. Naked, battered and bruised, as Rush entered they raised their heads and stared at him not uttering a sound. Bile had risen in his throat just like it was now.

"What?" Archer had demanded in a harsh whisper.

Rush opened the door wider.

Archer and Sterling entered and then swore. "Sterling, set them free." Archer whirled and gestured to Rush. "With me."

They went up the stairs and found Fisher and his cronies, men Rush didn't know, naked drinking cocktails while two young girls of far Asian descent were doing some kind of dance, their naked bodies gyrating to the club music. His gut churned and he'd wanted to puke. He raised his gun, his finger on the trigger but Archer reached out and pushed the gun down.

"Fisher," he'd growled. "This is over." It was all he said.

"You can't…" Fisher started to bluster but Archer gave him a steely-eyed look that shut him up instantly. One of his friends wasn't so smart.

"Who the fuck are you? You've got no business here. Get the fuck out!" The naked heavy-set man demanded. "I'll have you thrown out." He reached for his pants. "You're trespassing. This is my house. You can't just waltz in here and tell me what to do." He shifted his pants to the side to reveal a handgun underneath. Rush shot him between the eyes before he'd managed to pick up the weapon.

"Anyone else?" Rush asked.

The two other men shook their heads, while Fisher just glared.

Rush couldn't believe he hadn't been allowed to kill the rest of the assholes but Archer shook his head. Against the Society rules. *Fuck the rules*.

He'd demanded the keys to the chains from the shorter, skinnier man, who'd quickly grabbed a keyring full of keys off a dresser and gave it to Rush. After freeing the girls, he handed them blankets from the bed to cover themselves. He led them downstairs where Sterling appeared with five other girls in tow. All wrapped in blankets.

Seven girls in that hellhole and who knew how many more there were in other houses across the world? Just the thought made his blood boil. Rush had helped get the girls clothes and brought them in the back way to one of the Societies medical clinics. Archer had him put them on a jet and he sent them back to wherever they'd come from, each with a large duffel bag full of cash. It would never make up for what had happened to them, but it was the best they could do.

That wasn't strictly true. Archer could've let Rush kill Fisher and his friends. Rush had wanted to snap Fisher's neck. Still did, to be honest. Maybe whatever was going on here on the island involved Fisher. If so, he'd make sure the man went down for it. There was no need for scum like him to survive.

Rush had in the end avoided the Hub and wandered aimlessly through the paths trying to walk off his anger, but he'd just gotten more upset. He headed to the restaurant. He didn't want to be late for his date with Kat. Just the thought of dinner with her had a calming effect. Although, he needed to not think about it as a date. Job one was to find out what she was doing here and why she was lying. But he knew, knew implicitly whatever it was, it wouldn't be anywhere near the level of Fisher's shit. The only problem with being a monster hunter was that sometimes he wasn't allowed to kill his prey.

He entered the dining room and went back into the kitchen. Off the kitchen was the head concierge's office. Rush knocked on an open door and entered to see the man he needed sitting behind the desk. "Luke, I need some help."

The tall man looked up from his computer. "Of course, sir. What can I do for you?"

Ten minutes later, Rush was sitting at a table for two on a secluded part of the beach away from the restaurant. A privacy hedge surrounded the area on three sides, leaving just the beach side open. There was a bottle of Champagne chilling. It was a romantic table for two and two only. No one else could see them unless they came from the beach. Rush was looking forward to a bit of alone time with Kat. More than he should be. *Work, only.*

"Am I late?" Kat asked in a breathless voice.

He looked up and swore under his breath. She was stunning. Her black dress was held by thin straps covering her bare shoulders. The lacy material was fitted and stopped mid-thigh. Her auburn hair hung loose down her back, and she was carrying a pair of black high heeled shoes in her hand.

He stood. "Definitely worth the wait." He had gotten Luke to get one of his guys to bring him a fresh light blue button-down that he wore along with his jeans. "But now I feel underdressed."

She smiled. "You look good. Not underdressed at all." Moving closer to him, she lifted on her toes and gave him a peck on the cheek.

Fighting the surge of desire in his blood he pulled out her chair. As she sat her spicy, flowery scent surrounded him. *Much like her.*

Business. Just business, he reminded himself tersely. *Yeah right. Not in that dress.* He took his seat and offered her Champagne by holding out the bottle.

"Yes, please."

He poured for both of them and they clicked glasses. "To an interesting evening," he said.

She smiled and took a sip. "Thank you again for rescuing me earlier. I wasn't sure how I was going to politely excuse myself from dinner."

He set his glass down with a bit of a clunk. "When it comes to Fisher, you don't need to be polite."

"Sounds like there's a story there."

"Yes," he acknowledged, "and it's not a pretty one." The

thought of Kat being anywhere near Fisher... "Steer clear of that group, Kat. You'll be in over your head."

She hesitated but then nodded. "The talk of the treasure was interesting though. Do you really think it's still on the island?"

He studied her for a moment. Could that be what this was all about? Could she be a whacked-out treasure hunter? "It's possible, I suppose. But as I said, if it's here it belongs to the Society and Archer won't take kindly to anyone messing with it."

She took a sip of her champagne. "So how did you come to work for the Society?"

Rush sighed. He wasn't in the mood for making small talk. What he wanted was to know what she was doing here. Was there any kind of reasonable explanation for her lies? Anything that would clear her of wrongdoing? He hoped there was, even though for the life of him, he couldn't come up with anything.

"I knew someone who was already involved, and they asked if I would like a job here as well. It seemed like a great opportunity, so I took it." No, small talk wasn't what he had in mind. Taking that dress off Kat and making her scream his name as she came, was more like it but business and personal don't mix. *Remember Ronnie.*

"What about you? Why are you here really Kat? Why join the society?"

"Like I said before, I just needed a break." She immediately took a sip of Champagne and avoided his gaze. She'd never be a poker player. *Lies, lies, and more lies.* He hated lies. And liars. But she was so damn sexy, he'd be willing to forgive that fault. Only for her, though.

The waiter came around the corner and placed two seafood salads on the table. Once he disappeared, Rush leaned forward. "I asked the chef to prepare something for us based on your food preferences. I hope that was okay."

She glanced up at him, her eyes large. "That's more than okay. It was very thoughtful. I appreciate it." She took a sip of her sparkling wine. "I know it sounds crazy but sometimes I get tired of making decisions. Even something as small as choosing what to have for dinner becomes a monumental task."

"Why is that do you think?" he asked as he picked up his fork.

"Burnout, I guess. I make decisions all day long at the hospital, directing funds, deciding on programs to keep or cut, deciding on if we should paint the walls in the children's wing bright and cheery colors or soothing muted tones, going to meetings and having to decide between two factions as to what to do with a specific donation." She shrugged. "It gets a bit much sometimes. I always feel like I'm giving with one hand and taking with the other." She took a bite of her salad.

"Sounds like your job is very stressful."

"It can be. To be honest, I've been thinking about making a change for a while. Being around sick people all the time is depressing no matter how much I try to see the positive. Even though I'm in administration, I'm on the floors most days, attending meetings, chatting with other staff. It rubs off. And I think we're all burnt out from what's been going on in the world lately. There just doesn't seem to be any respite."

"You need a break. It's a good thing you're here."

"Yes, I guess so."

She didn't sound sure. He tipped his head. "You don't sound convinced."

She finished her bite of salad and then swallowed. "Still stressed, I guess. Takes a while to calm down."

Again, she didn't meet his eyes. *Another lie.* "Maybe I can help you relax."

Glancing up at him she smiled but then bent once again to eat her salad. Rush made a decision. "Stand up."

"What?"

"Come on, stand up."

She did as she was told, placing her napkin on the table. He grabbed her hand and pulled her over so she was standing in front of him staring out over the water. "Now," he said softly, "what do you see?"

"The sky is a beautiful shade of pink," she observed.

"Agreed but what about the sun?" He inhaled her scent, and blood rushed below his belt. He wrapped his arms around her waist. It was a mistake to get this close to her, but he was beyond caring.

"It's almost gone." Her voice sounded breathy.

"Yes. Now when it disappears, all your problems will be gone with it. You can think about them all again tomorrow when the sun comes back up. But just for now…for tonight…give yourself one evening without worry. One evening to relax and enjoy yourself. One evening to be free."

She let out a breath. "I…I would feel guilty."

"Kat," he breathed above her ear, "let yourself go even if it's just for one night. Everyone deserves one night of freedom from the stress and worries in their life." God knew he needed a night like that, in fact, he needed a lot of them. The sun was almost gone now.

She suddenly turned around, rose on her tiptoes, and brushed his mouth with a kiss. He tightened his arms around her and picked her up as he kissed her back, pushing his tongue between her lips, tasting her mouth. Their tongues danced as she wrapped her arms around his neck. Her soft curves against his hard planes sent more blood to his cock. He deepened the kiss, running his hands over her ass and hugged her closer to his body. She arched up against him in response.

"Uh hmm."

Someone cleared their throat, and he broke off the kiss and put Kat back on the ground.

"May I take the plates?" the waiter asked.

"Yes, thanks." Rush waited until the server was gone before helping Kat back to her seat. It was a damn good thing the waiter had come along or he and Kat would've been having sex on the beach right now.

Work. She was supposed to be work but those damn expressive green eyes were sucking him in. If he wasn't careful, Kat Rollings would be the death of him.

CHAPTER NINE

Kat couldn't believe she'd kissed him. Stupid. She was here to find her brother. It was all that talk of letting her worries set with the sun, of taking one night off from worrying, from the terror of losing her brother, of being alone. She'd fallen for it, mostly because she really needed a break. She spent her life worrying about everyone around her. Her father, who was always doing shady things and dragging the whole family down with him. Her mother, who loved her father and followed him willingly, no matter what it cost her. Her brother, who seemed to be taking after her dad.

She'd been the family worrier growing up until she'd said fuck it and went on with her own life. The four years at university had been bliss. Then, two days before graduation, her parents died in a diving accident, crashing her back into reality. The accident had been avoidable, and somehow her fault. Oh, she knew it was stupid to lay blame on herself, but if she hadn't given up worrying about them, she would've been there, monitored the situation, told them they couldn't dive because conditions were deteriorating. Instead, she'd been partying half a world away. That was ten years ago and the day they'd put her parents in the ground she'd gone back to worrying.

She and Rush had finished dinner chatting about all kinds of things, but Kat made sure to not share like she had before. Her nerves were jangling. He'd gotten under her skin so quickly. No one had been able to do that before. She almost didn't want to finish dinner. She wanted to run before she made an even bigger mistake. There was something about this man that made her want to tell him everything, confess her sins, ask for forgiveness and more, ask for help. She felt safe with him, and that had led her to letting her guard down. She couldn't do that again. It was too dangerous.

Dinner was over. The area where they ate was lit by tiki lamps and somehow music floated on the air. Rush took her hand and pulled her to her feet. "Dance with me?"

She wanted to say yes. To be held in his arms, feeling like nothing could hurt her, like it would all be okay. Instead, she knew she had to say no and leave. This wasn't going to get her anywhere good. She needed to find Danny and then get the hell off the island.

"I—"

A high-pitched sound, like a scream, pierced the air. The hair on her arms stood on end.

"What the hell was that?"

"I don't know but I'm going to find out. Stay here." He was gone before she could argue with him.

She waited as the sun sank fully into the sea. The sky was pitch dark now. Clouds had moved in, covering the moon and the light of the tiki lamps seemed dimmer than before. Five minutes passed, then ten. She wrapped her arms around herself.

One of the tiki lamps suddenly went out leaving only one small flame to light the space. Her heart rate ticked up.

Perhaps she didn't need to wait. She could head back to her cabin. Safer there anyway. She took one step forward and the other tiki lamp went out. She was surrounded by inky blackness. Her eyes needed a moment to adjust when suddenly someone crashed into her and hit her on the head. She cried out as she dropped to her knees. Whoever it was, took off down the beach.

Kat went down on all fours for a moment and tried to catch her breath. Her heart was hammering against her ribs and the pain in her head dimmed her vision. She got to her feet slowly and checked her head gingerly with her fingers.

No blood but there was a bump the size of a bird's egg back there. There was no way she was waiting now. Grabbing her shoes and she headed back down the beach toward the stairs to the dining area.

Twenty feet from the stairs, a man detached himself from the shadows and started down the beach. Reason said to ignore him and go up the stairs but there was something about him that was familiar. His walk. Was it her brother? He was wearing a groundskeeper's uniform. She wanted to call his name but knew that wouldn't be a good idea just in case. Instead, she ran to try and catch up. The pain in her head pulsed aggressively.

The man suddenly went left into the foliage. She ran to where he disappeared, but no one was there. Just a very small break in the hedge. She bit her lip, glanced around and then pushed through. She emerged on a narrow path. She swore when her feet came down on the path. It wasn't large flat stones like the main paths, or even the smooth pebbles of some of the smaller ones. It was roots and branches with lots of leaves and twigs. There was no way she could go forward. Her feet would be cut to shreds. Besides, she couldn't see anything. The branches overhead blocked out what little light the cloud-shrouded stars might have provided. She needed better shoes and something on her legs not to mention a flashlight.

Turning back, she came out onto the beach again. Making a mental note of where the path was, she headed for the dining area. She went up the stairs, put on her shoes and headed back to her cabin.

Her headache was getting worse. She could just take aspirin and go to bed…or she could go to the hospital. This could be her chance to get inside. There was no way she was going to find the man on the path tonight. If it was her brother then he was free roaming the island and that was probably a good thing, wasn't it? But if it wasn't her brother then this was her chance to see if she could find out what was what at the hospital.

She put on jeans and a black tank top and then made her way to the hospital entrance. The doors slid open and she approached the counter. A young woman with dark hair and a friendly smile sat behind it. "May I help you?" Her big brown eyes gave Kat the once over as if looking for any injuries.

"Um, I was wondering if someone could take a look at my head? I bumped it and I have a massive headache. I want to be sure I don't have a concussion or something more serious."

An immediate look of concern filled her face. "Of course. Your name?"

"Kat Sanders."

"Ms. Sanders, Dmitry will take you to an exam room."

She turned. A young blond man stood behind her with a wheelchair. She hadn't heard him come up. That was sort of freaky. It didn't help that it was after midnight and the hospital was quiet and dark. They had some sort of mood lighting going on and it wasn't helping the creep factor.

"Thanks, but I don't think I— "

"It's policy," the nurse said with a smile.

"I see." She sat down and Dmitry wheeled her through a set of double doors into the emergency area, which was much better lit. Everything looked state-of-the-art, the place much more like a major city hospital than a small island one. There was a massive nurse's station shaped like a horseshoe with room for at least eight to ten people to work. Only two people sat there, a man and a woman. Both were looking down so she could only see the tops of their heads.

Dmitry wheeled her into the second room on the left. He helped her out of the chair and then onto the bed. The room was a decent size and had all the usual monitors and equipment that she'd come to expect in a hospital room and they were all state of the art. She couldn't help but be impressed. Nothing but the best for the Society it seemed.

"The doctor will be in shortly." Dmitry smiled and then left.

A second later, the guy from the nurse's station walked in. He was on the short side of average and built like a fire hydrant. His light-blue scrub top pulled tight across his chest. He offered her a smile. "I'm Joe. I'm going to get your vitals and then the doctor will be right in."

"Okay." She was starting to have second thoughts about all this. Her head was banging and all she really wanted to do was sleep."

Joe stuck a pulse oximeter on her finger and then took her blood pressure. He gave her yet another smile when he was finished. "You're all good. The doctor will be in shortly." Then he disappeared out of the room.

What was it with all the smiles around here? It was way too late, or early for that matter, to be that friendly and happy. It was after midnight. And the smiles didn't feel genuine at all, more sinister horror movie than caring hospital staff.

She stayed on the bed and contemplated how she was going to get to poke around the hospital. If she tried now, for sure the doctor would realize she was missing. Better to wait until the doctor was finished. Her nerves fluttered when she realized the doctor on call tonight could be the dreaded Kyla. How many doctors could they possibly have on the island? Chances were high it would be her. *Ugh.* Was it too late to leave? Having Kyla check her over was the stuff of nightmares.

"Hello there, Ms... Oh! Hello again," Bear greeted her.

"Dr...." She suddenly realized she didn't know his last name.

"Walton, but please call me Bear. So"—he glanced at her chart as he approached the bed—"what happened?"

Kat wanted to be anywhere but there. She noticed how nice Bear was being even as she scrambled to think of a good story to tell him, instead of telling him the truth. The tension of the whole ordeal was causing a brain fog and nothing plausible was coming to mind. Letting out a long sigh, she finally just told him what had actually happened. "I was on the beach having a late dinner when the tiki lamps went out and someone crashed into me, hitting me on the head with something. Then they took off."

Bear frowned. "Did you report this to whoever is staffing the desk at this hour?"

"No, I really didn't want to cause a fuss."

"Security should be informed."

"No." She shook her head and winced at the sudden movement. "Really. The last thing I want to do is make a huge stink out of this. Chances are good someone was drunk and they crashed into me. I probably got nailed with their bottle of booze or something. I just want to be sure I don't have anything more than a headache."

He narrowed his eyes but nodded.

Bear checked the bump on her head and then asked her some questions while shining a penlight into her eyes. Satisfied with her answers, he declared that she might have a slight concussion at worst and most likely she just had a headache. He gave her ice for the bump and some ibuprofen for the headache. "You can stay here as long as you want. If it would make you feel better, you can stay the night."

"I don't think that's necessary."

"Okay then. I'll sign your paperwork and you can go whenever you want. But Kat"—he put his hand on her arm—"please come back if it gets worse. And be careful. If anything else happens, please tell Peter. You shouldn't have to put up with this type of thing."

"Thanks, Doc. I will," she assured him.

He walked out of the room, and she sat quietly for a moment, collecting her thoughts. If she did say she changed her mind and wanted to spend the night then she might have a little bit more time to explore. On the other hand, she would be on the nurses' radar and they would check on her all the time. It was probably better if she just did a quick search and see what she could turn up. She wanted to get down that locked hallway.

Decision made, she slipped off the bed and left the room. Joe was at the desk. She smiled at him and asked him where the restroom was. He pointed around the corner. It was down that hallway. *Yes!*

She followed his directions and then blew right past the restroom. Continuing down the hallway, she came to the nurses' station and recognized it immediately as the one she'd seen earlier. Turning left she sped to the end of the hallway and then turned right.

Elation bounded through her. The doors that had been locked earlier were now standing open. The hallway was dimly lit. She moved forward carefully, being as quiet as possible. It looked like any other hallway in the hospital. Rooms on both sides. The first couple of doors were closed, but then the next two, one on either side, were both open.

The beeping of an electronic vital signs monitor hit her ears and she decided to take the risk and go close to one of the doorways. She quickly peeked in but froze. A patient lay on the bed, more tubes and IVs sticking out of him than ever imaginable. One machine was breathing for him, and another was keeping track of his heart rate.

Kat swallowed. She recognized this hallway for what it was; The palliative care unit. The hallway where the terminally ill came to die. Some people went into hospice, some chose to die at home, but some put their loved ones in charge. Those unfortunate souls often lingered for ages while their families came to terms with their loss.

She backed away slowly and glanced down the hallway. The rest of the doors were closed, and the lights were off. Only two residents at the moment then. *Thank God for that.* She turned around, heading back the way she'd come. She moved as quickly as she could, figuring Joe would come looking for her at any moment.

Rounding the corner, she'd just started down the final hallway when Joe appeared from around the corner. "I thought we'd lost you there for a minute," he said.

"I'm sorry. I came out of the bathroom and turned the wrong way. Took me a minute to figure it out."

"Okay. If you're ready to go, Dmitry will give you a lift to the door."

She glanced behind her to see if he'd snuck up on her again but he was nowhere in sight.

Joe chuckled. "I know. It's kind of freaky how he appears and disappears without making a sound."

"I'm glad it's not just me who noticed."

They rounded the corner together and found Dmitry

leaning against the nurses' station. Her knees were wobbly, so she eased down into the chair. He wheeled her out through the lobby and back onto the path where she'd entered. She thanked him and started the trek back to her cabin.

It had been a long day and an even longer night. Her shoulders drooped and her gait was slow. This whole thing had left her feeling drained and more than a bit pissed off. She desperately wanted to go home and forget all about the Society with all its' weirdness. And she wanted to throttle her brother for dragging her into this mess.

Did someone try and kill her tonight because they'd discovered she'd lied to them? Or was it like she'd told the doctor, probably some drunk? It could have been aliens for all she knew. She shivered. At least her search of the hospital hadn't been a total bust. She now knew what was down that hallway. Since the building wasn't that big, it could still be possible her brother was there. But not probable. More likely she'd been right, and it had been Danny disappearing down that path right before she'd gotten injured. All she had to do now was track him down. So much easier said than done.

CHAPTER TEN

The day had dawned bright and cheery once more but Kat sure as heck wasn't feeling it. Traces of the headache lingered, but the pain had lessened from the defcon five level it had been last night. She'd met Remy and Tatum for breakfast, as agreed, but begged off spending the day with them, claiming her head was hurting too much. It wasn't a lie.

Reality was, she was getting nowhere fast in the search for her brother. The only possible clue she had was the guy disappearing down that path last night. She wondered where that path led. She would have to do a stakeout tonight. There was no way around it.

She made coffee, grabbed her mug, and took it out to her deck. Sitting in a glider, she stared out at the Caribbean Sea as she got a bit more caffeine into her.

"Good morning, Kat," a voice said.

She smiled at Peter. "Hi there yourself. How are you today?"

He came to a stop by her steps. "Feeling a bit better today. Got some much-needed rest last night."

"Glad to hear it." That made one of them.

"I hear you weren't so lucky."

"Um…" She cocked her head in confusion. "What? I'm not sure…"

He leaned on the railing. "Kat there's not much that happens on this island without me knowing about it. I'm so sorry someone hit you last night. You should've reported it."

Talk about feeling like a small child being called to the principal's office. "I'm sorry. I didn't want to be a nuisance or cause any trouble." Both were true.

"You can't cause any trouble, Kat. It's my job to help the members by knowing what's going on. I checked the security cameras but I didn't see anything. Whoever it was got away. Are you okay?"

She nodded. "I'm fine. Slight headache, but that's it. I appreciate your concern though."

"All right, but in the future if anything out of the ordinary happens, please let me know."

"I will," she agreed, eager to get him on his way.

"Have a great day," Peter offered and then started down the path again.

It hit her as he disappeared from sight, that she had no clue what the phone number was to reach Peter. She gave a mental shrug and had taken a sip of her coffee when one of the island staff came up her steps. *What the hell?* It was like Grand Central today.

"Can I help you?" she inquired.

"I have a message for you, ma'am," the young man said as he handed her an envelope.

"Thank you." She opened the envelope and pulled out the card. Rush. He was working today, but if she was free tomorrow, he'd love to show her the lagoon.

She looked up at the messenger. He seemed to be waiting for a response. He wasn't waiting for a tip because that was strictly forbidden at any Society location. She'd read it in the handbook last night when she couldn't sleep. "Please tell him that's fine."

The boy nodded and then left her porch and hurried down the path.

She sipped her coffee and contemplated what she was going to do for the day. Have a nap, she decided. The ache in her head had diminished, but this morning's coffee wasn't working its magic. A nap seemed like the best option. Maybe something would come to her in her sleep. At this point she was willing to try anything.

Kat pulled her hair up in a bun and glanced at the deep green scrunchie she had in her hand. Her brother had given the hair tie to her, saying it was the same color as her eyes. Suddenly she hated the idea of using it. If she lost it, she would be devastated. Stupid, but there it was. She secured her hair using a few extra pins and left the hair tie on the counter.

She'd laid down for a nap, but hadn't been able to relax enough to actually sleep. Finally giving up, she'd gone to the pool. There, the time spent in small talk and pleasantries moved at the pace of a snail. And she hadn't learned anything useful, except maybe she needed to up her sunscreen to a higher SPF. Giving up, she'd returned to her room mid-afternoon and managed to nap successfully.

Now it was just after eleven. She figured she had about twenty minutes before it would be the same time last night she saw the man who looked like her brother.

Cameras were a big worry. She hadn't seen any as she'd wandered around the island over the last few days. And she'd been looking. Based on all the other security features, the retinal and handprint scanners, it stood to reason the Society would have surveillance equipment. On the other hand, they were big on maintaining people's privacy so maybe they only had them in certain areas. At least that's what she was going with. She hadn't seen any on the beach when she was by the hidden path last night, although it would make sense if they had them looking out at the water to make sure no one came onto the island without them knowing.

And they probably had them around the public spaces like certain pools and the restaurants, but she didn't think they would have them on every path or around the outbuildings. Either way, the possible presence of cameras was a risk she was willing to take. She was almost positive the man who disappeared into the path was her brother. Maybe it was wishful thinking, but she trusted her instincts.

Stepping back, she took one last look in the mirror. She was wearing dark jeans and a black short-sleeved T-shirt. There was a nice breeze off the ocean. A storm was coming, or so Benny, the guy at the main pool, had told her earlier today. Made sense. It was summer in the Caribbean. It was supposed to rain.

She tied her hair in a high ponytail and pinned the loose hairs at the nape of her nape, then checked the mirror one last time. "You can do this," she repeated the mantra that had become second nature to her.

The pep talk didn't make her feel any better but she had no choice. She had to go. Stepping out onto her veranda, she listened for a moment. Only the sounds of the waves were there, keeping her company. She locked her door and then headed down the path toward the restaurant and the beach beyond.

It didn't take long to get to the beach. She clung to the shadows close to the hedge and made her way along until she found the opening she'd seen last night. Then she moved and took up a position in the shadows. She would give him some time to show up. Her brother was notoriously late for things.

Thirty minutes later, she was done waiting. Taking a deep breath, she pushed through the hole. This time, with sneakers on her feet, and jeans covering her legs, the going was much easier. From her back pocket, she withdrew the pen light she'd brought with her to the island, turned it on and kept the beam pointed downwards.

Her nerves were tripping like playing cards clipped to bike tires, and she hadn't done anything yet. She hated this type of stuff. *Danny, please be okay.* She moved as quickly and quietly along the path as possible. Then, suddenly, it ended at another hedge with a small break in it. She listened but heard nothing other than the sound of night creatures, cicadas, crickets, and the occasional sound that she couldn't identify. She didn't like to dwell on what creature was making it.

She pushed through the hedge and found herself on a wide pebbled path She peered into the inky blackness to her right. Flicking up her penlight, she quickly noticed a shed painted a dark color. Glancing left, the path curved, so there was only the bordering hedge along the path.

She turned to the right, and crept quietly closer to the shed, trying to visualize where this would be on the map. Nothing rang a bell. No large shed had been marked. *Note to self*, things on the map weren't to scale. Just another thing to make finding her brother more difficult.

The shed was painted a deep camouflage-green and faded into the foliage. Heaven forbid this place stood out. Society members might be offended. Scanning the roofline of the shed, she didn't see any cameras. Definitely a good sign. She peeked around the side and realized there were no windows.

The door on the other hand was going to be more of an issue. It was locked. She pulled out a set of lock picks. In one of her wilder moments, she'd bought the set thinking she'd learn all about lock picking and be aces at it. *Yeah, no.* Much harder than it looks in the movies. She blamed her father for even trying to learn. Every once in a while she did something that was like him and then she regretted it. Lock picking was the least of it. She put the penlight in her mouth…like a true professional…and picked up the padlock. Seven minutes later the lock popped open. Yeah, she might not win any competitions, but she'd gotten it done.

She took the penlight out of her mouth and opened the door. It was pitch dark inside. She let out a long sigh. Not that she'd thought her brother would be sitting in here waiting for her but still, she'd hoped he would be here, that she wasn't imagining things.

She took a step and immediately hit something with her foot. It made a metallic sound, and her heart rate accelerated. Cursing, she shone the penlight on the ground, illuminating a discarded trowel. She was tempted to move it but doing so might reveal someone had been there.

The penlight beam wasn't all that strong so it didn't reach the back wall but what it did show her was the shed was one large room and her brother wasn't in it.

She cursed silently. If this was what the sheds were like, then she could take all the other maintenance buildings off her list. They weren't going to keep her brother in a place like this. And he wouldn't stay in one because there would be too much foot traffic to stay hidden. No. Her brother had either found a bolt-hole somewhere on the island, or whoever was after the treasure was holding him some place and were using his supposed knowledge of treasure hunting to try and find it.

She took a few steps further into the shed and shone the penlight around. Nothing really stood out to her as she moved the beam slowly over the contents. Gardening equipment. Lawnmowers, hoses… Except one of the hoses moved.

She quickly put the light back on the moving hose. "Holy shit!" It was a long snake, and it was moving in her direction.

Kat turned tail and ran for the door. She bolted out and then closed the door behind her. As she tried to reengage the lock, she fumbled, her hands shaking too much, and she dropped it.

That's when she noticed the hole in the bottom of the door about the size of a fist. Big enough for a snake to get through. She snatched the lock off the ground, snapped it in place and hustled back to the path, tripping over some of the loose stones.

"I told you before, I don't have any money." The angry voice was one she'd heard before, in the outdoor shower. Humber. Why were these people all hiding in bushes to have conversations? Okay, this time she was the one hiding, but still. Couldn't people go inside to talk?

"Well, get some," a second voice hissed. It was a woman but not the same one she'd heard before.

He snorted. "How do you propose I do that?"

"I don't know but you need to be able to pay your bill. No one will take you seriously otherwise."

"You don't think I know that?" he demanded. "But the money is gone. The market—"

"I don't give a fuck about the market. You promised you would back me for the job. I am counting on you." The woman sounded pissed all the way off.

"Everyone is counting on me, including my wife, and guess what? I still don't have the money. So you can do what you want but I can't help you anymore. As a matter of fact, I want the jewelry back."

There was a yelp and then a gasp. She was pretty sure it was Humber that gasped. The woman snarled, "That jewelry is mine. Don't even think about trying to get it back or I'll make sure you're ruined not just with your family but all over the news."

There was another grunt and then the sound of footsteps on gravel. The hedge next to her moved. Kat turned and moved as quietly as she could back towards the shed. There was a break in the hedge on her left. It was another path, lined with soil not stones.

She darted through the hedge and kept moving as quickly as she dared without the penlight. The sound of footsteps on the gravel faded behind her. She kept moving forward thinking the path was bound to cross the main path at some point but it seemed endless. Where the hell was she?

Suddenly, the hum of air conditioning units broke the still night. She must have walked across the island again and was coming up behind the cabins on her side. She moved cautiously, hoping she wasn't going to burst out into some member's backyard or worse their outdoor shower.

The end of the path was in front of her. Moving very slowly, she peered through the foliage. Wait. That wasn't a cabin. Kat stopped moving and looked closer. Directly in front of her was a large gray wall. It was the side of a building. Sleek looking, definitely a modern design that didn't fit into the decor of the other buildings on the island at all. She moved slightly closer to the building hoping to see more but there were too many bushes.

The building was dark with no windows and she was tempted to step out on the other path that surrounded it. She glanced around looking for cameras. This seemed like a building they'd want to keep an eye on. Also, it could be a holding place for her brother. Or a portal to another dimension. With the Lock and Key Society, anything was possible.

The narrow path between the building and the bushes didn't offer her any clues as to the building's purpose and she wasn't about to risk getting caught. But one thing was for certain, this building wasn't on the map anywhere.

Turning, she headed back in the direction she'd come but much more slowly. She wasn't sure how far she'd come or where she was exactly so taking her time seemed important. As she retraced her steps, she debated turning on the flashlight. She'd come through so fast in the dark that it hadn't seemed so bad but now, going slowly she was getting a bit freaked out. Too many sounds that she didn't recognize and then there was the snake. It wasn't like there would be just one.

She swore softly as she stumbled in the dark. A root maybe? She glanced around as her eyes adjusted to the light from the break in the trees overhead. There on the left side of the path was an opening. It was a path with flat stones, so it was a main path. *Yes!*

She listened but didn't hear anything. Pushing through the hedge she came out on the main path. She turned and started walking.

"Where the hell did you come from?"

Rush was coming towards her but she hadn't heard any footsteps on the stones. "Um, sorry?" Her voice was three octaves higher than normal.

He stopped directly in front of her. "I didn't see you there a second ago. Where did you come from?"

She giggled. "It must be the dark clothes. I guess I kind of blend. Couldn't sleep, I thought I'd take a walk. I figured if I stuck to the main paths I'd be safe enough. You know how it is." She was rambling and needed to shut up. "What are you doing out here?"

He cocked an eyebrow like he wasn't buying her story but finally said, "I was dealing with an issue."

"Did you find the person who screamed last night?" She surreptitiously wiped her sweaty palms on her jeans.

"Not exactly. It's complicated," he said.

"Oh, well, I don't want to keep you. I'm sure you've had a long day."

She whirled around and immediately regretted it. Sucking in a breath, she put her hand to her head.

Rush reached out and touched her arm. "What is it? Are you okay?"

She tried to ignore the zing his touch sent through her. "Yeah. My head is still just a bit sore from last night."

His forehead furrowed. "Last night?"

She wanted to bite her tongue in two. Stupid. She should've kept her mouth shut. "Yeah, well I…" Again she couldn't come up with a suitable lie, not to mention Peter knew so it was likely Rush would find out sooner or later. So, Kat told him the truth about what happened.

He swore. "Are you sure you're okay? I'm so sorry I wasn't there to protect you."

She waved him off. "I'm sure it was probably some drunk guy. Plus, you had to help whoever was screaming."

He grimaced. "Truthfully, it wasn't a person. It was a box."

"I'm sorry?"

"It was a toy with an infrared beam. If the beam was broken, the toy let out a scream. Someone was being a jackass and scaring people."

Her stomach tightened. She knew exactly what he was talking about. Her brother used to have one and frequently used it to scare her. *Danny was here.* She let out a breath and her shoulders sagged.

"Kat, are you sure you're alright?" Rush put his arm around her waist. "I'll walk you back to your cabin just to be on the safe side. Do you want to go to the hospital?"

"I went last night. I'm fine." But his arm felt good around her and she wasn't going to turn down his help to get back to her cabin. She wasn't feeling so steady on her feet. Her relief was palatable. Her brother was alive and here on the island. She knew it in her bones. A shiver went down her back.

He wrapped his arm around her. "Cold?"

"It's the dampness, I guess." They rounded the bend in the path. "Well, this is me," she said quickly heading to the stairs of her veranda.

She was halfway up when Rush called her name in a soft voice.

She swallowed as she turned to face him. He picked a couple of leaves off her shirt. "I'm looking forward to taking you to the lagoon. I'm sorry I had to cancel again today. I need to clear up a few things. but I might be able to slip away tomorrow. I'll let you know."

"Er, sure," she managed to mumble.

His eyes darkened as he put his hand on the side of her face. He leaned in and kissed her softly. Then he rubbed his thumb over her lips. "It should be fun."

Her mouth had gone dry, and she was incapable of responding. He leaned in and kissed her again and then stepped back, murmuring, "Good night," before disappearing down the path.

She went up the rest of the steps of her veranda but her hands were shaking when she tried to unlock her door so it took a couple of tries but once inside she relocked the door and leaned on it.

That man was dangerous. If Rush kissed her again like he had on the beach last night, she'd be a puddle on the floor. Her knees were still weak. How the hell was she going to survive tomorrow?

"Damn you, Danny," she muttered. Now she was sure it had been him that she saw sneaking into the trees.

Letting out a long breath, she straightened and walked

over to the kitchen area. The wine fridge under the counter was calling her name. She pulled out a bottle and opened it. Giving herself a generous pour, she put the bottle back and took her glass to the bedroom. A hot bath and a glass of wine was just what she needed. There was no hope for sleep otherwise.

Walking into the bathroom, she set the glass on the counter. She walked over to the tub but then froze, momentarily disoriented. She looked back at the counter. The hair tie she'd left there was missing. She went back and stared at where she'd left it. What the hell could have happened to it?

Her heart rate, which had finally settled into a normal rhythm, shot back up, making it hard to draw a breath. Her hands shook. Had someone come into her room while she was out breaking into the shed? Were they on to her already? Her throat closed.

She darted her gaze over every surface in the bathroom while fighting the panic clawing its way out of her throat. Why would someone take a hair tie? It didn't make any sense. She scratched her neck and her fingers got tangled in a strand of hair pulling out one of the pins she'd used to keep it up. It hit the floor. She stooped to pick it up and immediately noticed the scrunchie. It had fallen under the vanity. How the hell had it gotten there? She grabbed it and the pin and stood up again. Placing them both on the counter, she took a deep breath and tried to steady her nerves.

The AC came on and a light breeze blew on her, giving her goosebumps. She rubbed her face with her hands and let out the breath she'd been holding. The AC must have blown the scrunchie off the counter. Boy, she needed to calm down. This whole ordeal was seriously stressing her out. *Get it together, Kat.*

Taking a sip of wine, she put the glass down with

unsteady hands and then walked over and turned on the bath.

Kat leaned against the vanity watching the tub fill. Tonight had been a disaster, plain and simple. If it had been Danny, where the hell did he go? He wasn't hanging out in the gardening sheds that was for sure. She recalled the snake and a shudder rippled through her.

And she was crossing the hospital off the list as well. The Lock and Key Society probably had specially designed prison cells and the only place they would be, as far as she knew, would be the sleek gray building she'd discovered. The question was…how the hell was she going to get inside without getting herself killed? "Damn you, Danny."

CHAPTER ELEVEN

Rush shifted his weight as he cocked his head. Was she talking to someone? Kat was just leaning against the vanity, staring at the tub. He strained to hear, but the only sound was that of the bath being filled. He peeked through the window, immediately feeling like a deviant. But this was the nature of his work. Spying, eavesdropping, collecting information like a little kid collected fall leaves. If the job called for spying on a woman through partially closed blinds, he'd do just that.

She was a fine-looking woman, beautiful in fact. Those lips. He shouldn't have kissed her on the beach but he hadn't been able to resist. Hadn't wanted to resist. If the server hadn't come along, they might have done a lot more than kiss.

There was something about her. Some spark in her deep green eyes that tugged a long-buried cord in him. She was… innocent or maybe naive was a better word. *Normal* might even be the best word.

The world he inhabited was not normal, but he wasn't

complaining. The Society provided him with a good life. It wasn't the life he'd envisioned but his time in the army had changed things. Changed him. He couldn't cope with normal. Not when he'd first come back seven years ago. Now? More and more normal was looking better and better. Sadly, a simple life would always be out of reach for him. He'd made a promise, a vow really, to Archer. He wouldn't go back on it.

But there was no point in denying it, he wanted Kat. Badly. She brought out something in him, a lighter side, that he liked. He wanted to be around her. But could he do that and still maintain any distance? Probably not. The smart thing to do would be to tell Archer to bring in one of the other guys to deal with this but the thought of not seeing Kat made his chest hurt. He was just going to have to find a way through. A way to spend time with Kat and still find out what he needed to know. It was his job which was not going well if tonight was anything to go by.

He clenched his fists against his thighs. The scream was machine-generated. As he'd explained to Kat, it was armed with an infrared beam that, when interrupted, the machine emitted a scream designed to scare the poor person shitless. He suspected animals were breaking the beam causing the thing to 'scream'. Otherwise, there would be people yelling about it or if it was one of the older members, someone would've dropped dead of a heart attack. The question was… Who put it up? And why?

Kat turned off the water and started peeling off her clothing. As much as he wanted to see her naked, this was not the way he'd imagined it. He moved back. A pervert he was not. She deserved her privacy. He would not intrude. There were some lines he just couldn't cross. The irony was not lost on him that he'd searched her place earlier.

Last night when he'd gotten back to the beach, she'd disappeared., He'd immediately come here to make sure she was okay. And then, not seeing her all day had been a little like torture. So he'd headed to her cabin to check on her. When she wasn't home, he took the opportunity to do a quick search.

She was definitely looking for something. A map of the island was spread out on the desk, and a quick study of her search history showed that she'd been trying to find blueprints for the buildings on the island. Was she after the treasure? Jesus what a mess that would be. She had Angel's token, but he was willing to bet Kat had nothing to do with Angel's death. She just didn't have it in her. He was sure of it.

The sound of splashing reached his ears. He leaned forward to check. Kat was in the tub, leaning back, with her eyes closed. A glass of wine was on the edge of the tub next to her. He let out a small sigh. It looked like she'd be there for the duration.

He'd still like to know where the hell she'd come from. He had just left her place when he found her on the path. There was no way she'd been there the whole time. She'd come through the hedge. The greenery stuck to her was a dead giveaway but so was the abject fear in her eyes.

The sound of a cell phone broke the silence. Kat jerked up, startled. "Shit," she said as she scrambled out of the tub. Rush moved away again, affording her some privacy. He twisted to see into the living room, where she appeared wearing a towel.

She picked up her cell. "Hello?" There was a long pause. "Who is this?" Another silence. "Where is he? What have you done with him?" Her voice sounded stressed. "What do you want from me?" she demanded. "But I can't. I have no idea where it is. I know nothing about it."

She disappeared down the hallway toward the bathroom. "I… I… hello? Hello? For shit's sake." She came back up the hallway and cursed some more. Then she went back into the bathroom and downed her wine in one big gulp.

Leaning on the vanity, she stared at herself in the mirror. "What the fuck am I supposed to do now?" she asked her reflection.

Slamming her hand on the vanity she straightened, then turned to let the water out of the tub. She stormed into the bedroom. Rush almost jumped at the sound of the door slamming. He waited another fifteen minutes, but she didn't appear to be leaving so he decided it was safe to go. What the hell was the phone call about?

Kat was just full of mysteries.

Ten minutes later he was back in the control room. Danton was off shift. Pierre had taken over. He wasn't sure he trusted Pierre. The man was supposed to be his lookout and let him know via text if Kat approached the cabin. He'd only just got out when she was suddenly on the path ahead of him. Was that done on purpose? Was Pierre the one behind the cameras being moved?

"What the fuck, Pierre?" he demanded.

"Dude, she came out of nowhere. One minute the path was empty and the next second, boom! she was there. No warning nothing. I even went back and checked the feed. I don't know how we could've missed her. She just wasn't there and then she was."

Pierre was a tall man with tan skin and deep brown eyes which were now pleading with him. Pierre was scared. Did that make him guilty or innocent? It was hard to tell.

Rush pointed to the monitor. "Show me."

Pierre brought up the footage and then got out of his chair. Rush took the man's seat and hit play. Damn if Pierre wasn't right. Kat wasn't on the feed and then she popped up coming out of nowhere. How could that... "Is there a blind spot there?" *Shit.* Another one?

Pierre glanced at the floor and then at the guy at the next station. "Um...there's sort of a small area that no cameras reach. But," he barreled on, "it's because there's a slight bend in the path and we'd have to hang a new camera to get everything. There are already a couple of birdhouses there. It would look suspicious to have that many in that one area. I can hang a camera but then we need to come up with another way to disguise them. People might catch on and I don't want to have to explain to Mr. Gray how that happened. He'll have my head."

Rush cursed.

Security hid the cameras in birdhouses and too many in one area would be noticeable. Archer would go ballistic because the members would go ballistic on him. Members visited this island because they all thought the island was totally private. And it was. It was just also very monitored. It had to be in order to keep everyone safe. All the Society locations were well monitored. They couldn't have anyone get upset and then have it come to blows, or worse, have someone whip out a gun and shoot another guest. And with some of the meetings that took place at Society locations that was a distinct possibility.

Rush pulled up the real map of the island and then zoomed in to see where this blank spot was located. Then he zoomed out to see where the hell she could have been coming from if she hadn't been coming down the main path. There were other paths, but they weren't that close and she would have had to push through the hedges that they'd grown to line every path. He zoomed out a bit more. "Fuck." She'd been here at the Hub or at least beside it. It was the only thing that made any sense.

"What?" Pierre asked.

"I think she might have been beside the Hub. There are a few narrow utility paths along the sides. If she took one of those, she might have found an opening in the hedge and come through to the main path."

Pierre looked at him and then back up at the screen. "Do you think she knew there was a hole in our video coverage right there? Did she plan this? Was she trying to break into the Hub? That's just crazy. Who would want to break into the security building of this island?"

Rush drummed his fingers. He didn't have a clue as to what she was up to. The only good thing was that Pierre knew about this hole in the camera view. It wasn't a new one, just one that needed to be fixed. He stood and took a couple steps towards the door and then stopped. "She got a phone call on her cell. Can you trace where it came from?"

Pierre nodded. "It might take a day or two, but I can get the information."

"Good. Let me know what you find out." Rush left the Hub and hurried back to his cabin. He glanced at the clock, it was just before two a.m. *What a freakin' long day.* After a quick, cold shower, he crawled into bed.

Twenty minutes later, he was still awake, watching the ceiling fan blades whir lazily above the bed. Just like his thoughts. Whatever Kat had been up to, it wasn't helping her case.

Rush grunted in exasperation and rubbed his face. What the hell had the phone call she'd gotten been about? Her voice had been desperate and terrified. If he was honest with himself, that was the real reason sleep eluded him. The terror in her voice triggered his protective instincts. No one should have to be afraid like that. He'd been afraid as a soldier but he'd always known his job meant he had to keep going. To be terrified because of a phone call was something different.

Something sinister. He needed to know what that call was about, and sooner rather than later.

Kat Rollings was a problem. And as sure as his name was Rushton Fletcher, he knew this could get much worse.

CHAPTER TWELVE

Kat eyed the path. After checking her map again last night she was pretty sure this path led to the gray building. It was a small walkway, obviously not for guests, and clearly off-limits. If someone questioned her, she could always say she got lost on her way to the main pool. She was dressed in a black and green striped bikini with a white linen cover-up over it. She even had a beach bag with a towel and sunscreen.

Fuck it. She started down the path. After last night's fiasco, she needed to make some progress. Her brother was either in the gray building or randomly running around the island at night. *Or dead.* No, she was convinced she'd seen him, so either he was under his own steam and hiding somewhere or the Society had him hostage. Either way, the sooner she found him, the better off they'd both be.

The phone call last night had rattled her. The caller ordered her to find the treasure. How the hell was she supposed to do that?

Kat's heart pulsed erratically, and she bit her lip. The path curved slightly so whatever was ahead was obscured. The air was scented with a divine aroma of the foliage in full bloom that lined the walkway. The plants were colorful, and typically she'd find their scent magical. But today, the blood-red flowers seemed more like a warning.

Kat did not have a green thumb but she'd always found it slightly depressing that flowers today were bred for their color, not for their scent. The flowers that she bought at the shop just down from her apartment, all looked beautiful but had no scent. It was such a shame.

Focus, Kat. Marveling at the flowers was distracting, and potentially dangerous.

She glanced at the ground. No need to bump into another snake. She shuddered. As she rounded the corner, the gray building came into view. Steps led up to a door. It had the same screen and eye scanner set-up as the entrance to the island, but this system looked like there were a few more bells and whistles on this door. There was a third scanner for what, she couldn't imagine and there was a camera over the doorway as well. What was this place? She was starting to like her theory of a portal to another world more and more.

"Kat, what are you doing here?"

She whirled around and put a hand to her chest. "Daisy, you startled me."

Daisy quickly approached and dropped her voice. "Honey, you can't be here. This area is off limits." The petite woman linked her arm through Kat's and pulled her back in the direction she'd just come. "If they see you here, you'll be in serious trouble."

"I was just looking for the main pool. I thought this was a shortcut." She tried to look convincing, not that it mattered. Daisy was practically dragging her back down the path while she kept her head on a swivel. The hair on the back of Kat's neck bristled.

"We need to get you back on the main path." Daisy tried to make her move faster.

"What was that building?" Kat asked in an undertone.

Daisy shook her head. "You must never ask about that building. Don't go anywhere near it." A rustling noise came from ahead, causing Daisy to stop abruptly. A second later a tall, raven-haired woman appeared in front of them. She was thin and obviously in great shape. Her cream-colored tank top showed off her biceps and her olive cargo shorts only served to make her legs look yards long.

"What the hell are you doing here?" she demanded.

Kat's mouth went dry. She had no clue what to say.

Daisy replied smoothly. "Kat and I were checking out the Clematis." She gestured toward the climbing purple flowers on her right. "She loves horticulture like I do."

"You know you're not supposed to be here, Daisy," the tall woman snarled.

Daisy drew herself up to her full height, such as it was. "I'm allowed anywhere on the island, as you well know. These Clematis are the only ones on the island in this deep purple color. Kat wanted to see them."

There was zero warmth in her gaze now. As a matter of fact, there was a distinct snarl on Daisy's lips. "Veronica, this is Kat, our newest member," Daisy said. Her face was a mask of calm now, no more snarl. "Kat, this is Veronica. She's in charge of fitness on the island."

It didn't take a genius to figure out these two women hated each other. Kat looked from one woman to the other. There were some serious undercurrents to this conversation and the whole exchange jangled her already frayed nerves.

Daisy smiled serenely. "Did you want to join our discussion, Veronica?"

Kat prayed Veronica said no. There was something about her that was upsetting. She seemed as prickly as a cactus.

Daisy was such a kind soul with a soothing energy, something Kat needed more of at the moment. So, whatever the hell was going on here, she was team Daisy and if Daisy said they were discussing flowers, then flowers it was.

Kat cleared her throat. "Yes, we were talking about the plant hardiness zones. The tropical and subtropical zones here make for a year-round growing season. Where I live in New York, it's zone five which means plants must be able to withstand cold temperatures. Do you live here or in another zone altogether, Veronica?"

The woman stared at her. "You need to get back to the path, now.

Kat's shoulders tensed as Veronica's voice went whispery rough and fully recognizable. She'd been the person with the man last night on the path. She was the woman who wanted money. The one with jewelry. Humber's mistress, or at least she used to be until he ran out of money.

"We were just on our way," Daisy said with an easy smile as she patted Kat's arm. "Weren't we, dear? Remind me to tell you about the lagoon and the bioluminescent plankton. They only appear at certain times of the year, but they are amazing. They make the lagoon glow at night. I think I have pictures. Drop by the office when you have the chance and I'll show them to you." She gave Kat's arm a squeeze. "I have so enjoyed our conversation, though."

Kat faked a smile and turned to Daisy. "I am enjoying our chat, too. Do you know what the lovely pink flowers are next to the main dining room, the ones on the hedge? I confess I haven't seen them before."

"Well, you probably wouldn't. They are a type of orchid and they only grow in warm temperatures."

Veronica crossed her arms over her chest and spread her legs a little wider. Her no-nonsense stance, flushed cheeks, and narrowed eyes made Kat happy she'd been discovered by Daisy.

"Daisy, I want to talk to you now, in private," Veronica demanded.

Daisy waved her off. "I don't think that's necessary. Kat and I are finished, though." She started walking again and as they moved around Veronica, Daisy tut-tutted. "You shouldn't get so upset, dear. It will give you wrinkles." They finished the walk in silence and emerged onto the main path moments later.

"There you are."

Kat turned to see Rush climbing from an electric golf cart. His blue t-shirt set off his eyes and wore a pair of sexy-as-hell black swim trunks. Kat's nerves buzzed for a much nicer reason. A picnic basket had been fastened onto the back of the cart.

"Rush," she blinked. "Ohmygod, I completely forgot. I'm so sorry. Did we set a time for today?"

He cocked an eyebrow. "I'm not normally someone people forget but I'll try not to be insulted. And no, we didn't set an exact time."

"Daisy and I were talking flowers and I completely lost track of time." She swallowed trying to keep the heat out of her cheeks. "Er, I assume you know—"

"Of course I know Rushton," Daisy said. "I haven't seen you since you arrived. How are you, dear?"

"I'm doing well, Daisy. Always a pleasure to see you."

"I was just looking for you but"—she glanced at the picnic basket—"it can wait. We'll catch up later."

Suddenly Veronica appeared on the path next to them.

Rush glanced at her. "Ronnie."

"Rush," she said as her gaze landed on the basket and her eyes narrowed further. "What are you doing here?"

"I could ask you the same question."

The undercurrents between the two of them rushed like river rapids in spring, and Kat was sure she was about to drown.

"Well," she said brightly, "if you two will excuse us. We have plans." She wanted to get the hell away from Veronica or Ronnie or whatever the hell her name was. She was bad news.

"What's in the basket, Rush?" Veronica demanded.

Kat was sure it wasn't her imagination. Rush's eyes had turned to ice chips. The temperature on the path plummeted.

"None of your business, Ronnie."

Veronica gritted her teeth. "No fraternizing with the guests, Rush."

"Stay out of it, Ronnie."

Kat didn't know what the hell was going on. She glanced at Daisy who immediately cleared her throat.

"Veronica," Daisy said, "I think we should leave these two. They obviously have plans." She let go of Kat's arm.

Daisy walked by Veronica. "It wouldn't do to upset one of the guests, dear."

Veronica remained still and glared…first at Rush and then at Kat. She opened her mouth to speak.

Rush cut her off. "Be very careful, Ronnie." Kat heard the warning in his voice. Rush wasn't playing.

Kat's knees were getting weak and her insides were quaking. What the hell was she in the middle of?

Veronica paled but sneered, "You too, Rush." Then she turned and stalked down the path.

Kat stared after her, twisting her fingers together.

Daisy smiled at Rush before reaching out and squeezing his arm. "Always good to see you, dear."

He kissed her cheek. "You too, Daisy." He caught her gaze. "Take care." It was another warning and if Kat didn't miss her guess, it was about Veronica.

"I always do, dear," she said and then she too traipsed down the path.

Kat met Rush's gaze. "What the hell was all that about?"

"How about we take the picnic basket to the lagoon first and then we'll chat? I don't know about you, but I could use a nice cold glass of something, preferably with alcohol."

"That sounds like heaven," she agreed. She settled in the cart and took a moment to collect herself. Her hands were shaking and her knees were gelatinous. She took a couple of deep breaths.

Rush gave her an appraising glance as he settled beside her. His eyes warmed up instantly. The temperature was definitely getting warmer. If he kept looking at her like that, it was going to be scorching. She willed the heat out of her face.

"You look"—he paused as their gazes locked—"amazing."

She didn't know what to say to that so she just smiled and he started the cart.

"It's a hot one today." It was an inane comment but she needed to get herself together. Between the look Rush gave her and being busted by Daisy, she was discombobulated. Thank God Veronica hadn't caught it. That would've been ugly no doubt. Her palms were damp and she took a second to wipe them surreptitiously on her beach bag. That had been close. Too close.

She was glad she'd put on sunscreen earlier. The sun's rays were fierce. The storm they were talking about seemed to still be a good distance away. "Does it always rain here in the afternoon?"

"In summer, yes. Just for a short time and then the sun comes out again. Although we're into hurricane season now, and it seems there's a storm off the coast. No one is sure yet if it will turn into a hurricane or not."

"I've heard that." She didn't know what else to say. As

much as she liked her little cabin, there was no way she'd trust it as a shelter during a hurricane. "Will they evacuate the island if the storm is bad?"

"Yes. We'll make sure everyone gets off in plenty of time to find a good place to ride out the storm. It's still a couple of days away."

She fell silent and tried to get her brain off the thought of a coming hurricane. *When it rains, it pours.* It seemed to take no time at all to pass all the buildings and make their way to the north side of the island. The boardwalk was covered by a thick canopy of trees, and manicured hedges blended into the green foliage. The plants here had been cut back but not manicured the same way. Like the bushes around the gray building, these were left to do their own thing. Just trimmed enough so people could traverse the boardwalk.

Rush pulled off the path and parked. "We have to walk from here, but you have to be very careful to stay on the boardwalk."

Kat gamely got out of the cart.

"The lagoon is just a few minutes up that way," Rush said as he gestured with his hand.

She looked over his shoulder. The boardwalk was a bit dark, and the sound of a branch snapping had her peering through the bushes. Suddenly going to the lagoon didn't seem like such a great idea. Should she even be alone with Rush? He worked there. Was he dangerous?

As if sensing her thoughts, he smiled. "Don't worry, I'll protect you from any predators." He took her hand and headed for the path.

But who would protect her from him? She walked next to him trying to act nonchalant, as if her heart wasn't racing. Her hand tingled in his. Natural. Their arms brushing set a thrill through her belly and lower. She needed to be careful with him. He could suck her in without even trying. Finding her brother was her priority, not an affair with this handsome man.

"Penny for them,"

"Sorry?"

He glanced at her. "Penny for your thoughts. You look like you're worried about something."

No shit. "Um, not worried exactly. Where are the sinkholes?"

"You can't see them from the boardwalk. They are in that direction." He pointed vaguely to the left. "There are underground channels of water that pop up on the surface unexpectantly sometimes as well. The excess water can cause issues. Heavy rains during the summer months can also make it more dangerous. A few years back, we lost a few workers after a hurricane. The ground beneath them just disappeared and they fell in the hole."

Another branch snapped somewhere off to their left and she jumped.

Rush chuckled. "Don't worry, you're fine. The light rain we've been having in the afternoons isn't enough to set anything off."

"Great." She searched around for another topic. What the hell was she allowed to ask about? "I have to ask; what was going on earlier with Daisy and Veronica? You could have cut the tension between them with a knife." Seeing his frown, she added, "But maybe it's something I shouldn't ask about. To be honest, I'm finding it hard to figure out the fine print with the Society and I don't want to piss anyone off. What am I allowed to ask about?"

"It's true; becoming a member of the Society can be a bit nerve-wracking but you'll be fine. You can ask me anything if you're too nervous to ask someone else. I'll always tell you the truth."

She looked at him and caught an expression flitting

across his face, but couldn't make out what it was. Did he just lie to her?

Kat closed her mouth and thought twice about asking any questions. The whole reason she'd agreed to see the waterfall with Rush was so she could ask questions and now she didn't want to. She wanted to go back to New York and pick up her boring life exactly where she'd left off. Steadily dull seemed ideal at this moment.

"We're almost there," Rush said as he gestured for her to go ahead of him into the clearing.

She emerged from the canopied path into the dazzling sunshine. The sun danced off the sky-blue lagoon, which had a deeper blue center. The entire body of water was surrounded by a ring of sugar-white sand. Water bubbled over a rocky cliff, frothing into the lagoon.

"It's stunning," she gasped.

The lagoon was about the size of an Olympic swimming pool but in free-form shape. Bushes growing beside the waterfall were bursting with color. Pinks and reds with a few yellows thrown in. Daisy would know what kind of flowers they were, but she didn't have a clue.

Rush dropped her hand. "It's one of my favorite places on earth."

She immediately missed the warmth of his grip. "Do you have favorite places in space?" she teased.

He turned to her and started to chuckle. "No." Setting the picnic basket down, he pulled out a blanket and smoothed it out over a shady patch of sand. He beckoned her to join him as he pulled out a bottle of wine. "I hope you don't mind if we sit in the shade. The sun is hot today and I'd rather not fry like an onion."

"Shade works for me." She kicked off her shoes and settled on the blanket beside him.

He handed her a glass of wine and then poured one for

himself. "Cheers. To the beginning of a beautiful friendship with a beautiful woman."

They touched glasses but there was just a soft click because the glasses were plastic. "Sorry about the glasses. Can't use glass here or by any pool."

"How come?" she asked after savoring the sip of wine.

"Glass is hard to spot if it breaks on the sand or rock but damn near impossible to spot if it breaks in the water."

"I hadn't thought about it, but I guess you're right."

He stretched out his legs and leaned back against the trunk of a tree. "Why'd you come to the island?"

Kat took a large gulp of wine. He'd asked her this several times before. "Like I said before, I needed a break."

He shrugged his shoulders "It just seems like it might be a bit more than that."

What the hell was he getting at? Did he know about Danny? She lied, "I think I just need to reassess my life. I find that hard to do when I'm in the middle of things. Do you know what I mean?"

Rush nodded. "Perspective is everything. What are you reassessing? Career? Family?"

"Everything." She took another large gulp of wine. That was true, too. "I've been keeping my head down and just doing my job for a long time now and suddenly I looked up and realized there has to be more to life." Why the hell was she telling him all this? Because she was drinking or because she was nervous?

"A little early for a mid-life crisis, isn't it? You're too young."

She offered him a playful smile. "I guess that depends on how long I live." *Shit.* That was a little too close to home. She glanced at her almost empty wine glass. She needed to slow down and get a grip on herself. She was already talking to Rush like she'd known him forever.

She put her wine glass down on the blanket. "You promised me details about what all that was back on the path."

Rush raked her body with his gaze. "Still interested?"

"Absolutely," she replied meeting his stare. She wasn't sure they were still talking about the scene earlier but at this moment she didn't really care. She'd already consumed too much wine way too quickly and on an empty stomach. She was up for pretty much anything this man had to offer.

He refilled her glass as he spoke. "Ronnie manages the fitness and sports centers for the island. She's ambitious and trying to move up in management. Muscle in on Daisy and Peter's jobs. She thinks they're too old to be effective. Daisy and Peter like their jobs and aren't interested in being pushed out. So, it's a power struggle."

"And how do you fit in?"

"Me?" he cocked an eyebrow at her. "I'm just a bystander. I think Daisy and Peter are good people, but they are getting on in years. Peter is…"

"Sick," Kat supplied. "Cancer would be my guess."

He nodded. "Yes."

She decided to push. "But there's obviously some underlying tension between you and Veronica."

"She knows I support Peter and Daisy." He sighed. "Ronnie is also my ex-wife."

Kat choked on her sip of wine.

"You okay?" Rush asked as he rubbed her back.

She coughed some more but then managed to wheeze out, "Way to bury the lede."

He grinned and his eyes danced with mirth. Too bad this was all such a mess. She could easily fall for Rush's charms.

"Go for a swim?"

She put down her wine. "Yes, I think that's a great idea."

He helped her to her feet, and she pulled off her hat and

cover-up. Turning she found him openly admiring her figure. Their gazes locked and Kat had to fight the urge to kiss the man. She cleared her throat and headed to the water's edge.

As she entered the water, she admonished herself for being stupid. This was not helping her find her brother. She waded in up to her knees. "Oh," she let out a breath. It was much colder than she expected. The drop off to the deep water was right in front of her.

"The water comes from underground as well as the waterfall. Keeps it cooler than the ocean at this time of year." Rush stood behind her, resting his hand on her hip.

She should pull away but she didn't. His touch set off a cascade of excitement across her body. It had been a long time since she'd reacted to anyone this way. If ever. She wanted to savor the moment. Pretend it was real and not some bizarre nightmare scenario.

"Can you swim?" he asked.

"Yes."

"Good," he said and pushed her off the edge into the deep water.

"You!" she said as she came sputtering to the surface. Rush remained on the edge of the drop off, laughing. His blue eyes danced as they crinkled in laughter. He was standing there in a pair of black swim trunks and nothing else. His chest was solid muscle with a six-pack the likes of which she'd never seen. He was stunningly handsome. Her heart lurched and her breath shallowed. *God, she wanted him. Right now.*

But he'd shoved her in the water, and honestly, wasn't turnabout fair play? Two could play this game.

She moved her arm through the water as fast as she could and splashed him.

He immediately stopped laughing and yelped.

"Not so much fun, is it?"

"This is war," he declared.

She started scissoring her legs to back away in the water. This was not good.

His eyes narrowed.

Kat turned and swam toward the middle of the lagoon. She glanced back over her shoulder to catch him diving into the water next to her. She increased the speed of her strokes but she was no match for him. He was on her in seconds, hands around her waist. He turned her to face him, their legs moving to keep them afloat.

She opened her mouth to plead for…whatever and he kissed her. She instinctively wrapped her arms around his neck and deepened the kiss. Their tongues danced while their legs moved. It was heaven until someone snapped a branch.

Rush broke off the kiss and looked over her head. His face froze. She turned to see who was there.

"Archer," Rush said. "I didn't know you were on the island."

"Obviously." The man standing at the edge of the clearing was wearing dark jeans and a black shirt. The look on his face made Kat's stomach drop to her knees. It had to be close to a hundred degrees in the shade and this man was cold as ice. She couldn't shake the feeling that she'd just met the devil.

CHAPTER THIRTEEN

Fucking Archer. Rush cursed a blue streak in his head. Why hadn't he said he was going to be here?

"Stay here," he said to Kat as he let go of her waist and swam back to the drop-off point and waded to shore.

"When did you get in?" He kept his voice low as he toweled off his face.

"A little while ago." Archer matched Rush's volume as he glanced over at Kat. "You making any progress... Besides the obvious?"

Rush didn't follow his glance. "You wanted me to do a job and I'm doing it. If you're going to check up on my every move then we're going to have a problem."

"I think you might already have a problem. She is the enemy. You need to keep your distance."

"Haven't you ever heard of keeping your friends close but your enemies closer?" Rush dropped the towel and started to turn back toward the water.

Archer snorted. "You don't have it in you."

"What?" he demanded.

"You don't have it in you to sleep with her and then kill her. That takes a special kind of asshole, and you aren't it. Trust me. I know from experience. Find another way." Archer turned then and headed back down the path.

Rush stared after him. Was his boss right? Did he not have what it took? He checked his gut and knew in an instant that Archer had nailed it. He glanced at Kat, treading water with a worried look. There was no way he could sleep with her and then do his job if the job required her to die. But that was a good thing, wasn't it? It meant he wasn't as far gone as maybe he'd first thought. *He might still be redeemable.* But what the hell was he going to do now? "Fuck," he mumbled as he waded back to the drop-off and dove back into the water, welcoming the shock of the cold water on his hot skin.

"Who was that?" Kat asked as he surfaced next to her.

"My boss."

"Oh shit. Are you in trouble?" she asked.

He gave her a quick smile. "Nah. It's fine. Want to see the cave behind the waterfall?"

"Sure." She gave him a puzzled look but gamely swam toward the waterfall without further questions. Which was good because he didn't have any answers.

He hadn't really planned what he wanted to do up here with Kat and he sure as hell hadn't planned to kiss her. As a matter of fact, that was why he pushed her into the water. When he'd walked up behind her and put his hand on her hip it had felt natural. He hadn't even realized he was going to do it until he was there. Seeing her in that tiny green bikini that made her breasts look so damn fine and made her eyes glitter like emeralds had detonated something in him. A desire he hadn't felt in a long time. He reacted. The kiss had been instinctive.

But now it was over. He needed this to be over. Kat was

too much of a temptation. Too hard for him to resist. She made him *too hard*. He was going to confront her. Once they were finished at the waterfall, he'd take her back to the Hub and confront her. He had no choice. He would savor these last few minutes and then it would be over.

Kat stopped swimming close to the bottom of the waterfall. "Do we just swim through it?" she half yelled over the roaring water.

He nodded. "It's easier if you go underwater. Follow me." He dove under and came up a second later in the cave behind the waterfall. He turned and treaded water, waiting for Kat to break the surface. Nothing. His chest tightened. "Kat?" he called. Did she not swim underneath? Was she waiting outside? "Kat," he called again. Louder this time. Still nothing.

Rush dove underwater and looked around. No Kat. He swam back under the waterfall and surfaced. "Kat," he bellowed. Had she gotten out of the water? The shore was empty. He dove down again and looked around. Still nothing.

The lagoon was very deep in the middle. So deep in fact, scuba gear was needed to get anywhere near the bottom. Could she have swum downward and gotten lost or knocked her head again? Rush surfaced one more time to get more oxygen before diving deeper.

He pulled himself downward, feeling the pressure build, but still no Kat. His heart pounded against his rib cage and his lungs were screaming for oxygen. He had to surface. Starting his ascent, he suddenly realized his miscalculation. He was deeper than he'd thought and now he was getting dizzy heading up. He was out of oxygen. Fighting the urge to draw a deep breath, he pushed through the water as hard as he could, he was still far below the surface.

He wasn't going to make it. All the shit he'd done, all the

bizarre and dangerous situations he'd been involved in during his life and he was going to die by drowning in a lagoon in the Caribbean. He wanted to laugh. Soon his mouth would open automatically in the desperate search for air that wasn't coming. His vision tunneled. He gave one more monster kick using all of his remaining energy but he still was too far from the surface. His only regret floated to the surface of his mind. He should've kept kissing Kat.

It was the choking that woke him. His lungs burned with the need for oxygen. The world spun as someone rolled him on his side, and he spewed out seawater. He coughed some more. His whole body hurt but his chest was on fire. He puked more water.

"Okay, get him on the stretcher. I want him at the hospital ASAP. Have Dr. Walton check him."

It was Archer's voice. Rush tried to open his eyes. They stung from the salt. He'd forced them open underwater looking for Kat. "Kat," he mumbled.

Hands were on him and rolling him onto something hard. He was being lifted. *Stretcher.* They were putting him on a stretcher. He forced open his burning eyes. Archer was next to him along with Daisy. "Kat," he wheezed out. "Is she okay?"

Daisey looked at Archer and there were tears in her eyes.

Archer shook his head. "We couldn't find her."

"How can that be? Where the hell could she have gone?" he croaked.

Archer ignored him and signaled to the attendants, The stretcher jostled as they loaded him onto the back of a tiny truck that served as the island ambulance. Rush wanted to argue but he didn't have the strength. He closed his eyes. How the hell could he have lost Kat like that? All she had to do was swim under the fucking waterfall. Hell, she could have swum through it and been fine. What the hell happened?

CHAPTER FOURTEEN

Kat had followed Rush underwater. With sure strokes, she pushed downward. The bubbling waterfall made it hard to see clearly, and the salt water stung. She went deeper. Rush was ahead of her. He was directly under the waterfall and had started to push upward. Following his path, she went under the waterfall when something tugged her leg. She kicked but it wouldn't let go. Turning she came face to face with her brother, Danny. He was wearing full scuba gear but she'd know those eyes anywhere.

Kat's jaw dropped open, and Danny shoved a regulator in. Instinctually, she cleared the line and breathed in fresh oxygen.

Danny! He was alive. She wanted to hug him and beat him up at the same time. She squeezed his hand. He squeezed back and handed her a mask. As she pulled it on, she tipped her head back and pressed the upper edge against her forehead, then lifted the bottom half away from her face and released a breath through her nose clearing the water from her mask. Her mind was going a mile a minute. She had so many questions. Why hadn't he called? Why hadn't he told her he was alive?

It was a good thing they were treading water because she was sure her knees wouldn't hold her upright. She was just so damn happy to see her twin. Handing the regulator back, she pointed upwards. He shook his head, his eyes trying to convey some message that she just wasn't getting. Now what the hell was the problem? Her stomach had finally relaxed at the sight of her brother but tightened viciously once again.

He pulled her down and she fought him. Where the hell did he want her to go? She needed more air. He handed her the regulator again. They'd done this growing up. Their father had made them learn to scuba dive when they'd been teenagers and then he'd made sure they knew how to handle themselves in case anything happened underwater. Sharing a regulator was just one of the things he'd made them learn.

She pointed up again and he shook his head. He drew a finger across his neck as if to say they would kill him. *He was not wrong.* The fight just went out of her. She was just so damn happy that Danny was alive. She relented. As she handed him back the regulator, she gave him a nod. He held on to her arm and tugged her down with him. She released some of the oxygen from her lungs to ease the pressure. She also squeezed the mask over her nose and blew out a bit to help her ears adjust to the pressure change.

Danny pulled her into a cave. This one was about fifteen feet down. It was completely flooded. He picked up a flashlight from the bottom of the cave and flicked it on. Then he handed her the regulator and she took in some much-needed air. When she gave it back, he tugged her farther into the cave.

The flashlight played on something yellow on the floor of the cave. Another tank. Danny swam toward it and then handed it to her. She put it on her back and cleared the regulator as she put it in her mouth. Danny motioned for them to go deeper into the cave. She swam behind him, keeping him in sight at all times.

The cave was large, maybe five feet high and about four feet wide. The walls were stone but not sharp. Years of water working on them made them smooth which was good. Scuba diving around sharp edges was never a good idea.

Kat kept pace with her brother but she was starting to wonder how deep they were going to go in this cave. And more importantly, why? Looking ahead, it became obvious why they were still going. It wasn't a cave. It was a tunnel. They were coming out of it. The water outside the mouth of the tunnel was light so they weren't super deep.

They left the tunnel and Danny motioned to her to keep swimming. The depth of the water wasn't much, maybe fifteen feet. She was sure they could be seen if any watercraft were around. It took another ten minutes to get to the point just below a boat. They took their time surfacing although it probably wasn't necessary, at least depth-wise. Danny had been under longer than she had been so it was better to be safe.

Finally, they surfaced, and Danny hoisted himself into the boat, helping her in immediately afterward. She took off her tank and hugged her brother, blinking back tears the whole time. She'd been so worried. So sure he was dead but never letting herself believe it.

"Oh Danny, you have no idea how good it is to see you. I was so worried. I thought you were dead."

When Danny pulled back, her own eyes were staring back at her. Danny was her fraternal twin, younger by five minutes. They had similar features although Danny was much taller at just a shade under six feet. His hair was darker than Kat's auburn and he had inherited their father's cocky grin, but there was no mistaking that they were siblings.

"I missed you, sis. I'm so sorry I worried you."

"Worried me? I thought you were dead! That goes beyond worry."

Danny had the grace to look sheepish. "I know. I can't apologize enough. You'll never know how sorry I am I got you involved in all this."

She frowned. "What is 'all this' exactly?"

Danny glanced around. "I'll explain, but it's better if we get a little further away from the island. Go below and get changed. You can use my shorts and T-shirts just like you did back in high school."

She gave him the eye, not quite trusting that she was going to get the truth later, but Danny was busy getting the power boat ready to go and didn't notice. And what a boat it was. An Azimuth 48 if she wasn't mistaken. A small yacht like this would be worth about a million bucks. There was no way in hell this was Danny's boat.

There was a flybridge above that no doubt had a couple of built-in sofas along with the captain's chair so the boat could be driven from up there. The main deck had a built-in sofa along the back and glass doors separated the inside cabin. The cabin itself had more sofas and tables. It also had a small table and a place to steer the boat. The whole place was done in neutral beiges, whites, and grays. Very classy looking.

Kat left Danny on the bridge and made her way to the bedrooms below. There was a main bedroom where Danny was sleeping. She could tell because his bed was unmade and there were clothes all over the floor. It, too, was done in neutrals with thick carpets and a separate bathroom. She grabbed some of his clothes. She had no underwear but once her bikini dried, it would do.

Going out of the main bedroom she picked a door on the right and went into that bedroom to find a set of twin beds and a small table in between. Not as luxurious as the main bedroom but not too shabby at all. Nothing like the floating shipwreck their father used to work on.

She took off her bikini and pulled on the tan-colored shorts and a black T-shirt. Going commando wasn't her favorite but she needed the bikini to dry before she could use it as underwear. Grabbing it, she went back up on deck. She put the bikini on the sofa so it would dry in the sun and headed up to the flybridge to her brother.

"So what gives?" she demanded.

He glanced at her from his position at the steering controls. They were heading out of the bay toward open water. He licked his lips. "We're almost there. Give me a few minutes. There's some food down below. I have sandwiches and stuff. We can talk over lunch."

She wanted to argue but she was starving and honestly, there was no point in pushing him. Danny only talked when he wanted to. Pressuring him for answers rarely worked. With a final skeptical look, she returned below to make a meal.

Ten minutes later, he joined her at the little table. "I just took us out a ways from the island. We can stay here without anyone paying attention." He picked up a sandwich. "Thanks for this. I'm starving." After swallowing, he said "Why does food always taste so much better when someone else makes it? This is amazing."

She took a bite of her own pastrami sandwich and had to agree, it hit the spot. After taking a sip of water she looked across at her brother. "You're stalling."

He swallowed and put down his sandwich. "I…don't know where to start."

"The beginning always works." She wasn't going to be swayed by his boyish charms. Her father had used them to get through life and Danny was no different, but their tactics had never worked with her.

"Okay, so Timmy said—"

"Jesus, Danny." She was instantly nauseous. "Timmy? Timmy Camerari? Timmy's been a disaster his entire life. How could you get involved in something with him? Haven't you learned your lesson by now?"

Danny scowled at her. "Do you want to hear this or not?"

"Timmy? He's been doing stupid things since he was in grade school. He does them and you take the fall. The time you got suspended for putting the frog on the cold cuts in the cafeteria. We all knew it was Timmy. You hate touching frogs. The time you got arrested for stealing that car and taking it for a joyride? You took the fall for Timmy because he'd be kicked out of his parents' house if he did anything else. Seriously. When has Timmy ever done anything good?"

Danny leaned back in the chair and crossed his arms over his chest.

For fuck's sake. She wanted to scream. They were in this mess because that fuck-up Timmy Camerari did something stupid and her moron of a brother followed him.

"Fine," she said through clenched teeth. "Tell me."

He stared at her a moment longer. "Fine," he said, his voice sullen. "Timmy was working for this guy, driving him around I think. Something like that. Anyway, they got to talking about that show, you know the one about the Oak Island treasure and Timmy tells him that he has this friend who knows how to find treasure. Like it runs in our family."

Kat gouged her nails into her palms. It always came back to fucking treasure with her family. She hated her father at this moment with every fiber of her being. She wished she knew a reanimation spell. It would be handy to bring her dad back to life so she could kill him all over.

"So, he tells Timmy he knows where BlackEye's treasure is, or at least where the general area is, but he doesn't know how to find it. Would his friend," he points to himself, "be interested in helping him out for a cut of the treasure?"

She closed her eyes and swore a blue streak. This was her worst nightmare come true.

"So, Timmy tells me about the guy and the treasure and then gives me the information that the guy has. I do some research and come to the same conclusion, BlackEye's treasure is on this tiny island in the Caribbean. The island is shaped like a kidney bean but it's private. So, I tell Timmy to tell the guy that I think he's right but it's a private island so there's not much we can do."

"Wait, why aren't you talking to the guy directly?"

He shrugged. "He doesn't want anyone to know he's involved."

"And that didn't, I don't know, ring any damn alarm bells for you?" Seriously? Was her brother truly this dense?

Danny closed his mouth and crossed his arms over his chest again. She raised her hands, palm out to placate him, and closed her mouth.

Danny leaned forward again. "Timmy comes and tells me that the guy can get me onto the island as a new member of the Society that owns it without a problem. But I have to be able to figure out where the treasure is and get it without anyone finding out. Timmy gave me the token thing in an envelope and told me what to do with it. He said he'd gotten it from the guy he worked for, Smith. That's the guy's name or at least the one he was using. I asked if I could get more help but Timmy said he only had one token and Smith wasn't going to give him more, so only one person could go on to the island."

"And you agreed to this?"

Danny looked down and scratched at the surface of the table. "I'm not that stupid. I said that was impossible. That I would need help and there was no way to do it totally in secret. If it was at sea, maybe but on a small island like this? No way."

She frowned. Her instincts said she was not going to like what she was about to hear. "Then what happened? How did you end up here?"

"Timmy disappeared. I got back to my car after work one night and there was a cell phone on my seat along with a picture of Timmy tied to a chair with a gag in his mouth and that day's newspaper on his lap."

"Shit."

"Yeah." Danny rubbed his face with his hands and then dropped them on the table again.

She reached out and squeezed her brother's arm. Timmy Camerari was an idiot, but he was a harmless idiot if you didn't count all the collateral damage.

"The guy called me and said I had to find the treasure or he'd kill Timmy. He said I had a few weeks to find it and he'd give me whatever I needed but it all had to happen quickly or Timmy dies." He looked over at his sister. "Kat, I've been at it for weeks and I'm no closer to finding it. If I don't figure it out soon, he'll kill Timmy and…you."

"Me?" her voice went up an octave. "Why me?"

"Once you arrived on the island, Smith started threatening you to keep me searching I guess. I'm so sorry, Kat."

"Jesus," she breathed. It was one thing to think it was a possibility that the Society might kill her for breaking the rules. It was another thing altogether to know that someone on the island was actively watching her and might kill her at any minute. Her hands shook as she ran them over her face.

She finally looked up and met her brother's gaze. "So why did you leave the token for me? Why not use it for yourself and then have access to the island full time?"

Danny shook his head. "Because then you wouldn't have any way of finding me or getting on the island. I needed you to come if I got into trouble. I told the guy I dropped the token and it smashed. He was pissed but he came up with this way to get me on and off the island so it didn't seem to matter much. In the end, he thought this was better anyway. He can control the security. What the cameras see and stuff like that. He directs me where to go so I won't be seen."

"But Danny if he can fix the cameras and stuff then he works on the island and he would know if I showed up with the token."

He ducked his head. "Yeah, I didn't think about that part. I thought he was just a worker but he's got to be high up in things considering all he's done. He knew you were on the island. I told him I needed your help. He wasn't happy, but he'd do anything to find the treasure."

She sighed. "He called me last night and told me I had to help find it and that time was running out." She closed her eyes and put her head into her hands. What the fuck were they going to do?

He shook his head. "I'm not surprised. This guy is twenty steps ahead of me at every turn.

"So then why can't he find the treasure?"

Danny shrugged. "I don't think he has a clue about how to locate it on the island. I think he thought I…knew more about finding treasure than I actually do. Like there's a science behind it that I'm supposed to know."

She frowned. There was a bit of a science to it. A shit ton of research needed to be done before anyone went looking. This whole thing had been a disaster waiting to happen from the get-go.

She sighed. "So, do you have any idea where the treasure might be?"

"No, and I have no idea what to do next. I've looked at all kinds of places on the island but nothing. I can't exactly dig up the ground though. I've been using a metal detector and ground-penetrating radar and running a grid pattern to search. I wear the same uniform as the grounds crew and no one pays any attention to me. Plus, I do it mostly later at night. Still nothing.

"Did you use that scream box to keep people away while you're searching?"

He grinned. "It worked well too, but then I got to a more secluded part of the island, by the hospital, and animals kept setting it off. I was damn lucky to get away the other night."

"You escaped via the beach, right?"

He frowned. "How did you know?"

She licked her lips. They tasted of salt. "I was there on the beach." She shook her head as if to clear it. "Get back to the rest of your story."

"Right. The guy told me if anyone found out we were looking for the treasure, he'll kill Timmy and you. He said the Lock and Key Society wasn't big on strangers knowing about them. They also aren't big on sharing so if they find out that the treasure's been discovered, they're going to want to take all the money."

"I know." He was not wrong. Kat leaned back and stared at her brother. Of all the outlandish, bizarre shit that Danny had ever gotten involved in, this one had to take the cake. "You'll have to show me your research. I'll take a look and maybe we can come up with some ideas on where you and I can search. But Danny, we're going to need some help. We can't do this on our own. The island is too well protected. I'm shocked you haven't been discovered yet." Hell, she'd been discovered and all she was doing was going down the wrong path.

"The guy said that he can run interference to a degree and if I enter through the lagoon, there's less chance I'll be spotted."

"That's true. Still, I don't know how we can find it and

then remove it without help." She suddenly reared back. "Holy shit! Rush." She hit the table with her hand. With seeing her brother and the whole scuba adventure she'd forgotten all about him.

"Rush?" Danny asked.

"The guy I was swimming with. His name is Rush Fletcher. He'll think I'm dead. I have to let him know I'm okay." She frowned. "Wait. How did you know I'd be at the lagoon? You said you usually go at night."

"Smith called about forty-five minutes ago and said you were going to be at the lagoon. He said the hunt was taking too long and that I should get you to help me. I got everything ready and waited behind the waterfall and then when you went into the water I waited below until I could grab you."

"Right. I have to tell Rush that I'm alive. Leaving him like that was a horrible thing to do. Just awful."

Danny's eyebrows went up. "Are you two dating or something?"

"Er, no." Not exactly. Although the idea was very appealing to her. That kiss was the best thing that had happened to her dating life in years. "He works for the Society. He was just showing me around. I just think I would feel awful if the situation was reversed. Do you have a cell phone?"

"But who are you going to call? You can't explain what happened. If he works for them, he'll tell whoever's in charge and they'll kill me and you. You don't understand who these people are. They'll kill us just because."

Her heart sank. Danny was right. She couldn't tell Rush she was alive because then she'd have to tell him the rest of it and that wouldn't be good. She closed her eyes again. This was just…so bad. If she'd met Rush any other way, she'd be actively pursuing him. He was sexy and dangerous and funny and warm all at the same time. She'd been robbed of the chance to get to know him because of all this mess and for that she was profoundly sad.

Sighing, she opened her eyes to see her brother eyeing his sandwich. "Okay finish your lunch and let me see what you've got. Maybe we can find this treasure and then get the hell out of here."

That brought a smile to her brother's face. He got up and gave her a hug. "I'll go get the research." He disappeared down the stairs. Kat stared after him. He had no idea that they were all dead. Timmy, if he was even still alive, Danny, and her. There was no way this Mr. Smith was going to let any of them out alive whether they found the treasure or not.

CHAPTER FIFTEEN

"I'm fucking fine. Stop asking and stop staring at me."

Rush got a beer from his fridge, then slammed the door shut. It was just after five p.m., and he needed a distraction.

Across the room, Archer studied him. "You shouldn't drink after almost drowning."

Rush arched a brow and made a deliberate show of twisting off the top.

"Whatever," Archer shook his head. "I know you're fine. I want you to continue to investigate these moving cameras. I want to know who is doing it. If it's Fisher, I'm gonna need that man's head on a platter."

"That I would be happy to do," Rush said and then took a gulp of the IPA, aptly named Island Pirate Ale.

Archer nodded. "Me too. I want you to run a full diagnostic on the island's security. Make sure there's nothing else, no other breaches."

Rush knew every Lock and Key location was checked on a regular basis, making sure the security was up to par and that the system hadn't been breached in any way. The process was ongoing and completely random. Twenty-four-seven, three sixty-five. If he wasn't mistaken, they'd run a check on the island not too long ago, maybe six months. Theoretically, it all should be secure but there was that hole on the path that Kat had stumbled onto and the reports of other off-kilter cameras.

Another thought hit him. "You aren't doing this just to keep me occupied, are you? I told you, I'm fine, goddammit. I barely knew Kat and you wanted her gone anyway."

Archer stood up with a scowl. "I don't assign busy work. You should know that by now. Don't insult me by suggesting it. I need this done. Are you up to it?"

Rush nodded once.

"Good. See to it. And be very thorough. Every single thing no matter how trivial."

"Understood."

Archer gave him a terse nod and walked out the cabin door, closing it behind him.

Rush lifted the bottle to his lips but paused as another thought occurred. Archer was worried. That was the only explanation. But about what? Not that he'd say anything unless he was absolutely sure there was an issue. Then, and only then, would he share his worry and ask for solutions.

Rush heaved out a long sigh. Archer's orders meant staying on the island for at least another week. There were a lot of details on this one. Lots of cameras and area to cover. He'd already made a lot of headway on the cameras, but a system wide diagnostic would take a lot longer.

Archer asking for a complete check struck him as unusual. Kat disappearing was another oddity. Rush hated this kind of abnormality. He'd learned in his military days that when something odd happened, he just had to brace for the other fucking shoe to drop.

He took a big swallow of his beer and sat down on his couch. Normally he would sit on the veranda and watch the ocean, letting the age-old rhythm soothe him. But he knew if he went out there tonight, he'd just scan the waves for Kat. In his brain, he knew there was no way she'd be found alive. Shit, he'd nearly drowned himself and he was a strong swimmer. But her likely demise wouldn't stop him from looking anyway.

He had to let go of her. Put her out of his mind. It was an accident. She got pulled under by the current. Rip currents from underground rivers and caves, where water flowed in and out of the lagoon, could be fierce. She could have been sucked into one. If only he truly believed that, then he'd be able to put it all behind him. But his gut was telling him there was more to it. A lot more and this security check just might lead him there. He needed to know what happened to Kat. He lied to Archer. He wasn't okay. His soul hurt. He'd thought that part of him had died a long time ago, but being with Kat had brought him back to life and now she was gone. He was definitely not okay.

He and Archer discussed sending divers down to find her but, in the end, Archer said leaving her wherever she was, would be the best for the Society. No need to speak to anyone. A body tended to need an explanation.

Except the way his gut roiled, and the hair on his arms stood up was proof he didn't like Archer's solution. If Kat's body was down there, it bothered him to leave her. She deserved to be brought to the surface. Buried properly. His knuckles were white as he gripped the beer bottle. He put it down on the coffee table and flexed his fists. He closed his eyes but immediately opened them again when an image of Kat immediately danced behind his eyelids.

He remembered the way she'd tasted when he'd kissed her; white wine and sweetness. The way she'd smelled of strawberries and sunscreen. Her smile and the way her expressive eyes alerted him every time she'd uttered a lie and, more importantly, when she hadn't. How could someone he'd known for such a short period of time leave such a mark on his life?

He swore and got up from the couch. There was no point in sitting there sulking, the outcome wasn't going to change. Work would keep him busy and his brain occupied until he was exhausted so he could fall asleep. He put the beer bottle in the recycling bin and headed out the door. He'd go to the Hub and start running diagnostics.

"Rush, I was sorry to hear about pretty little Kat," a voice said behind him on the path.

He turned to find Fisher and Davis walking towards him.

"Yes," Davis agreed. "Such a shame."

Rush wasn't in the frame of mind to deal with their bullshit. His tone was abrupt when he asked, "What are you gentlemen up to?" He didn't want Kat's name in their mouths, let alone talk to them about her.

"We're just discussing the treasure," Fisher said.

"And the storm." Davis scanned the clouds. "It's not looking good. Might be time to leave the island."

"Safe travels," Rush said and then turned on his heel and left.

"Hey, Danton," Rush said as he entered the Hub. "I'm going to be in that office for a while. I'm going to be running diagnostics." He nodded to Pierre who was sitting next to Danton. He had the impression that the two men were talking before he came in but had stopped because of him. What was that about? Was it because of Kat or because of something with the security? Danton had to be going off shift, so Pierre had to be coming on. Rush made a mental note to check the logs to see when each man was working. Who knew if it would be relevant but he sensed a curious vibe and knew something was up. He went into the office and closed the door.

A minute later there was a knock and Danton entered. "I just wanted to say I'm sorry about Kat."

He nodded. The man was not here to extend condolences or at least not only to do that although why everyone was offering them to him was a puzzle. Maybe he'd been more obvious than he'd thought in his feelings for her. He sighed. "What is it, Danton?"

"We've spent the last couple of days going over all the cameras with nothing standing out, right?" At Rush's nod, he continued. "This morning we overlaid the camera locations and their field of view on the island map with a sequence of events by date and time." He paused. "Can I show you?"

"Yes." He stood and moved out of the way so Danton could sit down at the computer.

Danton brought up a map of the island with camera locations pinpointed. He gestured to the screen, "Now watch what happens." He struck a few keys and the screen came alive, highlighting cameras that were off or out of focus by date. "Do you see it?" he asked.

Rush grunted as lines on the screen linked and stretched. "A grid pattern."

Danton nodded. "Someone is altering the cameras in sequence to create squares of blind spots. They're searching for something."

And he knew what. Fucking treasure. Davis, Fisher, Humber, and Valentine. One or all of them had to be behind this. "Good work, Danton. Go home and get some sleep. We'll talk more tomorrow."

Danton got up. "Thanks. See you in the morning." He left the room.

Rush stared at the screen. He hit a few keys and watched the sequence again. No doubt this was treasure hunters but if it was those four, then how were they doing it? They shouldn't even know the cameras were there, let alone know how to turn the birdhouse so the camera didn't catch what it was supposed to catch. It still came back to Rush's gut instinct that there was an inside person. He just had to figure out who the culprit was and make him pay.

He sighed and brought up the security cameras again. Besides the grid pattern were there any more holes? There was at least one blind spot. The one Kat stumbled onto. How many more could be out there?

Four hours later, Rush got up and grabbed his laptop and headed out. So far, he'd found two more blind spots which was interesting since they'd just done a diagnostic six months ago. They weren't real blind spots, more like the cameras just weren't set quite right. They were just slightly off in the direction they were supposed to be facing. Could just be that in the last few storms that hit the island, the cameras shifted due to high winds. Or there could be something more sinister going on. There wasn't any discernable pattern so the shifts might not have anything to do with the treasure hunters.

He was starving. It was just after nine and other than the wine he'd shared with Kat, he hadn't eaten since breakfast. He was headed down the path toward the dining room when he realized Daisy was headed toward him.

"I'm so sorry, Rushton. She was such a nice woman."

Her condolences hit him in the gut in a way the others hadn't. Visceral and aggressive.

He swallowed. "Yes, she was."

It seemed silly to say but he knew it to be true. There was something fundamentally good about Kat. Something that made him smile. He hadn't realized just how much he needed goodness in his life. Now a chasm yawned in his chest, as if he'd known Kat for years instead of days.

Daisy squeezed his arm. "Better days ahead," she murmured as she passed him and continued on her way.

But were there? Better days ahead? *Don't dwell*. He bent to pick up a piece of garbage that had fallen on the path when he noticed that he was in the area where Kat had appeared suddenly. He straightened and looked around. He walked back a few feet and located a camera. Then he walked forward and located the other one. There was a curve in the path and that's why they didn't overlap. That's what Pierre had said. Still, it was a bit odd. There were some larger trees around so another camera could be hidden in one of those to cover the whole. *Why wasn't that discovered on the last diagnostic?*

He headed back to his cabin and opened the fridge. There were sandwiches on a tray along with a salad. He'd requested to have food brought in. The kitchen staff was stellar and although it was only a sandwich, it was excellent. Roast beef with sprouts and spicy mustard. He chewed and then took a swig of beer. Exhausted lethargy seeped into his bones. Today had been an endless and traumatic day. He'd fucking drowned, for God's sake. He'd been through worse, but he was usually prepared for it. When shit happened out of the blue, the toll was always more.

He finished his sandwich and then sat down with his laptop. He was still too alert to go to bed. Instead, he started scouring the footage of Kat. He still had no idea what she was really doing on the island. There were answers somewhere and he was determined to find them.

CHAPTER SIXTEEN

Kat's eyes burned like they'd been scrubbed with sandpaper. She'd been up all night trying to figure out where the treasure was buried. Danny had been right. BlackEye had talked all about the kidney-shaped island which was obviously the Lock and Key Island, based on his description of where it was. He'd alluded to it a lot.

He'd also mentioned that the island presented the safest place to keep his treasure, but then the trail got murky. She didn't have the first mate's account so not many details were available. There were other accounts from sailors, some working as privateers and some in the military that mentioned something so frightening about the island that they avoided the place like the plague. She couldn't decide if that part of the story was real or made up. Sailors were notoriously superstitious, so her money was on made up.

She rested her chin on her hand. It wasn't like the children's stories where there was a map with an X or a clever little rhyming poem that told of the secret location. No, the knowledge died with the pirate, so how were they going to find it? If the booty hadn't been found by now, did it even exist? There had been a few reports of the treasure over time in other historical documents but honestly, it could all be just so much hogwash. Or maybe someone else had found it and just walked off with it. Anything was possible.

"I've been doing a grid search," Danny said matter of factly puffing his chest out a bit as he spoke. "I'm making some progress. It's slow but it's methodical and organized."

She glanced up at him. "Do you know how long that would take to do the whole island that way?" She hated that she was being so discouraging but he had to face reality. Seeing the defensive look on his face, she relented. "A grid search is the proper way to do it and being methodical about it is awesome. Much better than Dad ever did. I just don't think Smith is going to give us the time we'd need to do this right."

"I know," he agreed.

Encouraged she continued. "Don't forget, there are buildings on the island. A treasure chest could be buried under one of those and you'd never know it."

"Maybe," Danny commented, "but I don't think so. You've read his notebooks. Did BlackEye strike you as being lazy or stupid?"

She shook her head. Where was her brother going with this?

"Me either. The buildings tend to be on the outside of the island. I think BlackEye would have gone inland quite a bit. He wouldn't have wanted anyone else to know the treasure was there, so there was no way he'd risk burying it too close to the sea. With that in mind…" Danny pulled out a paper map of the island and spread it out on the table. "I think we can rule out this area." He ran his finger along the outline of the half of the island where the cabins were located. "I also think it's not going to be adjacent to the major resort areas, like pools, tennis courts, etc. The ground would've been dug up for that and it would've been discovered already."

"Okay," Kat rubbed her eyes. "So where have you been looking?"

He pointed to the larger untouched areas in the southern bit. "I've been doing a grid pattern on these areas. So far, nothing."

He'd covered the bit in the center of the southern tip where there were a few trails but nothing major, and by the hospital where there was more green space. Kat rubbed her temples. They'd been at this long enough that a headache was thrumming behind her eyes.

Danny went over to the counter and poured a cup of coffee. He added milk from the mini fridge and set it in front of her. She smiled her thanks and took a hasty sip, hoping the caffeine would work a little magic.

He returned his attention to the map. "I'm going to move to this area next." He pointed to the area just north of the center of the southern section.

"Um, no," Kat said and shook her head.

"What do you mean, no?"

She grimaced. "Have you been telling your inside guy where you're searching?"

"Yeah. That way he can manage the cameras and stuff."

Made sense. Pointing to the area on the map, she said, "The map doesn't show it but there's a building here. It's big and gray with no windows. It has serious security to get in. Not just the usual palm and retinal scan. Maybe DNA or some such. Anyway, there's no getting into that sucker. And there's no getting under it as well. If the treasure was there, it would've been found."

Danny leaned back in his seat. "Shit. I was really hoping."

"Yeah, I know. The reality is… I think it might be on the north end of the island."

"Why?" Danny asked and then took a sip of his coffee.

"Hunch."

Danny raised his eyebrows at her.

"Okay. Fine. The south end has been developed and not just by the Lock and Key. There was another group here before this one. They were some sort of missionary group trying to spread their religion to the region. It didn't work so well and in the early nineteen thirties, the Society bought it for a song. All the development has been on the southern part of the island though.

"You read up on it." Danny grinned.

"Of course I did. You said this was what you were going after and then you disappeared. What else was I supposed to do? I went to your place and read all your research and then did some more of my own."

"It's good. It's good. So, you think it's on the north end of the island?"

She nodded. "Unfortunately, it's also the unstable end. They say there are areas of sinkholes and sometimes chunks of ground have been swallowed up. They've even lost a few workers apparently."

"Shit." Danny rubbed his face with his hands. "I've been avoiding that end because the foliage is thick, and God only knows what lives in there. If there are also sinkholes it makes the chances of finding the treasure that much less." He met his sister's gaze. "What the hell are we supposed to do?"

That was a damn good question. "Part of me wants to run. Just run to the other end of the earth."

He shrugged. "I've been thinking the same thing. Just run like hell. To be honest, if I thought we'd make it, I might consider it. But this guy, whoever he is, he has access to the Society's resources. I don't think we can outrun the Society. I think he'd find us." He swallowed. "Smith also said he killed a member to get the token and I believe him."

She bit her lip. "I agree, he'd find us and I have no doubts he killed someone. These Society people seem very nonchalant about killing." She shuddered. "And there's Timmy, although he's the asshole that got us into this. However, being an asshole doesn't mean he deserves to die." She sighed. "I should've stayed on the island. Being on the inside gave me more leverage."

Danny put his head in his hands. "I know. I thought of that but I…I just needed you out of there. That place freaks me out. The other workers, I've heard them talking sometimes at night. I have to hide until they all disappear. They say some pretty creepy shit. They talk about members disappearing and weird sex parties." He shook his head. "I just didn't want you there on your own anymore."

She reached out and squeezed his arm again. If she were being honest, she was happy to be out of there too. The worst part was that they were both going to have to go back in. "You know, we're going to have to figure out a different plan."

"What do you mean?"

She rested her chin in her palm. "BlackEye's treasure hasn't been found in almost three hundred years. We don't have access to the island, or enough equipment to do a thorough search and we can't even look during the day. What do you think the chances are that we'll actually find anything?"

Her brother's shoulders sagged. "I know, I know. This whole thing was stupid and it's all my fault we're in this mess."

She wanted to argue with him, but in this he was right and the sooner he realized this the better. With any luck he would be different from their father and not make the same mistake again. She stood up. "I'm going to get some sleep.

We'll figure something out after I wake up. Start thinking and maybe making food." She gave her twin a quick hug. "We'll work it out. Have faith." Great. Now she sounded like their father. It was definitely time to go to bed.

Hours later, Kat sat on the deck and stared out at the water. They were anchored in a calm bay and the Caribbean was showing off its' beautiful colors The sun's rays bounced off the turquoise water. The sky was a deep perfect blue. A breeze came up and it seemed cooler than before. She shivered. Off in the distance, the sky looked darker. A storm was coming. *In more ways than one.*

Running really did seem like the best option but she knew there was no way she could live with herself and realistically neither could Danny. Timmy Camerari was not the best guy in all kinds of ways, but if they left him, he was dead. Hell, chances were good, they were all dead but at least now, at this moment, they had a chance, no matter how slim. It was still a chance.

Danny came up to the flybridge and handed her a cup of coffee. "Sorry I don't have any wine."

She offered him a smile. "I'm good, thanks. Coffee is what I need." She took a sip. Her brother was not going to like what she was about to suggest but she didn't feel like there was another choice. "Danny, I think I've found a way to make things work."

He met her gaze. "Why do I have the feeling I'm not going to like this?"

"This guy, Mr. Smith, he knows when you're on the island and where you're searching. He has Timmy. We are stuck because we can't outrun him, right?"

"Yeah, I guess."

"What we need is someone who can take care of him for us." She sat forward on the sofa. "The issue really isn't finding the treasure… it's rescuing Timmy and getting rid of Mr.

Smith. We need to work towards that goal instead of wasting time finding the treasure."

Danny stared at her. "And how do you think we're going to do that?"

"*We're* not. Someone else is going to do it for us."

"I'm not following you."

She stared down into her coffee cup, refusing to meet his gaze. This is where Danny was going to balk at her plan. "We need to tell Rush."

He shook his head. "Nuh-uh. Nope. No way. We are not telling one of those people. They'll kill us."

"Just hear me out." She shifted her gaze from him to the storm clouds building on the horizon, then back.

He sat staring at her, arms folded across his chest.

"Look, one of the rules of the Society is that you aren't allowed to tell anyone who isn't a member anything about it. And there's no way in hell you're allowed to smuggle someone into, or in this case onto, one of their facilities. Those acts are punishable by death, supposedly."

Danny paled.

"Mr. Smith told you and Timmy about the Society and has helped you sneak in. He's also altered their security system, which considering everything else, must at least be punishable by death if not followed by a lifetime in hell or some such. So, *we* don't need to do anything to Mr. Smith. We just need Rush to do something about him, once he finds out who he is. That solves our problem."

"But what about us? Won't they have us killed just for knowing about the Society?"

She'd been thinking of nothing else since the idea came to her. "I don't know. Maybe. But a maybe is better than a sure thing. There are extenuating circumstances. Maybe we can work out a deal or something. We can try and find the treasure for them during daylight hours with help. We'll figure out something. I just think we can't do this alone and the chance of us finding the treasure anytime soon, if there even is a treasure to find, is almost non-existent. We don't have much choice, Danny."

He stared at her intently, like he was seeing her, but his thoughts were racing, and then slowly, he nodded. "It's a really bad idea but you're right; I can't see another way out."

Her stomach unknotted a minuscule amount, and her shoulders sagged. She leaned back against the cushioned bench. "Okay then. Does Mr. Smith know you're going to the island tonight?"

"Yeah. I told him I was going to do one more pass over the last bit on the southern tip of the island."

She took a sip of coffee and swallowed. "That's good. I'm going with you and I'll find Rush." Her stomach fluttered at the thought. He was going to be pissed for sure but maybe, just maybe he might be a little happy to see her too. That would be nice. Another kiss would be better still.

Danny was on his feet. "How the hell are you going to do that without being seen? Everyone thinks you're dead. Smith will see you and then he'll freak out."

"I'm going to swim through the tunnel to the lagoon with you and then get out of the water after you leave. I'll go through the trees along the edge of the path back to the southern part of the island. I'll wear one of your landscaper uniforms with a hat. You have more than one, right?"

He nodded.

"Hopefully everyone will just think I'm another worker. As long as I stick to the less-traveled paths, I should be good." It was all bullshit but what else was she going to do? There wasn't much of a choice. She couldn't call Rush because she didn't have his number.

"I don't like it," Danny said as he paced.

"Join the club. It's not my favorite solution either but

there's not much choice, is there? We just have to hope that no one notices me."

Danny swore. "This really sucks," he said and then went down the ladder to the deck below.

"Tell me about it," she mumbled as she looked out over the water. The waves were getting bigger. Clouds towered on the horizon. The storm was getting closer. They were almost out of time. What she hadn't said earlier was that as a member, she might have some protection… that is… if they didn't kill her for lying to them about her name.

She also hadn't mentioned her backup plan. She and Danny had to wait out the storm on the island, but as soon as it passed, they could take the boat and disappear. People would chalk it up to the storm taking the boat and them with it. It meant they'd be leaving Timmy, but if Rush helped them to find Smith, then their longtime friend would be okay. She wasn't going to die over this, and neither was her brother. Not if she could help it.

CHAPTER SEVENTEEN

Rush tightened the screw and then jostled the housing. The camera was solidly in place. He grabbed his phone and checked the feed. It was running and pointing to where it should. The gap where the path curved was now covered by a camera.

"Rush, the cameras are still offline. Is everything okay on your end?" Pierre's voice sounded in his ear.

"Yeah. I was having problems with one of the screws. Fixed it. Refresh your feed and it should be back online. Let me know how everything looks on your end."

After a brief pause, Pierre responded. "Got it. Perfect here. You're right. Better resolution."

"Good," he grunted. "I'm going to take the ladder back and call it a day."

"See you tomorrow."

"Roger that," Rush responded and then took the earbud out of his ear. He carried the ladder back to the shed and walked along the deserted path to his cabin. It was late, and most of the guests on the island had retired hours ago. He'd known it was unlikely he'd encounter anyone, but the place was eerily empty. Checking an uneasy feeling, he turned on the lights in his cabin and then took a beer from the fridge. It had been a long fucking day and he needed sleep but, like last night, his brain wasn't going to shut off just yet.

The island's staff had been busy doing storm prep, which gave him the perfect cover for mucking about with the cameras. The storm was only a day or two away, depending on the shifting winds. People would begin to evacuate first thing in the morning. He'd grabbed a copy of the list of members who were leaving on the first boat. It didn't surprise him to see Davis and Fisher at the top of the list. They weren't fools. No point in sticking around.

He pulled his laptop out of the safe and booted it up. Pulling up a schematic of the cameras on the resort, he decided to finish his review of the remaining cameras he hadn't checked yet to see if they were pointing in the best direction. Might as well channel his disquiet and nerves toward something useful.

An hour and a half later, he found his first anomaly. He double-checked the camera angle and then the schematic. The camera was not pointing in the correct direction. He stared at the screen again and then at the schematic. He pulled up a detailed map of the property and studied it. What he should be seeing was a path and an open space that was in the southern part of the island. The only thing on his screen were trees, telling him the camera had been moved. The question was why? What the hell was going on that someone didn't want them to see? And when? He was sure he'd checked this camera earlier today and it was working fine. So someone must have moved it tonight.

He thought about calling security to check but that would alert whoever was behind this. Whoever was doing this knew about the cameras which meant they had to work for the Society and having the ability to know where each one was and then change the area it covered meant they had to be on the security team or be one of a handful of people that worked at the top levels in the Society.

He pulled himself to his feet. It was late but this couldn't wait. He hurried to the bedroom and pulled on a black long-sleeved T-shirt to go with his dark jeans. He also pulled out his gun and tucked it in his waistband, then pulled the hem of his shirt over the bulge.

He locked his cabin and then made his way over to the path where the adjusted camera had been. Ironically it was almost directly across from his cabin, just through the trees. He had to take an indirect route to get there, however, because he wasn't going to hack his way through the bushes at this point in the night.

Ten minutes later, he was moving as silently as possible toward the location. He'd stayed off the main path, walking a parallel path that was used by the groundskeepers and maintenance staff, so he wasn't on camera. He then quietly cut over to the camera where it only took a second to see it was facing the wrong direction.

Rush studied the whole area. Nothing stirred, not even a breeze. What was someone trying to hide? There was nothing there. It was just after one a.m. He squatted and rested his back against the base of a tree. He'd give it a while and see if anyone showed up.

The breeze finally came up and brought the smell of flowers. It made him think of Kat. She smelled like strawberries. *What a waste.* It didn't matter now that he'd been brought down here to find out the truth about her and possibly eliminate her if she was a threat. She wasn't. He didn't say it out loud because there was no point and because Archer would question his judgment, but he knew…knew in the very marrow of his bones, Kat wasn't a threat. That fact didn't solve the mystery of what was really going on, or how she'd gotten caught up in it. He hated the thought of her as collateral damage, but that's what this was shaping up to be.

After forty-five minutes, with his patience wearing thin, he detected footsteps crunching on gravel. And something else. Something being dragged. A few seconds later, a worker came into view. He was pulling some sort of machinery. What the hell was that thing? With the impending storm, it could be anything.

Suddenly there was a scream and then a burst of laughter. A woman came down the path with a man following close behind her. "You must be quiet, Donna."

The woman laughed. "Why? Why do I have to be quiet?"

"You'll wake people," the man said and stumbled. He grabbed a tree to keep himself upright. "Besides, you could wake your husband. Isn't your cabin around here somewhere?"

Donna spun in a tipsy circle. "I have no idea. I'm not sure where we are."

The man caught up to her and wrapped his arms around her waist. "We're at our spot. See the tree over there?"

She turned to look. "Right." Then she giggled. "Shhhh. We can't be loud then. Frank might wake up. He would be very cross if he knew I was out with you. I told him the affair was over. Not that I care. He lost all our fucking money. He's a moron. He keeps going on about treasure. As fucking if. He says he wants to stay on the island during the storm to give him a leg up in finding it. Stupid. I never should have married him. Daddy was right."

"Divorce him. Marry me," the man said and then kissed Donna. The two stumbled about until they came up against a tree and then things got serious. The man was quick to pull up Donna's dress and she responded by undoing his pants.

Rush glanced over to where he'd seen the worker but the man had melted away into the trees. That sounded like a good idea. Whatever was going on here, it wasn't going to happen now that Donna and company were screwing up against a tree. He contemplated fixing the camera angle but decided it would just alert whoever was behind this. It was better to just let things play out. He knew where to focus his search so he could check the cameras all around the area and see who turned up.

And now he knew Humber's wife was screwing around on him and he had no money left. But most importantly, he was after the treasure, and he thought he was going to stay on the island and look for it when everyone else evacuated. He was going to be in for a rude surprise.

Rush moved silently back through the trees to the service path and made his way back to his cabin. A complete waste of time but at least he knew for sure that someone was moving the cameras, so they weren't capturing footage from where they were supposed to. Now he just had to figure out why.

CHAPTER EIGHTEEN

Would these fucking people, literally, ever leave? Kat huffed out an exacerbated breath and softly cursed Danny. Her brother had left more than an hour ago but just after he'd gone, a couple showed up and decided to go skinny dipping in the lagoon. She was caught in the trees off to the side of the lagoon, too far from the path to try and head down the island. She was up against a mangrove swamp and she was not venturing through that at night without a light and a big ass gun. There could be gators and God knew what else in there.

She scratched her head underneath the ball cap. Who had wool hats in the tropics? She readjusted her shirt as well, trying to avoid getting bitten by whatever was around. She was fighting a losing battle on that one. She was wearing one of the groundskeepers' uniforms that her brother had. It was way too big but it offered the best disguise.

Moaning sounds reached her ears. *Great.* Now they were having sex. A shockingly short time later, they were finished and getting dressed. The woman was struggling with her clothing but the man was already heading back to their golf cart. He stumbled a bit. They'd had an entire bottle of wine between them which wasn't necessarily a lot, but by the look of the two of them, it wasn't the first one tonight.

An idea came to her. She quickly moved around the lagoon and then got on the path. She went through the trees on the outskirts of the path, hoping they wouldn't notice her. They were preoccupied with bickering about bug bites and the chick's missing shoe. She emerged onto the path ahead of the golf cart and then took a deep breath and cleared her throat.

"Oh," the woman exclaimed. "You scared me. Where did you come from?"

"I'm sorry. I didn't mean to startle you. Just doing the nightly rounds. It's really not safe over here at night. Would you like me to drive you back to your cabin?"

"Ish fine. I can drive," the man said and stumbled once more.

"You're drunk," the woman scolded. "So am I." She giggled. "Let the woman drive us."

The man crashed down in the back of the golf cart and slapped a hand on his neck. "Fine. Fine. Let's go. I'm gettin' eaten alive."

The woman got in and Kat slid behind the wheel. "What cabin is it?"

"Twenty-seven."

Kat took off down the path, keeping her hat low so it covered her face. Rush wasn't far from there. She pulled up by twenty-seven and then parked the golf cart. The man gave her a twenty and thanked her for the ride. She waited until they were inside and then got out of the golf cart and wiped the steering wheel down where she'd touched it.

Quickly she made her way down to Rush's cabin and then went around to the back. She walked onto the veranda and peeked in through the sliding glass doors. There was a light on over the stove but other than that the place was dark. She flicked on her pen light and looked at the lock on the doors. No way to pick that. It was on the inside. Now what was she supposed to do? She didn't think his front door was a good option since it was on the main path and anyone could happen by plus there could be cameras. A window maybe?

"Show me your hands," a voice said as what she assumed was a gun was pressed into her back.

"Rush?"

There was a beat and then he whirled her around. "Kat?" he growled and took a step closer.

"Hey."

"Hey? Are you fucking serious? *Hey*? I thought you were dead." The gun was still in his hand and pointed at her chest.

"Um, can we talk?"

"Give me one reason I shouldn't shoot you right now," he demanded.

This wasn't going the way she'd hoped it would. The way she wanted it to go. So much for being happy to see her. It was so dark she couldn't clearly see his face but his tone had dropped the air temperature around her to more glacial than tropical, and the gun made it pretty obvious she'd been wrong about Rush. *Maybe dead wrong.* "I need your help."

Rush turned her around and pushed her along the veranda until they came to the front door, his gun in her back the whole time. He unlocked the door and then pushed her inside. "Stand right there and don't move."

She nodded, arms still raised, standing just inside the door. It was hard to see because only the light above the stove was on, but he quickly closed every blind or curtain in the place.

Then he turned and walked back to stand in front of her, gun still drawn. "What the fuck is going on? Who are you and what are you doing here?"

He hadn't turned on any more lights so it was difficult to see his features in the low lighting, but his eyes glittered icily.

She shivered. "I'm here because of my brother. He…got involved in something and got in way over his head."

Rush leaned in so he was inches from her. "You're gonna have to do better than that."

She cursed her brother once more and then started at the beginning. "My name is Kat Rollings. My brother Danny and his friend Timmy Camerari got involved with a member of the Society. This member, they call him Mr. Smith or at least Danny does, wanted Danny to find BlackEye's treasure. It's supposed to be buried here on the island."

"Why your brother? What is he? Some kind of treasure hunter?"

She bit back a sigh. "He's a plumber. But my father was, so we were taught the basics. Timmy bragged about Danny being a treasure hunter and…it just all got out of hand. Danny had no idea what the hell he was signing on for. Now Mr. Smith has Timmy and will kill him if my brother doesn't find the treasure soon. He'll kill us all. We're running out of time."

The pulse in Rush's jaw jumped. "Where do you come into it?"

"Danny knew he was in over his head and tried to get out. Turns out, Timmy became a hostage. Danny left the token with me, told me where he was going, and then he disappeared. He was supposed to reach out to me in a few days but once he got down here, Danny didn't want to risk the call. Smith supplied all the provisions and the boat, anything Danny needs to find the treasure, but he can't get away. Not with Timmy being a hostage. When I didn't hear from Danny, I got worried, so I used the token and came down here to look for my brother."

"Where's he now?"

"He's here on the island, looking for the treasure."

Rush's eyes narrowed. "How is he on the island? Wait, is he wearing a uniform like the one you have on and is he dragging a piece of equipment that kind of looks like a lawnmower?"

She nodded. "Yeah. He comes onto the island at night. Smith stashed all the tools in the woods by the waterfall, including a ground-penetrating radar unit. My brother swims in and uses them and then swims out again."

"There's a tunnel in the lagoon?"

"Underwater, yes. When we went to swim under the waterfall my brother grabbed me, and we swam out." She wanted to apologize for scaring him and not telling him she was alive. In her fantasies that would've mattered and he would've kissed her because he was so happy to see her. In reality, Rush just looked extremely pissed off. His whole body was rigid as his eyes flashed at her and he clenched his jaw. Her heart dropped to her knees. She'd been hoping he'd be happy to see her. Instead, he was livid. Disappointment made her shoulders droop.

"I want you to get your brother to come here. We need to talk."

She shook her head. "I can't. Mr. Smith knows what my brother does. If he shows up here, he'll know we're trying to get you to help us and he'll kill Timmy. And probably us too. Danny doesn't know anything about Smith. He's just a voice on the other end of the phone. Someone with access to all the cameras and who knows the security here. I sneaked onto the island tonight. We used dry bags for our clothing when we swam in, but Danny went to look for the treasure and I waited and then came to find you. I was trying to figure out how to get into your place when you found me. Hopefully Smith didn't see me on the cameras or at least didn't recognize me if he did. I drove a drunk couple to their cabin and then walked here. Smith will know if Danny comes here."

Rush stared at her.

"Please, Rush, we need your help. I don't want my brother to die. He's a moron sometimes but he's the only family I have left."

"You know that by rights both of you should be killed for breaking the rules of the Society."

"Danny's not a member. He didn't break any rules."

Rush scoffed. "He came on to private property and is searching for something that doesn't belong to him."

"He was invited," she countered. "And he hasn't found anything yet."

"But you're a member and you lied on your application form. You faked your own death and came back on the island." Rush looked like he had more to say, his frown deepening. But whatever he meant to spit out, he swallowed.

"I didn't deliberately fake my death. But anyway, is that against the rules?" It wouldn't surprise her. The damn rule book was so damn thick.

"It's against the law," Rush supplied.

She snorted. "The Society doesn't strike me as being concerned with the law."

"No, but it's very concerned about you and now your brother. You're both in a world of trouble and you're not getting out anytime soon."

Her stomach dropped and a sharp shudder swept down her back. Danny was right. This was a bad decision. Had she just gotten them killed?

CHAPTER NINETEEN

It took everything he had to not crush Kat in a hug. His knees got weak when he turned her around and realized who it was. All the air left his lungs. He hadn't realized just how hard her 'death' had hit him until she was standing there in front of him, alive. He wanted nothing more than to take her to bed and not let her out again. His heart slammed against his ribcage as he tried to take in the fact that she was standing in front of him. He'd been thinking about how he'd missed his opportunity with Kat and that if he had it to do all over again, he'd make sure he did a hell of a lot more than kiss her.

Now though, he had to be professional. Do the job he was brought here to do. His impulse was to curse and throw things. How could she be so stupid as to lie to the Society? This whole thing was an epic nightmare. She was in so deep, there was no way out. And her brother, he was a dead man.

He stared at her while he fought a war internally. Did he march her over to the Hub where they had cells for this sort of thing? Then Smith, if he existed would know for sure. Or did he believe her, *trust her,* and hide her in this cabin with him instead? He knew what he wanted to do but he also realized he wasn't thinking with the head he should be listening to.

"Turn around and put your hands on the wall. Spread your legs." First things first. He'd search her and make sure she didn't have a weapon. She did as she was told and he tucked his gun in the waistband of his jeans. He ran his hands over each leg and then up over her ass. He did her back and her arms and then he did her front. His heart rate ticked up. She wasn't wearing a bra.

He struggled to control his breath and turned her around again. "Sit on the sofa." Again, she did as she was told, and he pulled out his cell phone. Archer answered on the first ring. "We have a problem. My cabin. Now." He hung up and then crossed the room and stood above her, arms folded over his chest.

"Tell me the whole thing one more time."

She sighed but repeated the tale she'd told him earlier. He didn't ask any questions, just listened to her words as well as her tone. He'd interrogated a lot of liars in his life, and he was positive she was telling the truth. Her story was simply too outrageous to be a lie.

A knock sounded at the door and he went over, letting Archer in. "What's the problem?" Archer asked and then stopped dead at seeing Kat on the couch. "I see." Archer's eyes turned a particular shade of cold that meant bad things.

Rush needed to get him to understand the story before he made any decisions on her fate. "Kat, tell him what you told me."

Kat scooted to the edge of the couch, twisted her fingers together and repeated her story.

Archer settled in an armchair and flattened his palms on the armrests, but that was the only outward sign that he was angry.

Rush had moved to the side of the room and leaned against the wall. Staying silent was hard, his instinct to protect Kat crowing like a rooster. But he knew if he answered any of Archer's questions for her, it would be worse for both of them. Archer would send him to some other location and take care of Kat and Danny himself. They'd be dead before daybreak. Rush had no idea if she understood that her fate was totally in Archer's hands, and it wasn't looking good.

Archer met his gaze. "You believe her."

"The story is just too bizarre to be made up," he justified. "More importantly, other facts that we know provide corroborating evidence."

Steepling his fingers, Archer said, "How did you get the token?"

"My brother gave it to me."

"Where did he get it?" Archer asked in a deceptively soft voice.

Rush's gut tightened. If she answered this question in a way Archer didn't like, this was over. She'd be dead and Rush would be—he didn't finish the thought. He crossed his arms over his chest and dug his fingers into his bicep to keep from jumping to her defense.

She frowned. "He got it from Timmy who got it from Mr. Smith."

"Are you sure your brother and Timmy weren't there when…Mr. Smith retrieved the token?"

"Pretty sure. Danny just said Timmy had gotten it from Smith and gave it to him. Why? Where did it come from?"

"A very dear friend of mine who was killed for it."

Kat blanched. "I-I know this looks bad, but my brother would never be involved in murder. Neither would Timmy. They may have been blinded by the prospect of finding treasure, but they aren't that stupid."

Archer remained silent for a couple of minutes and then asked, "The cameras?"

Rush let out the breath he'd been holding and nodded, glancing at Kat and back at Archer who gave him a slight nod. "I have found four cameras slightly out of position. A fifth one tonight. They were moved so her brother could search for the treasure without being seen and whoever put them back in place is just a bit sloppy so they don't always point as they should."

Kat opened her mouth but he shot her a look and she closed it again. Now was not the time for her to speak. She was damn lucky it appeared Archer believed her about her brother. Rush silently prayed she didn't push now. Archer was as pissed as Rush had ever seen him. Someone was doing something on the island that went against the rules and, the even bigger sin, they were doing it behind his back. And had killed something Archer considered a friend, in the process. Archer didn't call many people friend, so this was monumental.

Archer knew it all. Everything that happened. He was the devil, but he was also the Pope. He heard everyone's confessions and made sure they never came to light. Going behind his back to get the treasure was tantamount to mutiny. Someone had just significantly shortened their lifespan. They just didn't know it yet.

"Does your brother expect you to go back tonight?"

She nodded.

"You won't be. You'll stay here with Rush so he can keep an eye on you. More incentive for your brother to keep on doing his job. He will keep searching for the treasure while we track down Mr. Smith. What does your brother look like?"

Kat struggled with the answer for a second, frowning as if trying to figure out why he was asking. "Er, well, me. We're twins. He's taller and his hair is shorter, obviously, and maybe darker but we have the same features. His are just the male version."

"How tall is he?"

Kat bit her lip. "You're going to talk to him and you need to replace him on camera so Mr. Smith doesn't know."

Archer merely stared at her but she must have taken it as a yes because she went on to describe him in better detail. "Five-ten. He's lean as well and he's wearing one of these uniforms."

Archer stood.

"Please don't hurt him," Kat begged. "I know I have no right to ask that but he's my brother."

"No, you don't," Archer agreed. "I won't hurt him now. We need the charade to continue but I make no promises about the future. A price has to be paid for this web of deception."

He walked over to the door where Rush joined him.

Archer lowered his voice. "Keep your eye on her. I'll install someone on the boat that will look enough like her to satisfy Mr. Smith. And no, it won't be from here. We can't trust anyone on the island but I have other resources, as you know. If she says anything else of interest let me know. Otherwise keep her close to you at all times."

"Will do. Her brother is not far from here." He described the location and Archer nodded. "Keep doing your security sweep. Just do it from here if you can. I'll get you the equipment you need. Make sure no one sees her. With the coming storm, no one should find it odd that you are staying in your cabin."

Rush nodded and Archer left.

Turning back, he studied Kat. Her eyes had widened like teacups, and her hands shook slightly in her lap. "He won't kill my brother, will he?"

"Not tonight." That's all he could offer. "I told you before I don't lie. Archer will not kill your brother until this is all sorted but after that I make no guarantees."

"Will he kill me?"

It was the question he'd been asking himself all night. If it were anyone else, he'd say yes without hesitation. But he just couldn't let that happen to Kat. He'd have to find a way around it. Somehow. "I don't know." That was the truth.

She sniffled slightly and then shivered once more.

"It's late. I'm tired. You can have the bathroom first but, Kat, don't try anything. If I have to go find you and drag you back here, it won't be pretty."

Her eyes got even bigger and her mouth dropped open. "I—I'm not going to run. I want this all figured out. I want your help. I *need* your help. Running would be stupid and pointless."

His shoulders relaxed just a fraction. "Good. Then we're on the same page." He gestured towards the bedroom.

She moved past him into the bedroom, and around to the bathroom. "Do you mind if I have a quick shower? I'm salty from the swim in."

He gave her a quick nod, then closed the door. Part of him wanted to trust her but the logical part, the part that knew from years of experience that people often said things and then did something else, knew that the smart play was to go around to the outside shower and wait there, making sure she didn't change her mind.

He let out a sigh and then slipped quietly out the sliding glass door. There was a back door into the shower area. It was latched from the inside but the lock was pathetic and took him seconds to pick. He moved into the shower area and stood in the shadows. If Kat decided to make a run for it, she would run straight into him.

He waited and watched as she got ready for her shower.

She leaned over the sink. What was she doing? Crying. She was crying. *For fuck's sake.* His chest tightened and his hands fisted. He wanted to go in and comfort her. Tell her it would be okay but he didn't know if that was true. From where he stood, it didn't look good and that was causing him significant stress. He'd never experienced anything like this and he had better fucking figure his feelings out.

Suddenly she straightened and stared at the door to the bathroom. What was going on? He went to the glass door and slid it open. She whirled and stared at him.

What? he mouthed.

"Rush." Ronnie was calling his name from inside his cabin.

He glanced at his watch. It was after two a.m. What the hell did she want? He put his finger to his lips and slid out of the bathroom by way of the glass door. He went around to his patio doors and glanced in. Ronnie was standing in the middle of the room wearing a little black cocktail dress and what she used to call fuck-me shoes when they were married. Her hair was down and all of her assets were on full display. She'd come to seduce him.

Why though? If he had to guess because she desperately wanted to know what the hell was going on. Ronnie always thought she could use her feminine wiles and get any information she wanted by fucking someone. She'd been right, most of the time. It was sad. Rush thought once they were married, she'd realize she didn't need to be that way but instead, she'd just fucked other people for information. She always felt like she was on the outside looking in, no matter how many times he'd told her that wasn't so. It was her hang up and she loathed that more than anything on earth. She must have been feeling that now big time since she dressed to seduce him.

She called his name once more and then she walked

towards the coffee table. His laptop was sitting there, lid down. He opened the door just slightly so he could hear if she made any calls or spoke to anyone.

Ronnie lifted the lid. It was password protected and he wasn't worried about her gaining access, but he was curious about what she was going to do. She sat down and tried a few different passwords, but, of course, nothing worked. She swore and then stood up. "Rush," she said one more time and then headed toward the bedroom.

Why not ransack the place if he wasn't home? Maybe she'd find out something. Ronnie was a piece of work. He hadn't realized it during their whirlwind romance, but it came to light pretty quickly once they were married. He'd known early on that he'd made a mistake. He couldn't trust her, but the affair was the last straw. He didn't care what she wore, he still wasn't sleeping with her. Those days were over.

He went back around to the outdoor shower and slid into the shadows. Kat came out onto the deck and as she closed the sliding glass door, he put a hand over her mouth. "It's me. Don't make a sound."

She nodded and closed the door. He pulled her back into the shadows, her back against his front. He kept an arm wrapped around her but his right hand was by the butt of his gun. Ronnie was up to something. He was sure she was searching his bedroom. The bathroom door opened, and Ronnie tiptoed in. She gave everything a cursory glance, and then shrugged and left the room.

"Do you think she's gone?" Kat whispered.

He leaned down and spoke quietly in her ear. "I think she's tossing my cabin. She'll leave when she realizes there's nothing for her to find."

Kat seemed to relax back into him. Her body was suddenly plastered against his, taking his breath away. This wasn't supposed to happen. She was the enemy or, at the very least, she was work and the last woman with whom he'd mixed the two criteria was now tossing his place. He needed to get a grip.

The sound of the front door opening and the footsteps on the path reached them. "It's safe," he said and moved her away. "Go take your shower."

She turned and asked, "Are you going to watch?"

"Are you going to run?" he countered.

She shook her head. "I told you running doesn't work for me."

"Okay then, I'll trust you to take a shower on your own."

She walked back into the bathroom and he followed her, only pausing to lock the door behind him before going through to the bedroom.

"Do you have something I can sleep in?" she asked.

He turned and glanced over at her. She was right. She couldn't sleep in the uniform. "I'll find something. Take your shower." He closed the door and let out a long breath. This was getting damn complicated.

He pulled out a black T-shirt. It would have to do. He walked back to the bathroom but hesitated. He didn't want to invade her privacy which was just fucking weird. She'd turned on the shower, so he just opened the door slightly and hung the T-shirt on the knob then closed the door again.

Fuck, he *did not* need complicated. He'd lived it and had been miserable. Being involved with someone who also worked for the Society had been awful. But being involved with a member who broke the rules? That would be just as fatal for him as it was for them.

He went out to the kitchen and opened the oven. He pulled out his scanner and turned it on. Twenty minutes later he was sure the place wasn't bugged but he still had no idea what Ronnie had been looking for. Did she even know? Was she working with Mr. Smith? That was an interesting thought. He'd have to promise her something big, something worthwhile. Money was one possibility. Oh, she liked it well enough but what turned Ronnie on the most was power. If she was involved in this mess, then it was because someone had promised her more power.

The sound of a door opening brought him back to the present. He went into the bedroom and stopped short. Kat was standing in the middle of the room wearing his T-shirt and nothing else. Just the thought of that had his muscles tensing and a part of his anatomy with a mind of its own standing at attention . Her auburn hair was still damp and curling around her shoulders. There were shadows under her beautiful green eyes. Sadness lurked there.

He cleared his throat. "You can sleep on the left side. If you get up in the night you better tell me why."

"We're sharing the bed?" she croaked.

He glared at her. "Yeah. I'm exhausted and I want to be comfortable. You have to be close by so I can keep an eye on you. I could handcuff you to something"—a bedpost—"or you could sleep on the floor. Sharing a bed with me would be more comfortable. So I suggest you get in the fucking bed on the left side." His last words slipped through tight lips, but the tension was more from the idea of what he'd rather do with this woman on the downy soft mattress than from anger.

She stared at him for a long moment, anxiety and interest shadowing her face, and then she climbed into bed.

Forcing his shoulders into a more natural position, he headed into the bathroom to brush his teeth. When he came out and stowed his gun under his pillow. He peeled off his shirt and jeans, leaving only his boxer briefs. After a final check on the cabin to make sure it was locked up tight, he returned to the bedroom, turned out the lights, and crawled into bed next to Kat.

Lying in the darkness, his thoughts raced. He tried to come up with who Smith could be, but Kat's scent wrapped around him and made it hard to concentrate. Her breathing wasn't even so he knew she was awake also. He wanted to reach out and offer her comfort in the form of mind-blowing sex, but that idea would earn a top spot in the museum of bad ideas. If only he could get it out of his head. Turning on his side, he practiced some breathing exercises he'd learned in the military. A few minutes later he drifted off to sleep.

An odd sound woke him. He remained motionless, not daring to move until he identified what had woken him. He was on his back and Kat had shifted in her sleep, rolling over to curl up to him, her head resting on his chest. She fit perfectly and he was loath to move her but now he needed her to roll off.

The odd sound came again. *Fuck*. Someone was trying to pick the lock on the sliding glass door in the living room. He shoved his hand under his pillow and brought out his gun just as the door slid open. He eased Kat off his chest and got up, grabbed his jeans, and yanked them up his legs. Moving silently, he crossed the room. Someone was walking across the living area. He moved into the hallway and slowly made his way to the other end. He took a quick peek into the living area. Someone was picking up his laptop. They straightened.

"It won't do you any good to steal it, Ronnie. You'll never crack the encryption."

"Shit!"

He hit the light switch beside him and the overhead light came on. Ronnie stood there glaring at him. Only she could be pissed at him for catching her.

"I dropped by earlier and I saw it was out. I was worried it might get stolen since you weren't around."

"So you came to steal it?"

"To take it for safekeeping. You seem preoccupied these days. I didn't want you to get in trouble."

He chuckled. "Do you really think anyone is going to buy that story? I realize you're just testing it out on me but I gotta tell you, it's lame."

"I was only looking out for you." She attempted to look indignant but failed.

"No, Ronnie. You were only looking out for you." He grabbed a T-shirt that had been on the back of a chair and pulled it on then crossed his arms over his chest. He didn't want to send any mixed signals. "I don't know what the hell is going on, but you need to put the laptop down and leave. Now. You were stupid not to take it with you the first time you tossed my place if you wanted it. You could've blamed it on a break-in but no one comes back twice in the same night. That's sloppy."

She seethed at him, "Bastard. Why won't you help me? I'm just trying to move up. Build my career. A good word from you and Archer would give me a better position. I'm sick and tired of being here. I want to go back to New York. It's your fault I got sent down here."

He shook his head. "We were done and dusted by that time. That was all on you. You slept with a member's husband. The wife requested your transfer and Archer had to accommodate her. I had nothing to do with it and you know how you know it wasn't me? Because if it was me, I would've sent you to our location in the caves in Algeria. You're in the Caribbean. It's not even a demotion. Just a lateral move. So don't bitch to me.

"Now, put my laptop back and get the fuck out. If you try something like this again, I will tell Archer and your career will take a nosedive. Don't be stupid. Make the right choice."

Hatred flowed from her eyes and her upper lip actually

curled as she slapped the laptop back down on the table. "This isn't over." She turned and stomped out of the cabin by the front door, slamming it after her.

Rush locked both doors again. This time he put a stick in the track of the sliding glass door so no one could open it. He also set a stack of glasses by the front door so that if anyone opened it, they would fall and shatter. It was unheard of that he had to do this type of thing in a Society location. Things really were falling apart.

Ronnie was a fucking disaster. She'd reached the end of the line, only she didn't know it. He was going to have to inform Archer about her action tonight. She was a serious liability, and they didn't need any more of those.

"Rush?" Kat called in a soft voice. "Is everything okay?"

"Fine," he responded.

He went back down the hall turning off lights as he went. Kat was standing just inside the bedroom door. Her green eyes were big and a tremor ran through her. She was so damned sexy, it was killing him. He should stay away from her. She was business but, oh God, how he wanted her to be pleasure.

He meant to brush by her and go back to bed but somehow his arms closed around her and she was leaning on his chest. She wrapped her arms around him. "Tell me it's all going to be okay."

"I…I can't promise anything. I'll do my best to help you." How was he supposed to tell her that he'd been brought down here specifically to take care of her, which included killing her?

"That's all I can ask. Thanks, Rush."

Her words crushed his heart. It made his chest physically hurt. He pulled back and met her gaze. "I…", instead of confessing he swooped down and captured her lips.

CHAPTER TWENTY

He was done denying himself. He'd crushed his personal needs for the job too often. And ever since Rush had met her, he had been fantasizing about this moment. She was absolute perfection as their tongues intertwined in a fierce dance. His hand roamed to her breasts and cupped the soft fullness, rubbing circles with his thumb over her nipples. Kat moaned in response, and he pulled her closer, and lifted her, so that her thighs wrapped around his hips. Her enticing warmth seeped through his clothes, rushing blood to his cock, making him hard as steel. He wanted her more than he'd wanted any woman.

She arched against him and whispered his name as he kissed down her neck. His name on her lips was sexy as hell. The way she swallowed his groan as the juncture between them heated and boiled over. His fingers wove into her hair as they once again locked lips. Kat began to rock back and forth as he moved his hand up under her shirt to caress her breast.

A low moan escaped from her lips, and he ran his hands down to cup her bottom. She put her hands in his hair as their tongues moved together. He needed to feel her, skin to skin.

As if reading his mind she whispered, "Rush, take your shirt off." He complied instantly, tossing his shirt away, then kicked off his jeans and boxer briefs, before reclaiming Kat's lips in a scorching kiss. She broke the kiss to pull off her T-shirt and dropped it to the floor.

Her breasts were so round and high. He ran a thumb over her nipple and her eyes turned a deep green. Heat radiated from her body. She wanted him as much as he wanted her.

He cupped her breast and kissed each nipple before he asked for her to say his name once again. She complied, her voice barely above a whisper as she spoke.

Lifting Kat into his arms, he placed her on the sofa. His lips dropped gentle kisses along her jawline while his hands roamed her body. When he finally reached her delicate throat, she wound her fingers through his hair and opened up to him.

A thong was all that remained between him and heaven. He felt desire rush through his veins as he moved his hand over the fabric. She responded by biting down on her lip and lifting her hips, seeking his touch.

Rush went back to sucking her nipples and teasing them with his tongue until he began trailing lower, across her hip and then down to the wet warmth between her legs. When his mouth reached its destination, Kat gasped out his name. He grabbed the sides of the thong and pulled it over her hips before tossing it away from them. He watched her watching him intently as he lowered his mouth to taste her.

She was slick and wet for him, driving him wild with desire. He lapped leisurely at her with his tongue before making circles over her clit. Her hips gyrated as she gripped the couch cushions. Her breath came in sharp gasps each time his tongue laved the bundle of nerves at the apex of her thighs. He inserted one finger inside her, then two, moving in a delicate pattern while stealing glances at her face.

Her head was thrown back over the arm of the couch, lower lip between her teeth, swaying to his every touch. If he'd thought he was hard before, seeing how much pleasure he was giving her made him feel fucking invincible. He added another finger and quickened his pace, matching the rhythm of her undulating hips while holding her captive with the pressure of his tongue. Her body clenched and she clutched his hair. An instant later, she shouted out his name as she came undone in a glorious climax. The sight of her lying there on the sofa afterward stirred something primitive within him - an urge to protect and claim this beautiful red-haired goddess as his own.

Kat motioned for Rush to lie down on the sofa and then climbed on top of him. His eyes turned a deep blue. Placing his hands on her hips, he tried to guide her onto his cock, but she laughed and batted away his hands, guiding them to her breasts instead. "Not yet," she said right before she sucked the flesh of his neck between her lips and ran her fingers all over him.

"You are a work of art," she murmured against his skin, taking delight in exploring every inch of his body. Chuckling at each of his groans. He bucked beneath her. She laughed at his obvious pleasure before taking his nipple into her mouth and teasing it with her tongue.

He cursed in response, and then she continued her journey lower. She wasn't sure what had come over her. Normally she was a quiet woman, willing to take but never demand. When had she become such a sexual being, using her teeth and tongue to torture him? The only difference was him. Her intense desire for Rush had turned her into this…this woman willing to take his cock to the back of her throat. Her mouth hovered over his cock, and she licked slow circles around the head, swirling her tongue up and down in a tantalizing manner, and cupping and releasing his balls until he was almost screaming her name. God, she was almost climaxing again with need for him.

Rush started to move his hips, and she matched his rhythm, working faster and harder until he begged for something else. " I want to come inside you."

Kat smiled. "Condom?" she asked, pulling away from him momentarily so he could get it from his wallet. He complied quickly, tearing open the package before sliding it down over himself.

He started kissing the back of her neck while she turned around in his arms; he grabbed her breasts from behind and she moaned. Rush guided her until they were kneeling on the sofa together. She loved that he was behind her. She was unable to think straight anymore from desire.

Rush caressed one breast while the other hand moved lower, his fingers expertly playing at her center. Her hips kept in time with his touch as he wedged himself between her ass cheeks and rubbed up and down.

"God, Rush. I want you inside me. Now." She pleaded, needing him inside her; he complied and entered her slowly. But she couldn't take it slow; she wanted more—she wanted him as wild and abandoned as the storm consuming her. She pumped her hips, meeting him stroke for achingly hard stroke. Within seconds, they both came with a shared ferocity that she'd never experienced before.

"That was…" there were no words as far as she was concerned.

He smiled. "Shall we move to the bedroom and see if we can top it? I have a few ideas."

"I like the sound of that," she murmured and then kissed him.

Kat opened her eyes and smiled. She was on her side and Rush was curled around her. *Safe*. He made her feel so safe as if nothing could reach her. It only that were true. She glanced at the clock. It was already eight a.m. They'd left the curtains partially open, but the light in the room was dim. Intimate.

Rush had checked his phone right after they'd showered together. Archer had found her brother last night, but she wanted to call him and make sure he was still okay. They'd brought the burner cell phone from the boat in waterproof bags.

She slid out of bed, careful not to wake Rush and then made her way to the bathroom. Slipping on the robe from behind the door, she pulled the burner cell that her brother had given her out of her pants pocket which were still on the bathroom floor and padded quietly to the kitchen. The robe was ginormous on her but was as cozy as a warm hug. The sun was a bright blur behind the dark clouds on the horizon, and a strong breeze ruffled the fronds on the palm trees around the cabin. The wind looked stronger than it had previously. Maybe they were right, and the storm was headed towards the island.

Hitting the redial number on her phone, she bit her lip waiting for her brother to answer. After the fourth ring, there was a groggy hello on the other end. "Oh, thank God. I was worried."

"Hey, sis. I'm okay. Just tired. That Archer guy made me

tell him the whole thing not just once or twice but like five or six times. He's friggin' crazy and scary."

"Yeah, I know what you mean. Where are you?"

"He's got me in a huge cabin. I think it's his. It's toward the north end of the island, not far from the hospital." His voice dropped. "He locked me in the room and told me if I tried to jump out the window, he'd kill me. He was serious."

"Yes, I don't think Archer jokes around at all." The fear in her brother's voice made her chest tighten. She wanted to make him feel better, but she had no idea how. What could she say? "Rush is going to work on finding out who Mr. Smith is. They have people on the boat pretending to be us during the day and then you'll keep working at night. We have to keep up the charade."

"Yeah, that's what he said. I gotta tell you, I'm getting tired. I mean seriously tired."

She swallowed hard to dislodge the lump of unshed tears building in her throat. "I know, me too."

There was a long silence and then Danny asked, "Where are you?"

"Staying with Rush."

"Did they lock you in as well?"

How the hell was she supposed to answer that question? "No, not exactly but I can't go outside either. Listen, keep the phone handy and check in when you want. You might as well go back to sleep. Get all the rest you can."

"Okay, you too, sis." There was another silence. Then in a quiet voice, Danny said, "I love you."

Her heart cracked. "I love you too, little brother." Then she clicked off the call. She wanted to go see Danny and give him a hug. This was all so friggin' out there. Just ridiculous. She missed her predictable, comfortable, boring life. And she had no doubt that Danny missed his too.

"How's your brother?" Rush asked as he walked into the kitchen area.

He'd obviously been listening to her side of the conversation but didn't want to interrupt her. At least he gave her the illusion of privacy. She'd been hoping last night had changed things for them. That Rush would trust her but maybe she'd been wrong. It had certainly changed things for her. She knew that she cared for Rush. Might honestly be falling for him but apparently, he wasn't necessarily feeling the same.

She met his gaze. "Are you making breakfast? I'm famished."

He grinned. "I guess I could do that. All that exercise last night make you work up an appetite?"

"Of course," she said and then immediately turned and started making coffee. She wasn't hungry in the slightest, but she needed normalcy and breakfast would help. Plus, she wanted Rush to relax around her. Domestic chores were sort of relaxing in a weird way. Maybe making breakfast would help.

"Any thoughts on who Mr. Smith might be?" she asked as she sat down across the island from him and waited for the coffee to finish.

"A few, but nothing concrete. There's more work to do that might help figure out who it is. Are you up for helping?"

She perked up. Did he trust her after all? "Sure. What can I help with?"

"I'll explain after breakfast. First, why don't you pour me a cup of coffee while I make you eggs and bacon with toast."

"Deal," she said as she hopped off the stool. She moved by him, and he stepped back, catching her and dropping a kiss on her lips. Then he pivoted and started getting ingredients out of the fridge.

CHAPTER TWENTY-ONE

"I've been over the whole list twice," Kat groused. "These are the only names that were here the entire time my brother has been down here. Both members and employees." She flopped back on the sofa and rubbed her eyes. Then she rested her head in her hands.

"Headache?" Rush asked. The fatigue around her eyes was noticeable.

"Yeah," she admitted. "I've gone over all of the records for the last six weeks and compiled a list of twenty names of people who have been on the island the whole time."

He took the paper she'd handwritten.

"The majority are employees, which is to be expected," she pointed out. "But there are a few members who've been here as well." She looked over at Rush. "Do you think it could be a member?"

He shrugged. "The chance is remote, but we have to consider it. I also think we have to consider that Mr. Smith might not have been here the whole time."

Her jaw dropped. "Are you insane? I just went through

all those names twice to make this list and now you think it could be anyone?" Frustration dripped off every word.

He lifted his gaze from his laptop screen and looked over the top at her. He didn't blame her for being frustrated. "I said it's a possibility. Not a probability. I think it's someone who's been here the vast majority of the time, so your list is the perfect place to start."

They'd been at it for hours. After finishing breakfast, they had cleaned up and then got dressed. Rush had someone bring over her 'effects' under the guise that he was going to do a thorough search of them but since he wasn't feeling well, he couldn't go out to her cabin. He'd opted for the *I'm sick* scenario, instead of the *I'm scared of a little old hurricane* explanation. After he'd searched her bags, and then let her at them, she'd danced giddily to the bathroom to change. When she returned dressed in shorts and a floral top, she'd kissed him soundly. He'd returned the kiss, but then forced himself to break the seal of their lips so they could get started. They'd been at it all afternoon.

"What are you working on?" she asked.

"Cameras. Just making sure there aren't any stray ones out of alignment somewhere else on the island." He didn't tell her what he was really working on. Tracking her brother's movements to make sure what he'd told Archer was true. So far, so good. And if he was telling the truth about that, then maybe he was telling the truth about Angel's death. Smith was most likely the killer, but he couldn't totally rule Danny out. Not yet. Any evidence that backed up what Danny had told them was a step in the right direction of getting him and by extension Kat, off the hook.

"And are there any?" she asked.

"Not that I've found. I'm also running background checks on the employees whose names are on your list. You gave me the first few a while ago."

"Right. Well," she said as she stood up. "You made breakfast, so I'll make dinner. Any ideas on what you'd like?"

He was back to staring at his screen. "Surprise me."

She wandered over to the fridge and looked inside. She stood immobile for almost a minute.

"Is there something wrong?" Was she okay? Did her head hurt that much?

"Hmm, what?" she asked as she turned around to face Rush.

"You've been staring into the fridge for a while. I was wondering if everything is okay."

"Oh." She frowned. "Yeah fine. Just worried about my brother."

"He's fine. Archer will protect him until Mr. Smith is found."

"But what happens after that?" She stared at him.

He wanted to make promises, but in good conscience, he couldn't. She was so beautiful and vulnerable and naïve, and all those things were incredibly appealing to him to the point that he was even thinking of ways to help her and her brother escape, which would be a colossally stupid move.

The lies and half-truths were eating him alive. He'd been trying since he woke up curled around Kat, to find a way out. A way to tell her the truth without her hating him but there wasn't one. And he needed her to know the truth. The real reason he was here.

She'd gotten under his skin. Sleeping with her hadn't been a mistake, but it was an error in judgment. He just lost the power to resist any longer. Now she was about to find out the truth and she would hate him. His spirits sizzled into ashes.

With his lack of answer, she switched gears. "How do you feel about sandwiches?"

"Sure," he agreed.

"Where do you think Mr. Smith is holding Timmy? When I was looking for my brother, I thought he was either at the long gray building or at the hospital. What do you think? Is he on the island? What is that long gray building?"

"That's the Hub. It's where we run the security for the island, and everything connected to that. And no, he's not there. I think he's dead."

She paled. "That's harsh. Why do you think that?"

"Because if it were me, that's what I would do. Your brother isn't asking for proof of life, and he's already here and so are you. You would be all the threat I would need. I would tell Danny that I would kill you if he didn't do what I said. Find the treasure or your sister dies. That would be the best motivation. The moment you stepped onto the island, he no longer needed Timmy."

Kat stared at Rush. "You seem to know a lot about all of this type of thing."

This was as good a time as any. God, he'd cracked open the door and she'd thrown it wider. He had to just rip the bandage off. She'd hate him but he couldn't survive like this. Lies ate at him. They always had, but after Ronnie, he just couldn't tolerate them at all. He wanted to help Kat but that meant going against Archer, tossing away everything he'd worked toward for years. It meant death. Hers. And maybe his. He closed his laptop and leaned back. "What is it you think I do, Kat?"

She frowned. "You said you solve problems…" Her voice died and suddenly she went pale.

He held her gaze and made his expression as blank and cold as possible.

"You're a what… a hitman?" Her voice barely rose above a whisper.

"I'm a monster wrangler. I keep the real monsters in line, and I bring justice to those who break the rules."

Her skin was the color of chalk and she swallowed convulsively. "Were you brought here…for me?" she whispered.

"Yes, Kat, I was brought here to deal with you." His chest ached as the words left his lips. Hurting her was agony but she had to know the truth. Had to or he couldn't live with himself.

"Why?" she pleaded.

"Because you lied on your application. Because you presented yourself as someone you're not and because we knew you weren't here just to relax. The fact that you had Angel's token set off a chain of events that culminated in me."

Her green eyes were wide, and all the blood had drained from her face. "But…you seduced me. Was that part of your plan?"

This was killing him, but he had to be honest. He didn't have much else in this life but his word was something he took seriously. "No. But once I met you, I was attracted to you and decided if I got close to you maybe you would tell me the truth."

She stood. "I need to leave."

"You can't. You must stay here with me."

She looked around wildly. "I can't. I need to get away. I need space. I…"

"Kat, sit down. You're not going anywhere. You're stuck here until we figure out the mystery of Mr. Smith."

"And then what? And then you kill me? I'd have to be crazy to stay here with you. How do I know you won't kill me now?"

"Kat." He kept his voice even. "Use your logic. You are no good to us dead. We need you to keep your brother in line just like Mr. Smith does."

She collapsed onto the couch. "I can't believe it. I...I... You bastard."

The color was coming back into her cheeks now. *Yes.* Anger was good. Anger would keep her distant. It would keep her focused. He needed that. Because he was going to help her. It might cost him everything, but he just couldn't let her die. And he sure as hell couldn't kill her. His heart hurt too much at the thought. He would never get over her death. Better he died than live with her death on his conscience.

He got up from the chair and went into the kitchen. Filling the kettle, he proceeded to make her a cup of tea. His hand shook slightly as he poured the boiling water. Kat must never know how much she meant to him. It would be dangerous for both of them.

His cell rang and he looked at the screen. "Danton, what's wrong?" he asked by way of a greeting.

"We're having problems with the evacuations. The storm shifted and now the island is in its direct path. Wind gusts have picked up and people are starting to panic. I need your help getting everyone onto the boats and off the island."

He glanced over at Kat. She was curled into a ball on the other end of the sofa as far away from him as she could get. He understood it but it crushed him to see it.

His phone beeped. "I'll call you back," he said and then answered the other call. "Archer, do you want me to help with the evacuations?"

"Yes. People are panicking. I don't want anyone to be left behind in the mayhem."

"What should I do—"

"Leave her there. She's not going to get on a boat and no one is crazy enough to scuba dive now."

"Understood." He clicked off the call. And shut down his

laptop. "I have to help with the evacuations. You need to stay here. Do you understand me?"

She glared at him. Her eyes were red-rimmed and she sniffled but she nodded.

"I'll be back as soon as I can." He got up, pulled on a rain jacket and left the cabin. He knew there was no way Kat would be there when he got back. He just hoped she would find a safe way off the island.

CHAPTER TWENTY-TWO

Kat listened at the door. No sound. She peeked between the blinds, but the night was dark, and visibility was almost non-existent. The wind had picked up with the approaching storm. Glancing at her watch, she knew she had a choice to make. Stay or go. Such simple concepts, but words fraught with repercussions. If she remained in the cabin as instructed, Rush would walk back inside soon. Leaving meant she wouldn't see him again, which should be okay since he'd been sent to 'take care of her'.

And he'd truly taken care of her last night. In the best possible way. Her body still tingled from the attention to detail that probably made in freaking awesome at his job.

She closed her eyes against the pain in her chest. How the fuck could she sleep with the one man who'd been sent to kill her? Bad luck just didn't even come close to covering it. She shook her head as if to chase away the harsh reality. Asshole.

Decision made, she picked up her cell, she hit the button for her brother.

A moment later he answered. "Kat."

"Can you get out? Does Archer still have you locked in?"

"He does but I think I can get out. Honestly, all he's done is lock the door and threaten to break my leg if I break the window. I don't think he's overly concerned about me escaping with the storm. Only an idiot would go out in a boat at this point. So, either I stay here or I die on the water. I get the feeling it doesn't really matter to him. Otherwise, I'm just running around the island and he'd find me eventually no matter how good I am at hiding. The island isn't that big and it would be hard to really hide if there was a group of people looking for you."

Her brother's assessment of the situation sounded pretty accurate to her. Archer probably didn't care if either of them lived or died. They were just a complication at this point. He'd heard their stories. He needed nothing else from them. It wasn't like the movies where they were going to court or testify or anything. Realistically as far as Archer was concerned, they'd served their purpose. And that's what made it so damned scary.

"Good. Meet me by the path on the north end of the island. I'm going to make my way up there, but it might take me a bit. I need to move without anyone noticing."

"Why? What's going on?"

She narrowed her eyes. "Where are you exactly?"

"At the south end by the hospital. That's where Archer's place is."

That put him just through the woods from her. "Okay, stay where you are. I'm coming through the woods towards you. Stay on the line and I'll find you."

"Kat, what's going on?"

"Just do what I say, Danny."

He grunted, "I've got to call you back."

She slipped quietly out the back door. A blast of wind temporarily stole her breath. Bracing as best she could, she crossed the deck and hurried into the woods. She tried to maneuver through the trees, but it was tough going.

Her cell rang. "Danny?"

"Yeah. Where are you?" She explained her location and he said, "Just keep coming until you hit the small path and then turn left. You should see me after you start down the path. Don't worry… no one can see you."

A minute or so later, she came out onto a small path. She turned left and moved swiftly.

The wind rushed through the leaves. The storm was getting closer by the minute. Evacuations would continue until everyone was gone. She and Danny weren't going anywhere but with everyone leaving it might make it easier to get around the island unobserved. After the storm, they might be able to use the boat Danny had been staying on to get away quickly. Especially if she was right about the treasure.

"Kat," Danny said as he stepped out of the trees next to her.

"Ahh!" she yelled and then clamped a hand over her mouth and froze. They both stood still and listened. Nothing. "You scared me," she whispered.

Danny just shook his head at her. "All I did was say your name. What did you expect me to do?"

"I didn't expect you to come out of the trees at me." She immediately bit her tongue and took a deep breath. It didn't matter how old they got, she and her twin always bickered like they were kids again.

"Listen, we need to get to the other end of the island. Can you get us there without being seen?"

"No, but I can get us there in a way no one will bother to notice us."

She shrugged. "That will have to do."

He was in the groundskeeper's uniform so he would

blend in, but she was wearing jeans and a black T-shirt. She had no idea how he was going to make this work, but she decided she needed to trust that he could mostly because she didn't have the energy to fight with him.

"Follow me." He started back into the woods but then he turned and stopped again. "Stay really close and don't say anything if anyone speaks to you." He flicked on a small flashlight.

She wanted to point out that it wasn't exactly cocktail hour. They shouldn't run into anyone roaming around at three-thirty in the morning. At least not with any luck. Instead, she just nodded.

Danny went into the trees and she followed him. They stepped onto a small path, different from the one they'd just left. This walkway was narrow, and like the path by the beach, the base was forest floor, not stone. She followed her brother, trying to dodge some of the thorny branches on either side of her. Whatever this hedge was, she was pretty sure it wasn't natural to the Caribbean. None of them were. One branch scraped her as Danny let it go, and she bit her tongue to keep from yelping. Damn bushes reminded her of slightly less-prickly holly.

Suddenly, they emerged on the beach. "That's better," she said as she wiped a particularly nasty scratch on her arm. The storm surge had started. Waves churned against the shore. They were much higher than she'd ever seen before. If they didn't move quickly, the sand would be swallowed up and they'd be in danger of getting swept out to sea.

Danny turned off his flashlight and shook his head putting his finger to his lips and then nudged her back into the shadows.

What now? She tried to telegraph that thought to him, but he just kept staring off into the darkness. There was just a sliver of a cloud-shrouded moon, so it took her eyes a moment to adjust.

Then there was movement. A man. Walking on his own down the beach. He didn't seem to see them or even look in their direction. Danny had stopped moving and she followed suit. Holding her breath, she waited until the man had passed and was quite a bit down the beach before turning back toward her brother, but Danny had vanished.

What the fuck? Where did he go? She stayed in the shadows and moved up the beach towards the dining venue. She came to the edge of the hedge bordering the dining area but didn't want to leave the relative safety of the shadow. There were outside lights here and there was no way she wanted to be seen.

"Here," her brother said as he came up behind her and tried to hand her a piece of cloth.

"Seriously?" she hissed. "You scared the life out of me again."

"Well, if you paid more attention to what I'm doing then I wouldn't have to scare you."

Kat contemplated smacking her brother upside the head but decided it wasn't worth it. He wasn't going to change, and neither was she.

"What's this?" she asked as he shoved his hand against her belly.

"It's an apron. The servers and kitchen crew all wear them. With your black T-shirt you look like part of the kitchen staff. Black hides the stains better."

She pulled the apron over her head and tied the ties around her waist. She glanced at her brother, and he gave her a nod of approval.

"Not that we're likely to run into anyone else out here at this hour but this should work for any cameras we might encounter. That guy we saw on the beach walks every morning at around this time, so I knew to look out for him."

Danny turned but Kat reached out and touched his arm. "I know I'm hard on you a lot of the time," she smiled. "Maybe all the time, but I'm proud of you, little brother. This is a brutal situation and you're holding up."

"It's my fault we're in this mess."

She wanted to argue with him but that was the bald-faced truth. She shrugged. "We all make mistakes."

It was easy to be magnanimous now that she'd been seduced by the man who'd been brought here to kill her. Suddenly, Danny's lapse in judgment seemed much more understandable.

Danny squeezed her hand and then backed up a bit. He turned and headed out towards the water before heading up the shore again.

Kat followed, the soles of her shoe sinking in the sand. Her brother was smarter than she gave him credit for. He'd made sure they avoided the lights and cameras. He was quite good at sneaking around. She shouldn't be surprised considering the amount of trouble he got into when they were young. Surprised didn't cover her emotions, but impressed did.

They were quite far up the beach, past the dining area when Danny cut back into the trees to another narrow path and flicked on his flashlight. Two minutes later, they emerged onto the boardwalk. It only took a few minutes more to arrive at the lagoon. Danny flicked off the flashlight as he walked around the right edge of the lagoon to where he'd left their diving equipment.

"Are we going back to the boat?" he asked.

She shook her head. "I need you to help me get suited up and then keep watch."

"I don't understand. Where are you going?"

"Danny, I think the treasure is at the bottom of this lagoon."

"What? No way!" He shook his head. "I would've seen it. I've been diving in that lagoon for over a month."

She nodded. "I know but you've been diving through the lagoon. Did you ever go to the bottom of it?"

He folded his arms across his chest. "I checked it out the first couple times and I didn't see anything at all to say the treasure was there."

"I heard the end of the story about BlackEye. It's not well known but one of the Society members saw the first mate's diary. He said that when BlackEye came back for the treasure, he and some of his men were found with rashes and respiratory issues. Then they died without ever saying where the treasure was. Daisy mentioned that the lagoon sometimes fills up with bioluminescent plankton. If someone goes into the water—"

"They get rashes, and it can make them very sick and possibly if it's bad enough, kill them," her brother finished for her. "Shit. And if the lagoon glowed, it would be the type of thing that sailors back then would have terrified superstitious sailors. Making this the perfect location to hide the treasure. Son of a bitch, Kat."

The anger was now gone, and his eyes took on a glow of their own. Treasure fever. She'd seen it enough times with her father to recognize it. It was why he was staying up here and she was going down to check it out. If he got his hands on the treasure, who knew what he might suddenly decide to do. Treasure clouded people's brains.

"Why don't I dive, and you wait here," he suggested.

She braced herself for the argument that she'd known would come. "You know the island better than I do and if you have to run, you have a better chance of getting away.

We need you alive to deal with Mr. Smith. I'm the logical choice because I'm more expendable."

It was all true, but it wasn't the real reason. She knew her twin. The gold, if it was down there, would prove too much for him and he'd do something stupid. Better to limit his access until it was absolutely necessary.

He narrowed his eyes and she thought he was going to argue but he merely shrugged. "Okay, I guess. Just be very careful. We don't have a ton of oxygen. There's enough in the tank for this dive but it will be impossible for both of us to make it out without getting another tank."

She grimaced. "Yeah, I was thinking that. We might have to steal one from the dive shop. With the evacuation going on, there will be fewer people and that should make it easier."

"Okay then. Let's get you suited up."

Ten minutes later, wearing only her bra and underwear under the wetsuit, Kat slipped into the water. She grudgingly issued a silent thanks to her father for making her and her brother learn how to dive when they were teens. She'd fought him at the time but it was sure coming in handy now. She gave herself a few moments to get her bearings, then flicked on her underwater light, flipped upside down and started pulling herself downward. The deep part of the lagoon was a circle as if someone had taken a massive drill bit and hollowed it out. It was probably about twenty-eight or thirty feet across. The walls were limestone. The coming storm was making the water choppy but the lagoon was pretty insulated.

She shone her light over the walls seeing the layers of stone. Nothing stood out to her until she was about halfway down. There was a ledge. It wasn't huge but it stuck out into the center about a foot and a half. The edge was slightly jagged but had been smoothed over time.

How had BlackEye gotten the treasure down here and how in the world did he expect to get it back up? That question haunted her as she scanned the outcrop. The answer became clearer. The ledge was at about twelve feet. He could have easily lowered the treasure onto it using a rope and a tree branch as a pulley system.

If the ledge then broke and the treasure hit the bottom then when he and his men came back for it, they'd have no way to get down to it. The bioluminescence would have made it that much worse. It must have been so damn frustrating to know his treasure was there but there was no way to get to it. Maybe he wasn't even sure if the treasure was still there.

It had better be. She arrived at the bottom of the lagoon and shone the light around. Nothing jumped out at her, just like Danny had said, but she knew about the shelf or at least suspected about the shelf so she lined herself up underneath where the treasure might have fallen if it had been on the outcrop of rock, and then started searching.

There were a few lumps on the bottom that she gently waved the sediment away from, but they were rocks or bits of rotting wood. She searched the area for any sign or clue but there was nothing. She glanced at the watch Danny had loaned her. She'd been down for about ten minutes. She only had another twenty minutes of oxygen.

She shined the light upwards and stared at the edge. Was she wrong? If the shelf didn't exist then it could be anywhere in the circle and it would take quite a few more dives to find it because the circle had to be fifty feet across at the bottom. The whole thing had gotten wider as she'd descended. They didn't have time for more dives. Smith said they were running on empty and if they didn't come up with something soon, Timmy would be dead. What he hadn't said, but she'd understood, was they would both be dead too. If only Rush could figure out who Mr. Smith really was.

She waved the light around some more and then back up at the shelf. It was the only thing that made sense. The treasure should've fallen exactly where she was. Then it hit her. If the shelf was significantly bigger than she thought it was, the treasure would be behind her.

Turning, Kat swam about ten feet back from where she'd been. She aimed the light toward the bottom. Nothing. Flat. She moved the light around and still nothing. She tried again. There, to her left a bit. A series of lumps covered with sediment. She drew closer. Wood. She brushed some of the sediment away making the water murky. Swearing long and low in her head, she waited a moment for it to clear a bit.

A hinge. There was a hinge on the wood. She brushed away more sediment and debris and something flashed in the beam of her light. Gold. She'd found it. The long-lost treasure of BlackEye. She wanted to be thrilled or even excited. Instead, her gut churned. It might be their only way out, but treasure always made her uneasy.

She wiped away some more debris and sand. The flash of gold was doubloons. Lots of them. Millions of dollars' worth in fact if the lumps that were here were all chests of gold. She picked up five coins and put them in the pouch she'd brought with her. Then she slowly rose toward the surface, allowing time to readjust although it wasn't strictly necessary. Hopefully, this would be enough to get them out of the situation they were in. Buy Timmy's life and theirs too. She didn't think it was likely, but she had to try.

Surfacing she looked around for her brother. He stepped out from the bushes and turned on his light. She pulled herself out of the water and started removing her gear.

"Did you find anything?" he asked.

She debated for one second not telling him the truth but

she knew she didn't have a choice. "Yes." She held up the pouch and he looked at it under his pen light.

"Holy shit! You did it, Kat! That's amazing! You're amazing!" He was practically yelling.

"Danny!" she barked in a harsh whisper. "Quiet. Don't get too excited. This has to go to Smith to get Timmy back. It's not something we can keep." She didn't add that she was hoping that Rush would find Smith and take care of him so that she could use the treasure in another way. Regardless they weren't going to get to keep it.

The gleam in Danny's eyes made her uncomfortable as she peeled off the wet suit. She asked for help, and he finally put the pouch in his pocket. Kat immediately vowed to get it back. She was not trusting her brother with this. He did get them into this mess, but she was going to make sure they got out… or die trying. Which was a very real possibility.

CHAPTER TWENTY-THREE

Rush's patience was shot. He was done. "Get on the fucking boat, Ronnie."

She crossed her arms over her chest. "I'm not going if everyone else is staying."

"Everyone else *isn't* staying. Everyone else is evacuating." It was like dealing with a small child. They were standing on the jetty arguing while members climbed into the boats. "Ronnie, get in the goddamn boat!"

She shook her head and started walking toward the office.

"Fine. Suit yourself." He wasn't going to chase her which is probably what she wanted. He just didn't care enough. "I won't be coming to your rescue," he muttered as he strode over to Danton and Pierre. "Where are we?"

"This should be the last set of boats going over to the other island. There are enough jets to fly them out, but the window is closing." Danton cast a worried look around. There were still quite a few members on the jetty.

Rush nodded. "Okay. Are we missing anyone?"

Pierre and Danton shared a look.

"For Christ's sake, spill it." He did not have time for this shit.

"Valentine and Humber haven't shown up. Humber's wife split earlier. She said her husband had decided to ride out the storm here on the island."

"Fucking great. And Valentine?"

Pierre shrugged. "Not sure why he's staying."

Rush inhaled a long breath between his clenched teeth. The wind buffeted his T-shirt, making it flap around his torso. He knew why Valentine was staying. He didn't want Humber to find the treasure. But staying in the path of a raging hurricane seemed extreme. There must be more to it. There was something about this treasure, some clue he was missing. What could be so important that made it worth it to risk their lives?

"Do what you can to get everyone off and then get back to the Hub and lock it down," he had to shout over the wind. "Everyone will be safe there. I have to go check on some things."

They nodded and Rush started down the jetty. *Fucking treasure.* What in the hell was going on that made smart men do such dumbass things? No treasure was worth it, as far as Rush was concerned. There had to be something he was missing.

He entered the reception area and found Archer with Daisy and Peter. "Are you guys going or staying?"

"Staying. You boys will need all the help you can get with clean up," Peter said and then sat down behind his desk.

"What about you, Daisy?" Archer asked. "Are you sure you want to stay?"

She nodded and patted her husband's shoulder. "We'll be fine."

Rush turned to Archer. "Got a minute?"

He nodded and they went through the door to the island side.

"What?" Archer demanded.

"There's something up with this treasure thing. Ronnie is staying and so are Humber and Valentine. Seems fucking stupid to me so there has to be more to it. You got any ideas?"

Archer stared. "I am mystified."

"That makes two of us, and that's not good. This is all gonna turn to shit. I can feel it in my bones."

"Any clue as to the identity of Smith?"

Rush shrugged. "It's got to be either Valentine or Humber. My vote is Valentine. He's the smarter of the two or at least the less desperate. I thought it could be Fisher or Davis as well, but they've left."

"They don't have to be here to run things," Archer pointed out.

"True. But it seems a little hands-on for either of them, doesn't it? I can't picture Davis or Fisher making threatening phone calls. They would have henchmen for that."

"What a shit show. See if you can find Humber and Valentine. Keep eyes on them. I want to know what the hell they're up to."

"On it."

CHAPTER TWENTY-FOUR

"Do you think they'll let us keep any of the treasure?"
Danny's question came as the sky grew darker even though it was morning. The wind picked up as the storm rolled ever closer. They'd spent the night not far from the waterfall in an old shack that Danny had found. Kat was tired and hungry, not to mention cold. She was also so done with everything. It needed to be over. At least she'd managed to get the pouch with the doubloons back from Danny.

"I doubt it."

"Still," Danny said. "It's so cool that you found it."

They came around the side of the shack and headed towards the boardwalk. "I guess. Hopefully, it's going to save our asses. Then I never want to hear the word treasure again."

"I hear ya. Can I see the doubloons one more time?" Danny asked.

She just didn't have the energy to say no but she wasn't stupid. She gave him one.

"Wow, it really is beautiful. How many do you think are down there?"

"A lot." She didn't feel like discussing the treasure

anymore. "We need to find Rush and see if he has any lead about who Mr. Smith is. If he doesn't, then we'll call Smith and start negotiations for Timmy."

They reached the boardwalk. Danny frowned. "I hope Timmy is okay. He would freak to see the gold doubloons."

"I knew it!" a voice barked out. They turned to see Veronica waving a gun at them. "I knew you found the gold. I saw you on camera. While the whole world was trying to get off the island, I got into the Hub and spotted you two on the security feed. I knew sleeping with Pierre would eventually come in handy.

"Now, give me the doubloons." Veronica shook the fist holding the gun, then pointed the barrel directly at Kat's chest. Kat's heart skipped a beat or two. No doubt the other woman would drop her in her tracks if provoked.

But she couldn't comply. If she gave away the gold, she gave away the only leverage they had to bargain for Danny's life. "I can't." The wind gusted and the first few drops of rain hit her face.

"You don't think I'll use this?" Veronica waved the gun.

"I'm sure you will, but I still can't give you the gold." Kat's voice came out remarkably calm, given how her heart was clattering.

"I want that gold. I deserve that gold." Veronica's voice rose above the wind. "I've worked my ass off for this place. I've *screwed* my way to the top. I even spent years married to Rush to get closer to Archer but still nothing. This gold is *mine*. It's my reward for all the shit I've gone through. I want it now."

The rain was falling steadily now, slanting in sideways in the wind. The storm everyone had been preparing for had arrived. Danny shifted beside her, and she didn't have to be his identical twin to know he was about to do something reckless.

She kept her voice low. "Danny, for once in your fucking life do exactly as I say. Keep your mouth shut." The weight of his gaze made her stomach roll but she wouldn't coddle him now. Their lives depended on it.

She cleared her throat and yelled above the storm. "What about Humber? I thought you two were a thing."

Veronica let out a bark of laughter. "Humber is a fucking idiot. I thought he had money and could get me what I wanted, but the jokes on me. Turns out he just wanted to screw me." A smile spread across her face that gave Kat goosebumps. "I fixed him. I told his wife about the affair and gave her pictures, not that she cared, but the gossip mags in New York City did. I got well paid for those shots. They're all over the internet now. There's nowhere he can hide. Not from this. His father-in-law can't save him now."

"You bitch!" came a scream from the trees to their left. Humber burst out of the woods, hand raised, gun glinting in a flash of lightning. "You fucking bitch! You ruined my life!"

Veronica laughed. "I told you that not keeping your promises was a bad idea."

"You fucking ruined me, and you weren't even that good of a lay," Humber screamed over the wind. "Valentine, get your ass out here."

Valentine sauntered out of the trees. He met Kat's gaze but remained silent.

"Who the hell is he?" Humber demanded, pointing the gun at Danny.

"My brother," Kat supplied.

"They know where the treasure is and it's mine," Veronica moved slightly so she could point the gun at both groups of people.

"The fuck it is, you bitch. That treasure is mine." Humber glanced at Valentine. "Ours. We've been looking for it."

Valentine's face was blank and he remained silent.

"Right?" Humber glanced at Valentine to get his confirmation.

The rain was coming down in sheets. Veronica had been standing off the path. The rain had formed a channel in the hard-packed sand and water rushed over her feet. She tried to step onto the wooden path but stumbled, lurching towards Humber who jumped back and pulled the trigger. The roar of the gun was lost in the storm, but Veronica's eyes got big and a large red stain spread over her chest. She dropped to her knees and then went face first into the newly formed stream.

"Oh my God!" Humber screamed. "Pick her up! Pick her up!" He waved the gun at Kat and Danny.

"Don't bother," Valentine said in a calm voice that cut through the noise of the storm. "She's dead."

"Fuck! I didn't mean to kill her. I thought she was coming at me! She had a gun! It was self-defense!" He'd found the right answer and kept repeating it. "It was self-defense. You all saw it. You all saw it."

"Shut. The. Fuck. Up," Valentine snarled. He turned to Danny. "Where's the gold?"

Danny glanced at Kat. "Um, I-I can't tell you."

"Tell me or I will shoot your sister." Valentine pulled a black handgun from under his blue button-down.

Did everyone have guns on the island? Maybe it was mandatory, a rule that she didn't know about since she hadn't read the massive rule book. Laughter was bubbling up in her throat. She bit her lip to keep it from escaping. She swallowed and found her voice. "Don't tell him, Danny. He can't kill us if he wants to know where the treasure is."

"Wrong. I can't kill both of you, but I can kill one. So, who will it be? Who will give up the location of the treasure to stay alive?"

"Don't say anything, Danny," she warned as she wiped rain out of her eyes. Icy water streamed down her face. Valentine was right of course. He could kill one of them and still find out where the treasure was. She glanced at her brother. He'd been under extreme pressure for a long time now and it showed. His skin was blotchy and his eyes were glassy. The lines around his eyes that used to be fine were now deeper. He'd aged enormously in the last few months, and she wasn't sure he could take anymore.

She reached out and took his hand. He turned to her. "You can do this." She turned to Valentine. "We're not telling you where the gold is and if you kill either of us the other won't say anything for sure."

"Then there's no point in keeping you alive," he said simply.

"So, if you can't have the gold, no one can?" she demanded.

He smiled. "Now you're getting the picture."

"Valentine," Humber grunted, "let's not do something stupid. I'm sure we can negotiate a deal. We can split the gold with them. That still leaves plenty for us."

Valentine turned to Humber and shot him directly between the eyes.

Danny's hand jerked in hers. She squeezed it as she tried to suck air back into her lungs. This man was serious. He wasn't going to let them live. She broke out in a cold sweat that mixed with the rain and her stomach churned. How the hell was she going to get her brother out of this mess? Valentine would kill them both no matter what.

Valentine pulled out his cell and made a call while pointing the gun at them. "It's done. Humber's dead. I want my money." He listened for a second and then hung up. "Now, who wants to die first?"

"You think you can find the treasure?" she snarled.

Valentine smiled. "I think I have a better chance now, knowing you've already found it. If you don't want to play ball, I'll still get it. It will just take longer." He raised his gun and pointed it at Danny's chest. "Last chance."

She wanted to scream, to attack Valentine but she knew she'd be dead before she made it one step. He was going to kill them no matter what so telling him would be stupid but she couldn't let her brother be killed in front of her.

"Fine," she yelled. "Kill me first and he'll tell you." It was the coward's way out but she couldn't stand to see her brother die. She just didn't have it in her.

"No!" Danny yelled. "Shoot me." He tried to pull free of her grip, but she squeezed tight. The look on Danny's face was pure regret. "I got you into this mess. I should've listened to you, but I thought I knew better. You were right. I'm just like Dad and his passion for treasure got him and Mom killed. I won't do that to you. No way."

"How fucking touching," Valentine snarled. "One of you tell me where the treasure is and then I'll kill you both."

Kat squeezed her brother's hand. He returned the pressure and gave her his best smile. "It's—"

There was a loud crack and a tree off to the right started to fall. "Run!" she yelled, and she took off running in the opposite direction, off the path and into the trees. The sound of a gunshot reached her ears over the storm.

She glanced over her shoulder and realized Danny wasn't behind her. He'd run in a different direction. She kept running and prayed that Valentine hadn't killed her brother. Moving through the trees, she had to slow down as the undergrowth got thicker. A couple of minutes later she came to a small clearing. Just a large hole in the foliage. She took a moment to rest. Bending over, gasping for breath, she reached out to balance on a tree when the ground literally disappeared beneath her. A scream ripped out of her throat as she plummeted down.

Landing on her back, she had the wind knocked out of her and she struggled to catch her breath. The whole was rapidly filling with water but it was moving. An underground river. She'd landed in it and the water was washing away the soil all around her.

Looking up, she calculated that the surface was about six, maybe seven feet over her head. She got to her knees in the water and then tried to get to her feet. She struggled to gain her footing and fell face first into the water. Pulling herself back to her knees, she coughed and coughed until she could breathe again.

Fatigue hit her. She'd been running on adrenaline since Danny had first given her that damn token. It was like her tank was suddenly empty. She sat in the water. Was this it? Was this the way she died? Her thoughts flicked to Danny, and she whispered a quick prayer for his safety.

Rush. She'd been hurt by him. Her naivety had been her downfall there. She'd thought he cared for her like she cared for him. And she did care for him. She might even be a little in love with him. She started to laugh. "I'm a goddam idiot," she yelled at the top of her lungs. How stupid was she? Falling for a man whose job it was to kill her. Ridiculous.

The storm raged above her. The water ran over her. Maybe it was time to admit defeat. Then another sound reached her.

"Kat? Kat!"

Someone was calling her name. With the storm she couldn't tell who it was. If it was her brother, she could be rescued. But if it was Valentine, she'd be dead. *Fuck it.*

She got up on her knees one more time and then struggled to her feet. She leaned on the wall of the hole and put her hands above her head, searching for something...

anything to grab on to, any way that she might use to pull herself out. Her hands hit on a root. When she looked up the falling rain blurred her vision.

"Here goes nothing," she said as she pulled on the root and tried to climb upward. She made it a few steps up the wall but then the root started to give. "No. No. No," she yelled as she started to slide back.

A hand grabbed hers. Then two hands. She looked up but the driving rain made it impossible to see. But she was being pulled up. She tried to use her feet to help climb the wall. What seemed like an eternity later, her head came over the top of the wall and with a final yank she was on top and laying on the forest floor.

Rush stood over her. "You can't lay here. The ground could give way." He jerked her to her feet. "Can you walk?" he asked. She nodded and then stumbled. He caught her and set her upright. "We need to move." Grabbing her hand, he set out at a fast clip. She had to run to keep up with his long strides.

Ten minutes later, they broke through the trees. They were near a cluster of cabins and Kat realized that they were on the opposite side of the island from her cabin, more towards the middle of the island. The force of the rain and wind had lessened here. Rush didn't let go of her hand and practically dragged her along. They stopped in front of the fifth cabin down and he pulled her up the steps. Seconds later, they were inside.

"We'll stay here to wait out the storm."

She shivered as she stood in the middle of the room. "W-w-will we be okay in here? T-this doesn't seem hurricane proof."

"It's not, but this is only a tropical storm. So far. It probably won't reach hurricane strength."

"C-can't we go to the Hub? I-it seems like a much

stronger building." After everything she'd been through, she really just wanted to be safe. Not to mention, being alone with Rush wasn't on her list of things to do. Unfortunately, that scenario was still on her list of things she craved.

Rush was shaking his head, his brows drawn into a straight heavy line. "I'm not sure who's behind all this. It's someone with access to the Hub. I'm not putting you in any risky situations until I know more."

She frowned as she wrapped her arms around herself. "W-why do you c-care? I-I thought it was your job to k-kill me."

He stared at her, his jaw working. Finally, he said, "Go take a hot shower. That should get you warm. Do not turn on any lights. There'll be a robe behind the door for you to change into. You can put your clothes in the washer. It's in the closet in the hallway".

He spun away from her and walked into the kitchen area.

Kat stumbled down the hallway and peeled off her clothes dropping them into the washer. Then she went into the bathroom. Normally, she'd tell him off for his pompous orders, but she was fundamentally exhausted and worried out of her mind for her brother.

There was so much to tell Rush, but she needed to get warm first. Or that's the excuse she was using. Really, she just needed some time to gather her resolve. Facing someone who was supposed to kill her, someone she cared about, was a soul-sucking endeavor. She needed all the time she could get to be ready and that still wouldn't be enough. She was starting to think that she truly was supposed to die on this island. At least she could be warm and dry when it happened.

CHAPTER TWENTY-FIVE

The urge to pull her into his arms and kiss her until neither of them could breathe overwhelmed him. Even after drawing on years of military training, he struggled to resist. He couldn't believe it when he saw her run from that tree. She'd moved so fast he'd lost her for a few minutes. The beating of his heart slowed to glacial speed and hadn't normalized again until he'd seen her hands clawing on the root by the sinkhole.

When he'd discovered Kat was gone, he'd checked the cameras and found her and her no-good brother on the north end of the island with Ronnie, Humber, and Valentine. His gut still reeled as he thought about what could have happened.

Rush opened the fridge, but it was empty. He searched the cabinets and found some canned soup and crackers. It would have to do. Not something they usually had on the island. Someone must have brought it with them. Whatever. It would keep them from starving.

Working to calm his jangled nerves, he focused on heating the soup and arranging the crackers on a plate, anything to stop him thinking about almost losing Kat. Twice. *Jesus.*

He couldn't take it. He had no idea how this woman had gotten so far under his skin in such a short period of time. His attraction to her was crazy, and at the same time so damn right. He had no clue how to explain it to Archer.

He ran his hands over his face. The bastard had it right. There was no way he could kill Kat. Not after sleeping with her. Hell, not after meeting her, if he was being honest. There was just something about her from the first moment he'd met her. He tried to write it off that she was normal, and normal was sadly lacking in his life. But he couldn't lie to himself. Normal wasn't what attracted him to her No, Kat was… home. She grounded him somehow. She made him feel safe, which was ironic considering it was his job to keep everyone else safe from monsters. She just made him feel…human. And he'd missed that. Craved it, in fact, but hadn't realized it until she'd come along.

"I have a lot to tell you," she said as she walked into the room. She sat down on the stool in front of him. "I'm so sorry… Veronica is dead. Humber shot her. It was by accident, really. He panicked when she fell towards him but she did have a gun so I don't know, I guess it could be self-defense."

Rush stood stock still. Ronnie was dead? He waited a beat, expecting some emotion to hit him, something like pain or sorrow. Nothing. No, not nothing. Relief. His shoulders sagged and his gut unknotted just a bit. He was relieved that his ex was dead. She'd caused him pain and anxiety not to mention anger for years and now that was over.

"I'm so sorry," Kat said again. "I know you must be very upset."

He cleared his throat. "Actually, I feel… if I'm being honest, I feel relief. Ronnie has been on a dark road for a long time, and I was worried…" that he'd have to kill her or have one of his teammates do it. Ronnie had become a liability. Hell, she'd always been a liability. More, she was a mess who needed a shit-ton of therapy which she would never get. He'd asked Archer to keep her on in the hopes that it would stabilize her and help her keep her shit together, but it had the opposite effect. Maybe that was on him. Yeah, there was definitely going to be some guilt over Ronnie. It was already nipping at what was left of his conscience. He pushed it aside.

He glanced up and their gazes locked. "There's more isn't there?"

She nodded.

"Tell me," he said as he stirred the tomato soup.

"Valentine and Humber were working together to find the treasure. When Valentine threatened to kill Danny and me if we didn't tell him where it was, Humber tried to get him to negotiate. Said we could all split the treasure. Valentine shot him right between the eyes. Then he called someone and told them it was done. Humber was dead and he wanted payment. I have no idea what that was about."

Rush froze. Any kind of relief he'd felt vanished in a heartbeat. Frank Humber was a board member. His death left a vacancy on the board. Would someone kill him for a seat at the Society's table? Absolutely. But who? He had some ideas.

Suddenly what she said hit him. "Wait. Do you know where the treasure is?"

She nodded. "Yeah." She reached into her robe pocket and pulled out five gold doubloons. They clattered melodiously when she set them on the counter.

He stared at them. Then back at her. "Let me guess, Ronnie wanted the gold too."

She nodded.

"What happened to Valentine?"

Kat shrugged. "I don't know. A tree started to fall and I took off. I yelled at Danny to run…" her voice broke, and she bit her lip. Her nostrils flared and her chest rose, but then she continued. "I don't know what happened to him."

"I was there for the last bit. Danny flew down the path. Since he's been lurking around the island for the last couple of months, I would assume he knows it much better than Valentine. Frankly, probably better than me."

She grimaced. "I'm worried about the cameras."

Rush grabbed a bowl and started ladling soup into it. "What specifically are you worried about with the cameras?"

"Well, whoever this Mr. Smith is, he has access to the cameras and can track Danny and us. What if it's Valentine? He could find and then kill Danny or come after us."

He set the bowl down in front of her. "It's not Valentine. He wouldn't have access to the Hub to get access to the cameras. Like I said before it has to be someone on the inside. Valentine isn't on the inside."

She sank her spoon into the soup. "What about Fisher or Davis?"

Rush filled his own bowl and then came around the island and sat down beside her. "Again, they shouldn't have access."

"Shouldn't?"

"Fisher is not a likely candidate. He doesn't have enough pull as a member to have any kind of access and I don't think he's liked enough for anyone to help him. He could've bribed someone, but I've been looking and can't come up with anything on any of the employees. Archer has a team on it back in New York and they've come up blank as well."

She swallowed another spoonful of soup. "What about Davis?"

"You think Davis is behind the search for the treasure?"

"He suggested the game."

Rush tasted the soup and tried not to spit it back out. Canned tomato soup was only good with a grilled cheese to dip in it. "But if he already had your brother working on finding the treasure, do you think he'd call attention to it? Ask others to try and find it? It would only mean sharing the treasure if by some miracle…" he turned to look at Kat. "I guess some miracle did happen. You know where the treasure is."

She merely nodded and kept eating her soup.

He heaved out a breath. "Anyway, my point is the game meant he would have to share the treasure with more people. He would have no chance of getting away with hiding that he found it from Archer if all these people knew. Nope, him as Mr. Smith just doesn't make any kind of sense."

Kat persisted. "But he has the pull to get into the Hub?"

"Not into the Hub, but he has a better chance of influencing someone to do it for him. Davis is a bit out there in his beliefs. He encourages some of the conspiracy theory crap and if he found a true believer here, they might do it for nothing."

"But you don't think so." She met his gaze.

"No. As much as I would love it to be Davis or Fisher because I would love to kick them out of the Society with prejudice, I don't think Mr. Smith is either one of them."

"So, we're right back where we started."

"No. You have the treasure. You can bargain to get Timmy back."

She frowned. "I thought you said he was dead. You don't think he is anymore?"

"He's dead but Mr. Smith doesn't know you know that so you can bargain with him. Tell him you will tell him where the treasure is if he lets Timmy go. We can set it up so we're there to see who it is."

"We? You're going to help me?"

He lifted his head and looked at her. "Someone on the island is breaking all kinds of rules and fucking with the security system. There's no way I wouldn't work on this with you. It's my job."

"Just like killing me."

Those words sliced deep into his heart. "I wouldn't have done it. Couldn't have in fact, and Archer knows it. You were never in any danger from me, Kat."

"But Archer would've sent others to kill me. I mean if he thought it was necessary, right?"

He wanted to lie to her but that moment had passed. He had to be honest. "In this situation, Archer wouldn't have sent anyone. He would've done it himself."

She bit her lip. "What do you mean 'in this situation'?"

"I mean…" he paused. He hadn't told anyone that he cared about them since Ronnie. Hell, he hadn't even come close. This was not the conversation that he wanted to bring it up in, but he wouldn't lie to her. She deserved the truth.

"Archer knows I care about you so if he deemed it necessary to kill you, he would've done it himself. That way none of my friends are responsible and I would know your death would be as clean and painless as possible." It sounded so harsh, so cruel but he'd seen too many people die slow agonizing deaths when he was in the military that a quick, clean death was all he hoped for.

Having no idea what her reaction to his revelation would be, he waited. His gut knotted and he bounced his leg on the stool. He hadn't fidgeted so nervously in many years, so long that he couldn't remember the last time.

This woman brought out so many things that he thought were long dead inside him.

"And that's okay with you? You would let Archer kill me?" She stared at him open-mouthed.

"No." As soon as he said the word, he knew it was true. There was no way in hell he was going to let anyone hurt Kat. His kitten. No. Way. In. Hell. "That's not what I said. In the current situation, should Archer think it was necessary, he would attempt to kill you himself. That's all I'm saying. I won't let that happen. I won't let him kill you, Kat." The monumental power of those words punched him in the gut. He was willing to go against Archer for this woman, throw away the whole life he'd built. Risk his very existence. And yet, he knew he'd do it in a heartbeat.

She stared at him. "You'd be willing to go against Archer for me?" She sounded doubtful.

He didn't blame her. He'd done nothing but toe the party line since he'd arrived on the island. But not on the inside. That's what he wanted her to know. On the inside, she'd captured his heart the moment she'd tripped in those too-big shoes and fell into his arms. Silly and trite but also true.

"Kat," he swung her stool until she faced him, "I'd be willing to go against the world for you. I know I didn't tell you what you wanted to hear when we were at my cabin. I… if I admitted the truth, it would make me vulnerable, and I have spent my life doing everything I could to avoid being… unprotected. But I am defenseless when it comes to you. You make me vulnerable because I care about you. A lot. Hell, I might even be in love with you. I'll do whatever it takes to keep you safe, baby. I promise."

"I want to believe you." Her eyes glimmered. "I need to believe you. Otherwise, I'm just racing toward my own death… and I don't want to die. But it's difficult to trust you. You were brought here to 'deal with me' whatever that entailed. Your words. Do you know how scary that is? How am I supposed to trust you?"

He took her hands in his and pressed them against his chest. "What does your heart tell you? What do your instincts say to you about me?" It was a gamble. He could only hope that her instincts told her to trust him, to believe he told her the truth. And that she trusted what her heart said.

She bit her lip while her eyes searched his. Then she slipped off the stool and into his arms. She captured his mouth with hers and slid her arms around his neck.

She felt so damn good in his arms, so right, but he had to ask. He broke the kiss. "Are you sure?"

"Yes. I'm overwhelmed, stressed out, and logic tells me to run far away from you. But my heart… My heart says that you're a good man. You energize me. The things you do, you do because you live by a moral code. You wrangle monsters and I feel better knowing you are out there keeping the monsters in check. But I feel even safer knowing you are here. With me. We feel…right. I have no idea what's going to happen or how the hell we're going to survive this, but I know I want to be with you for as long, or as short, as we have."

He kissed her then. Their tongues communicating all the spoken and unspoken words between them. She tasted sweet and sexy at the same time. He moved one hand up to hold her head while he deepened the kiss. He wanted to touch and taste every inch of this woman.

She wrapped her arms around his neck and brought her body in full contact with his. He cupped her ass and pulled her hips against his rock-hard erection. His nerves were jumping all over the place, knowing where this kiss was leading. Once wasn't ever going to be enough. He was a fool to ever think that. A lifetime still wouldn't be enough, but he'd take what he could get. Any amount of time he could spend with Kat. His kitten.

He dragged his lips down her neck. She let out a moan and tugged on his T-shirt. He leaned away from her and pulled the shirt over his head with one hand. He dropped it on the floor and immediately pulled her in and reclaimed her mouth.

Her fingertips trailed down his chest and she started to undo his jeans. He moved back and loosened the belt on her robe, letting it fall open.

She shivered.

"Cold?" he questioned.

"Not even a little."

He swore and then circled one of her nipples with his tongue. He kept his hands on her ass and flexed his fingers into her flesh as he tugged her closer. She moaned as he nipped her with his teeth.

"Rush. I need to feel you. Skin on skin." Her hands were on his belt buckle, but he brushed them off again.

He stood and started pushing her backward until she hit the wall next to the fridge. He grabbed both her wrists and held them in one hand above her head. The fact that she was here with him was blowing his mind. He'd thought he lost her. Now he couldn't imagine being without her ever again.

He claimed her mouth, their tongues tangling, heightening his need for her. He kissed her from neck to nipple. The hard bud peaked for his tongue. When he nipped the other one with his teeth, she sucked in her breath. She tried to squirm out of his grasp, but he held her fast. "If you keep trying to get your hands free, I'll stop what I'm doing," he whispered against her flesh. She whimpered and he grinned. He loved that she wanted him just as badly as he wanted her. "Say my name," he demanded.

"Rush," she whispered and then arched against him as he sucked her nipple once more. She groaned. "I want to touch you."

He wanted that too but first he wanted her to yell his name as she came. He turned her around, so she was facing the wall. Then he let her hands go and pulled her robe off, quickly recapturing her hands and pinning them again. He kissed her neck as he rubbed his hard-on against her lush ass.

"Rush," she whispered, her breath ragged now.

He reached around her hip and stroked the apex of her legs.

"Yes," she moaned.

Her hips started to buck. She pushed back harder against him. He worked her clit with his fingers. She was so wet it was driving him crazy. She pushed her ass back against his pelvis. He worked his fingers faster and faster until her hips rocked wildly. Then he drove his fingers inside of her and she swore as her orgasm rushed around his fingers.

He turned her back around and let go of her hands. She reached for him, but he stepped back. Flushed with desire for him, she was magnificent. She was his. And only his.

He pressed his whole body against hers, trapping her bare ass against the wall and kissed her once again. The feel of her skin against his chest sparked an insane throbbing inside him. He had a hard time keeping himself in check. When he touched her hot center, her hips bucked again. He kissed her neck while he brushed her clit with his finger. Then he got down on his knees in front of her.

"Rush," she said as she brought her hands down to his shoulders. "I want you inside me."

"Not yet," he said with a slow smile. He blew on her hot center, and she sank her fingers into his hair. He licked her and relished the sweet taste in his mouth. He swirled his tongue around her center and deep inside, and she moaned breathlessly.

He gripped her ass and held her in place as he sucked and licked her, driving her higher and higher with lips, teeth, and tongue. Then he eased one finger inside her tight sheath. She arched to meet him. He added another finger while he sucked her clit. She flexed her hands on his scalp and draped one leg over his shoulder, opening her hips to meet his fingers and mouth. As he increased his rhythm, she rocked with him. This was so fucking hot. He loved that she was losing control. He swirled his tongue and kept her right on the edge until he nipped her clit with his teeth. She called his name as she came.

Her knees buckled, and he caught her, hugging her hips tight. She combed her fingers through his hair as her breath evened out.

"Jesus, that was even better than the first time," she murmured.

He grinned as he stood, picking her up as he did. His cock jerked as her hip connected with his groin when he lifted her. Walking with his dick like steel was hard, but he managed his way down the hall to the bedroom. He tossed her on the bed. "Let's see if we can make round three even better."

CHAPTER TWENTY-SIX

Kat patted the bed next to her. She wasn't going to hear any argument. She needed to touch him. To *taste* him. He started to climb onto the bed, but she braced a hand on his hip, really wanting to drag her thumb across the hard line behind his zipper. But wanting the barrier gone more. "Take the rest of your clothes off first."

Once he was naked, she pushed him until he was lying on his back on the bed. She moved on top of him and kissed him. Hard. Then she worked her way down his neck to his chest. She used her teeth on his nipples, and he swore. He grabbed her ass, but she wiggled him off.

"Kat" His low voice rumbled under her body, sending shivers across her skin. His physique was something to behold. Chiseled and steely, as if carved out of granite. Not an ounce of fat anywhere, which might have been damned annoying if he wasn't so fucking hot. She went back to his nipples and then headed lower.

He swore in response, and she moved farther down his body until her mouth hovered over his cock. She touched the tip with her tongue and then laved small circles on the crown, first one way, then the other. Slowly, she drew more and more of him into her mouth, sucking and twisting her tongue.

Rush growled her name; his rough voice ignited sparks in her girlie bits. She wanted him inside of her, but first she wanted him to yell *her* name. His hips started to move, and she matched the rhythm with her tongue.

"I won't last if you keep that up."

She stopped and glanced up along his sculpted ab muscles to catch his gaze and hold it. "No, you won't. I'll stop if you don't control yourself."

"Fuck, Kat," he said through gritted teeth. "You're killing me."

She licked her lips and let them curl up into a sly smile. She liked that he wanted her so damn badly. Almost as much as she wanted him. She was wet and ready. She crawled up and hovered over his body once again. She started to lower herself on top of him, but he flipped her over and suddenly she was beneath him, face down on the bed.

"You seemed to like it from behind," he said, his voice just above a whisper in her ear.

God help her, she did. He was so fucking hot. She was drenched and oh so ready.

He pulled her hair out of the way and kissed the back of her neck. He cupped her breasts from behind. The heavy length of his shaft nestled along her ass. She moaned and arched into his hands. She was so turned on she couldn't think anymore.

Rush brought her up onto her knees and tweaked her nipple with one hand as he moved the other down to stroke her clit. "You're so fucking wet."

"Yes, Rush and I want you inside me. Now." Her hips started moving in time with his fingers as he played with her.

He wedged his cock between her ass cheeks and rubbed it up and down, driving her wild.

"Fuck me, Rush," she demanded.

He bent over her back and entered her. The slow stroke was so luxurious. She wanted to feel him all the way inside her. Her body vibrated with desire for him. He started moving slowly, but she pumped her hips faster.

She needed more. "Please, Rush." He increased his speed. She moaned, "Yes, oh God, yes."

Rush slowed down. "You need to wait until I say it's time," he ordered, slapping her ass to punctuate the demand. "You're mine."

He slammed all the way inside her, hard and fast. And she loved it, thrusting her hips back to meet his. She nearly wept as he drew out. Then he slowly entered her again, making her cry out in frustration. She wanted it all now. "Rush." She didn't want to beg, but she would if he didn't hurry the hell up.

He reached around and played with her clit as he pumped into her again and again.

"I'm gonna come," she said and bit her lip.

He increased his speed. "Yes, honey. Come hard."

She threw her head back as he slammed into her and yelled his name as she came again. A few strokes later, he was right there with her.

He leaned over her back. "Jesus, Kat, you're so fucking amazing."

Her arms and legs were shaking with the lingering release, her chest and belly quivering. "The feeling is mutual."

The sound of the wind woke her. It was really howling. She had doubts that the cabin would hold together. She glanced over at Rush but he was asleep beside her. He looked so peaceful she decided not to wake him. Instead, she slipped quietly from the bed and padded into the main living area. She grabbed the robe off the floor and put it back on, tying the belt around her waist.

She moved to the kitchen area and realized the power was off. The generators, or whatever the island used, weren't working. Looking around, she realized she no longer had her phone. She must have lost it in the sinkhole or maybe even before that.

Looking out the window, a hollowness formed in her chest as anxiety crept back up her spine. Danny had to be okay. He just had to be. After all this shit, after everything he'd been through, he just couldn't be taken out by the storm. He would have found somewhere to ride it out, wouldn't he?

They seriously needed to figure out who the hell Mr. Smith was and where he had Timmy. The wind whipped the palm trees so the fronds almost blew horizontal. The rain made it almost impossible to see anything besides the front porch and the trees in the front yard.

She suddenly wondered about the treasure. Would it survive the storm? *Well duh*. It had been there since the seventeen hundreds. Chances were excellent it would withstand this storm as well. The bigger question was, would she? *Can I survive the storm raging inside me?*

She wanted to be with Rush but she couldn't see a viable way to make that happen. Archer was likely going to demand her death for lying to the Society and helping her brother who he thought might have something to do with Angel's death. He obviously would want her brother dead too. Even if she found a way around that, Archer wouldn't let Rush leave the Society. Was that the oath or whatever? Did he even want to leave the Society? Fundamentally, he was doing good work. Keeping the monsters in line. If he left the Society what else could he do? Security work somewhere maybe but it probably wouldn't be as fulfilling. Did his job make him happy? There was so much she didn't know about him but she desperately wanted the time to find those things out.

A loud thump came from the side of the cabin and she jumped. Probably a downed branch. The rain was not letting up. On top of everything else, the storm had her completely freaked out. The cabin groaned in the wind.

"Don't worry, honey. It will hold," Rush said as he walked into the room. He was fully dressed holding the clothes she'd thrown in the dryer. "They're a bit damp but better than they were."

"Thanks," she said taking them from him. "Are we going somewhere?"

"Not just yet, but you have me thinking about who might know where we are. I just want to be prepared if we have to move in a hurry."

"Do you think someone will want to kill us?" She pulled on her underwear. When had her life become a surreal parody where it was normal to casually discuss who might want her dead as she got dressed? It was all so out of control, but she was too tired to panic anymore. Resignation had set in. Now she had to see it through.

"Treasure makes people do crazy things." His gaze softened. "As you know." He squeezed her arm.

Sighing, she finished getting dressed. "It occurs to me that I have no way to reach Smith to tell him I know where the treasure is. Danny had his number and unless Danny turns up with his cell, we've got nothing."

"I've been thinking about that. I might have a solution." He wrapped his arms around her waist.

The look in his eye had her stomach rolling. "What? What is it?"

"As much as I hate this idea, I think we're going to have to use you as bait."

She took a step back. Being in his arms was fogging her brain. He wanted to use her to lure the man she would prefer to avoid at all costs. *This is to save Danny.*

She leaned against the wall and crossed her arms over her chest. "Explain."

"We know Smith has access to the cameras. What if you go in front of one and hold up one of the doubloons? Then he'll know you've found the treasure."

"Okay but then how do we set up a meet? It's not like he can talk to me through the camera. And won't that alert everyone else that I have the doubloons too? The people in the Hub?" She paused and then murmured, "And Archer?"

"Smith will know. The only people in the Hub at the moment are Pierre and Danton, the two heads of shift. If one of them is Smith then this play kills two birds with one stone. But you're right, Archer will know because I'm going to tell him. There's no way around that. It would be signing our death warrants if we didn't tell him."

Her heart started racing. "But aren't we doing that anyway?"

Rush's gaze bored into hers. "Do you trust me?"

Oh, that was a big one. He'd been assigned the job of killing her and now here she was sleeping with him. Did she trust him? Deep in her heart, she did. Logic said she was probably dead either way but she truly did trust Rush. "Yes," she whispered and then cleared her throat. "Yes, Rush, I trust you. It's probably stupid to do so but I do." She shrugged.

His shoulders seemed to drop a bit and a huge grin lit his face. He came forward and kissed her hard. "Good, because I trust you and I will do everything in my power to keep you and your brother alive."

Her heart lifted with his words. He cared about her. She

knew it. That was enough for now. Maybe forever. Her forever might be a wee bit short. If they'd met outside of all this, she'd want him to say he loved her. It would almost be worse now if he said it, knowing that she was quite possibly going to miss the life they could've had together.

"So, what are we going to do about Archer?"

"Leave it to me. I've got a plan. I'll tell you all about it once we finish with Smith."

She shrugged. She could argue the point but he was right. First things first. She had to make sure Smith didn't kill her and her brother and then she could worry about Archer killing them. Hysterical laughter burbled up and she fought to quell it.

"How will we keep Smith from knowing you're at the meet? Won't he be able to see us both on the cameras?"

"Once you show the doubloon to a camera, I'm going to pull the plug."

She frowned. "I don't get it."

"The island's electricity runs off massive generators and solar power. They would've switched off the power to most of the island for the storm in case downed trees caused power line breaks. I'm going to take the generators offline making the cameras inoperable."

"Won't they just turn them back on?"

"Not with what I'm going to do to them. They'll have to wait to get a part to repair them."

"Oh," she said. He was going to sabotage them. Great. Just another thing Archer could use against them. Still, it wasn't like they had a choice.

The lack of sound penetrated her thoughts and she turned to look out the window. The sun had risen and the wind had died. The storm was over, and it looked to be another perfect Caribbean day. If only. "What time do you want to do this?"

Rush glanced at his watch. "I'll head over in about an hour. At exactly 9:30 a.m. I want you to leave here and walk to the hospital. When you get there, stand outside the entrance until 9:45 and then hold up a doubloon to the camera. Say the words 'pool bar'. Wait two minutes and then head over to the main pool and sit at the bar. I'll turn off the cameras at 9:47 and follow you over. You won't see me, but I'll be there. Promise."

"Won't Smith expect that?"

"Yes, but I'm guessing he's not as experienced in the art of warfare as I am. Don't worry. I'll be there to protect you."

"Okay." She looked out the window. "I wish I knew where Danny was. I'd feel a whole lot better."

"I know. I'm going to go over to the Hub shortly and see if I can locate him on the video feeds. We'll find him."

She gave him a quick smile. It would be nice if Rush were right but she wasn't so sure it was all going to work out like he thought. It wasn't that she didn't trust him or even that she didn't have faith in him. It was more an instinct. Just a feeling, but something told her this was going to be a shit show and she'd be lucky to escape with her life.

"In the meantime," Rush said as he pulled Kat into his arms and then kissed her.

CHAPTER TWENTY-SEVEN

Rush hated leaving Kat alone but he didn't have a choice. As he hurried to the Hub, he assessed the storm damage. It didn't look too bad. Some downed branches and destroyed flower beds. Only one structure he passed had any damage and that was from a large tree branch breaking a window. It would probably only take them a few days to clean up before they could invite members to come back to the island.

He snorted. As if he was still likely to be here. Archer was either going to banish him forever, which was the likely scenario if his plan worked out, or Archer would kill him and possibly Kat. His gut churned as he considered that possibility. Personally, he wasn't afraid of death, but the idea of Archer hurting Kat gnawed at him. He couldn't let that happen.

He arrived at the Hub to find Danton and Pierre studying the screens. "Hey," he greeted them as he entered. "It doesn't look too bad out there."

Danton nodded. "I thought the same thing. Nothing too bad on any of the feeds either."

Pierre pointed to a screen on the top right. "That looks like the only significant damage." It was one of the cabins. A tree had fallen on it and damaged the roof."

"Did you notify Archer?"

"Sending the report now." Danton's fingers moved quickly across the keyboard.

"Have you guys seen any groundskeepers on any of the screens?" Danny had to be out there somewhere.

Pierre frowned. "I thought they all left."

"One was left behind. I'd like to find him if I can."

"Let's do a scan."

The three of them backed up the video feeds for the cameras until daybreak and then started scanning. A half-hour later, nothing. Danny really knew what he was doing. Or Valentine had killed him. Rush prayed it wasn't the latter. He'd have to worry about it later. Now he had to go talk to the devil.

"Where's Archer?"

"His cabin," Pierre said.

Rush nodded his thanks and left. He followed a wide pathway to Archer's bungalow. Twice the size of the regular cabins with an excellent view and lots of privacy. He walked up the steps to the veranda and Archer opened the door before he had a chance to knock.

"Status?"

"Island looks good. Not too much damage."

"I wasn't asking about the island." Archer was standing there in jeans and a white T-shirt. He looked tired and harassed. *Great.*

"Make me some coffee and I'll tell you what I know."

Archer backed up and let Rush into his place. Then he closed the door and walked over to the kitchen. The bungalow had the same general layout as the other cabins, just much larger. Rush sat down at the large kitchen island

and Archer placed a cup of steaming hot black coffee in front of him.

"I think I have a plan to lure out Smith, assuming he's still on the island or even if he's not."

"I'm listening," Archer said as he leaned against the stove and crossed his arms over his chest.

Rush took a sip of coffee and swallowed. "You should know, Kat found the treasure."

Archer's jaw dropped. It was the first time Rush had ever seen surprise on his boss's face. "Seriously? After all these fucking years?"

"Yes," he said and stalled by taking another sip of coffee. "She currently has a couple of doubloons as proof. She's going to hold them up in front of a camera at precisely 9:45 this morning and say the words 'pool bar'. Then"—he set down his mug and met his boss's gaze—"I'm going to take all the generators offline."

"You're stopping his camera access," Archer surmised.

He nodded. "I'll go directly over to the main pool bar area and set up. Smith will eventually show his face and we'll get him."

Archer rubbed his jaw. "He'll know it's a trap."

"I'm counting on it."

Archer tipped his head and cocked a brow.

Rush had definitely gotten the man's attention. The coffee scalded Rush's tongue as he took a bigger gulp. "Smith is desperate. He won't leave without the gold, not after all this. I'm counting on that. I expect he'll be extra cautious and try to either do something to get Kat away from the pool bar, or more likely, create a distraction somewhere else on the island to lure me away."

"You want me to take care of the distraction."

Rush nodded. "There are only a few people still on the island. My guess is Smith will light something on fire or blow something up. Maybe even do something to the Hub."

Archer was nodding slowly. "And when we're all dealing with that, he'll grab Kat and try and get the location of the gold." This is why they paid Archer the big bucks. The man caught on fast.

"I'll have you radio me with orders to head to wherever the problem is. I'll tell Kat I have to go and that Smith isn't on the island yet. I'll tell her to stay there until I get back. Hopefully, Smith will be watching and believe I've left. Then I'll wait and get him when he comes out." Rush sighed. "It's not the best plan but we really don't have much to work with."

"Agreed." Archer stared at him for a moment, eyes darting around as he apparently weighed the options. Finally, he sighed. "Go get set up. Do what you have to, and I'll radio you once whatever the distraction is, happens. Get a radio from the Hub once you knock the cameras offline."

He finished his coffee and stood.

"Rush." Archer's tone was serious. "This is not over. Kat and her brother are not out of trouble. There are rules in place and they have to be followed to keep order."

Rush met his gaze. "I know that."

Archer nodded once. "Besides, Danny cut open the thatch in his bedroom to escape, the little fucker. My floors are ruined from the rain."

Rush grinned. "Resourceful little shit, isn't he?"

A small smile played at the corners of Archer's mouth. "Yes, he is."

Rush took his leave and went back to the Hub. His plan was weak but it was all he had. If Smith didn't go for it, they were all in trouble. He actually uttered a silent prayer as he entered the Hub. This had to work. Just had to. Otherwise, he and Kat weren't going to make it off the island.

CHAPTER TWENTY-EIGHT

Kat hustled along the path that led to the hospital. She'd fallen asleep after Rush had left and now she was late. Very late. She was about to break into a run when her brother stepped out onto the path in front of her.

"Jesus, Danny! You scared the crap out of me." Then she threw her arms around her brother and hugged him tight. "I'm so glad you're okay. I was worried. I thought you were behind me at the lagoon, but when I looked back you were gone."

"It's good to see you too, sis." He returned the hug and stepped back. "I...uh...panicked and ran the opposite way."

"Tell me all about it in a few. We have to get to the hospital. I'll explain everything later. Just come on."

They took off at a jog and arrived at the bend in the path at 9:45. "I have to do something. Stay here. I'll be back to get you shortly." She ran up to the camera and held up a doubloon and said, "Meet me at the main pool bar." She waited a bit and then glanced at her watch. 9:47. The cameras should be dead now.

Walking back around the bend, she grabbed her brother's

arm and headed towards the main pool bar. "So where did you go? What did you do? I can't believe you're all in one piece." She squeezed his arm.

"I know. I thought I was a goner after that tree fell. Then I ended up getting lost in the trees. It took me a while to make my way back to the waterfall. I spent the night in the cave behind it. I knew the water wouldn't rise that much and no one would come looking for me in there."

"Smart thinking."

He smiled. "Thanks. Where did you end up?"

"I ran through the trees and then fell into a sinkhole."

Danny stopped walking. "Oh my God, I'm so sorry. I—I just panicked. I should've stuck with you."

She shook her head. "It's fine. Rush pulled me out. I lost the phone though so I couldn't call you."

"Yeah, me too."

"How did you find me then?" she asked.

He shrugged. "I didn't actually find you. I was heading to the hospital. It was the only place I could think of that you might have gone. And if you were hurt…"

"Right," she said.

They arrived at the pool area but the bar was closed. The shutters were down and the stools were gone. There was nowhere to sit. The pool itself was littered with storm debris. She walked over to the bar area and went around to the side. The door was locked and she didn't have her lock picks with her.

"Here," her brother said, "let me." He picked up a rock from the edge of the path and smashed the lock.

"That works." She pulled off the lock and opened the door. In a few minutes they had the bar shutters up and the stools out front. She sat on a stool and Danny stayed behind the bar.

"What'll you have?" he asked.

She laughed. "It's a bit early, isn't it?"

"Is it?" he countered. "After everything we've been through?"

"You're right. I'll have a rum punch."

He grinned. "I have no idea how to make that, but I'll try." He put a couple of glasses on the bar. "Timmy is dead, isn't he?" he said as he poured out a measure of rum in both glasses.

"Rush thinks so."

He grabbed a couple of bottles of juice and poured some in each glass. "What do you think?"

She slowly nodded her head.

"I was afraid of that. He's probably been dead this whole time."

Not wanting to break her brother's heart any more than it already was, she remained silent. Timmy had probably been killed just after that picture of him was taken. Smith hadn't needed him after that. Danny was doing what he said and Smith could always threaten Kat if he needed to.

"Why then are we still on the island?"

An excellent question. She said, "We need to know for sure Timmy is dead and we need to catch Smith."

Danny frowned. "Why? Why do we need to catch Smith? Why can't we just take the treasure and run?"

She stared. He had a valid point. Closing her eyes, she cursed silently. She opened her eyes as her brother put her drink in front of her. "We can't just run because we won't get far. Archer Gray won't let us live. Not if we steal the treasure, not to mention Smith seems to have some reach as well. We'll be running for the rest of our lives."

Danny shrugged. "Just thought I'd ask."

She studied her brother. He looked so defeated. So damned tired but something else. He looked calm. She gritted her teeth. "You moved the gold, didn't you."

He blinked. "What? Who, me? No, I didn't." He ran a hand through his hair. "I swear—"

"You're lying Danny. I can always tell. You moved it. Where the hell did you put it?"

"Really sis, you're getting paranoid."

She slammed her hand down on the counter. "Tell me," she demanded.

He swallowed. "Fine. I moved it." His tone was sullen.

"Jesus, Danny, why? Why the fuck couldn't you leave well enough alone?"

"Because it's a fucking fortune in treasure! Why should I leave it? We found it. It's ours. I'm not giving it back."

She couldn't believe it. He still didn't get it. "You…" She took a deep breath. "Danny, that treasure is the only thing keeping us alive. Fuck with it and we die."

"You should listen to your sister," a voice said from Danny's left. Valentine entered the area behind the bar, gun up and pointed at Danny's chest. His hair was messed and the clothes he had on were torn. It looked like he'd weathered the storm outside. There were dark circles under his eyes. Tell me where the treasure is, and I'll let you live. Stay quiet and I'll kill her and then you."

"You're Mr. Smith?" Danny asked raising in his hands in the air.

"I'm whoever I need to be. Tell me about the treasure."

Danny swallowed. "What about Timmy? Is he alive?"

Valentine snarled. "I'm not messing around. Tell me where the treasure is. I want off this island and I won't go empty handed. I've wasted too much time as it is."

Danny looked at Kat. She didn't know what to say.

"How about I show you where the treasure is," Danny offered.

Valentine's eyes narrowed. "Just tell me."

"You won't be able to get it on your own," Danny countered.

"You're bluffing."

"I'm not. You can't get it on your own. You'll need help. If I'm lying and the treasure isn't there, you can shoot me."

"Danny!" Kat said, her voice full of warning. What the hell was her brother doing?

"Okay. But your sister comes too."

"No." Danny shook his head. "Not part of the deal. I moved the treasure. She doesn't know where it is. Hurt her and you get nothing."

Valentine gestured with his gun. "Fine. Move slowly towards me."

"Danny," she said again. This couldn't be happening. Where the hell was Rush?

Danny walked over to Valentine and then brushed by him. Valentine jabbed the gun into Danny's back and marched him out of the bar. They came out to the pool area and Danny stopped in front of his sister's stool. "It's okay, sis. I've got this."

"No. Please. Valentine. He'll give you the treasure but you have to let him go."

"Up to him. If he tries anything then he's dead. If he gets me the treasure, I might let him live." Valentine pushed the gun into Danny's back. "Move."

Kat reached out and grabbed Danny's hand. Her heart was in her throat, blocking her airway. Where the hell was Rush? Why wasn't he here saving Danny?

"It's okay sis. I promise. I've got this."

"Enough," Valentine barked. "Move."

Danny squeezed her hand and then let it go and started walking across the pool area.

Rush came out from behind the towel cabana and put his gun to Valentine's skull. "Drop it."

Valentine froze.

"Drop it. This won't end well for you."

Danny turned and stared at Valentine.

Valentine started to smile. It grew into a laugh; not an ordinary laugh but a weird high pitched one. It made Kat's hair stand on end. "I should've known," he sputtered, drawing in a ragged breath. "I shouldn't have trusted them. I should've gone with my gut." He still hadn't turned around. Instead, he stared at Danny. "Let that be a lesson. Trust your instincts. Don't let greed override them." In one quick motion, he turned the gun away from Danny, put it to his own temple, and pulled the trigger.

Kat screamed as he dropped to the ground.

Danny stood there shocked, blood spatter all over his clothes and face. Rush kicked Valentine's gun away from this hand even though it was obvious the man was dead.

"You okay?" he asked Danny.

Danny stared at Valentine.

"Danny!" Rush barked. "You okay?"

He nodded but he was obviously in shock. Kat got off the stool and stumbled. She wasn't sure her legs could hold her but she tried to walk over to her brother. She tugged at his chin. "Danny, stop staring at him. He's dead."

Danny slowly shifted his gaze to Kat. "I…I just didn't expect…that."

"No. No one did," she said gently. Rush put his hand on her shoulder and squeezed. She brushed her cheek on the back of it and then straightened again. "Danny, let's go. Rush will deal with this." Glancing in his direction, he confirmed her supposition with a nod of his head. "We'll go…" Where?

"Back to my place," Rush said. "I'll deal with this and meet you there." He handed her the keys.

She nodded. That was good. Rush's place. Her clothes were there. They'd be fine there. She started walking and gently tugged her brother along. He came but his eyes were still wild. Shock for sure.

"I'll be there as fast as I can." Rush gave her a small smile and then she started walking faster.

Ten minutes later they got to Rush's. She let them in and got her brother into the shower. She pulled out a T-shirt of Rush's and a pair of sweats. That would have to do for now. Going back to the kitchen she made some coffee for herself and poured a glass of whisky for her brother. He was going to need a shot of something to bring the color back in his face. She stared at the bottle and poured a glass for herself as well. It had been the day from hell and it still wasn't noon.

CHAPTER TWENTY-NINE

"What do you think?" Archer kept his voice low as Pierre and Danton put Valentine's body on a stretcher.

Rush ran a hand through his hair. "I don't know. Valentine as Smith would mean either he was some kind of hacking genius, or we have a mole on the inside to help him."

"Neither scenario makes me feel any better about this situation," Archer declared.

"Me either."

"Gentlemen, take Mr. Valentine to the morgue. Tell Dr. Walton I'll be over shortly." Archer waved his hand toward the hospital.

"Yes, sir," Danton said. "I just want to apologize again for the cameras going down. We're working on it, and we'll have them back up as soon as possible." The man's eyes darted around and he shifted his weight from foot to foot as he spoke.

"I know you will, Danton."

They wheeled Valentine away on the stretcher.

Archer sagged onto a stool at the bar. "You okay?"

"Yeah." Rush had wiped his face earlier but longed for a shower. He also wanted to hug Kat but that would have to wait. "Why do you think he shot himself?"

"What choice did he have? If he didn't, you would've killed him. If not today., then one day soon. He broke the rules. Killed a fellow member on Society property. That can never be allowed."

"I guess." But Rush wasn't sure he was convinced. "Valentine said something about trusting the wrong people and being greedy. What do you think that was about?"

Archer shrugged. "He did work for the Bratva."

"Russian mob? Interesting. I didn't realize."

Archer nodded. "No one did. He was the bastard son of one of the top members. He kept a low profile so he could have access to legitimate businesses that the Bratva would normally be shut out of. Valentine would go in as a legit investor and then slowly take control, turning it over to his Bratva compatriots to run afterward. He was slick but who knows, maybe he pissed one of them off, or triggered a rival faction. Maybe he skimmed off the top. There are lots of ways to piss off the Bratva."

"And pissing off the Bratva might make anyone want to eat a bullet rather than face the consequences. Still…"

"Yeah." Archer went silent. Then gave a small shrug. "I'll poke around a bit and see if I can find out more. In the meantime, if you're good, go put the cameras back online. Danton is sweating bullets."

Rush grinned. "Will do. Be thankful I didn't do physical damage to them like I'd planned."

Archer shook his head. "Good help is so fucking hard to find," he muttered as he got up from the stool and walked off.

Rush chuckled and made his way to the Hub. He liked

Archer. A lot. He was a good man in many ways but, more importantly, he was always fair. His gut churned about the next part of his plan. He came to the fork in the path and grinned at the irony. The fork in the road. The spot where he had to make a choice.

If he took the right path, he would go to the Hub and fix the cameras. That path led to them all staying to face the consequences of their actions. Kat, Danny, and him. If he took the left path, he'd go back to the cabin, put the two of them in a boat anchored at the jetty and get all three of them the hell out of there. He had enough money socked away to let them live out their days in comfort if not peace. They'd always be looking over their shoulders, but they'd be alive. It was a hard choice.

It dawned on him suddenly that he was burned out but he genuinely liked his life. It suited him. He liked being an enforcer of rules. A monster wrangler. He liked Ryker, Cash and Lachlan. Archer was a friend as well as a boss.

But he also admitted that he loved Kat. More than he ever thought possible. Ronnie had been a distraction. An attraction he let get out of control. Kat was…home. Love. The person he wanted to build a life with. The person that made his life worth living.

He stared at the fork in the path and then started walking. There was never a question in his mind, not really, about which choice he would make.

CHAPTER THIRTY

"It's over. It's really over," Danny said then drained his whiskey.

"That part of it is, yes."

He looked at his sister. "What do you mean that part?"

Kat took a deep breath. "Danny, I'm not sure Archer Gray is going to let us off the island alive."

Danny swallowed. "What if we leave the treasure? Just go. He wouldn't bother to chase us, would he?"

She exhaled. "I…I think he would. I think it's a matter of principle for him. He can't really just let us go. Me anyway. I'm a member. It means there is a different set of rules I have to follow. I think I might be able to get him to leave you alone."

"Nope. No way." Danny slammed his tumbler on the counter. "I won't go without you, Kat."

She smiled. "Just don't worry about it for now. I've got a plan and with any luck, it will work. We could use some luck right about now, right?"

He nodded and she poured him more whiskey. There was

a knock at the door. Rush. She'd locked the door after they'd gotten there.

She went over and opened the door. "Oh, hey. What are you doing here?"

"Kat! You're alive!" Peter stood there. "I was looking for Rush. Does he know you're alive? What happened?"

"It's a long story."

"Can I come in?" Peter asked. He leaned on the door jamb. His color wasn't great.

"Of course." She stepped back and let Peter into the cabin. "Peter, this is my brother."

"Hi, Danny. It's nice to meet you," Peter said and the two shook hands. Peter sat down on the stool next to Danny. "Oh, can I have some of that?" he asked as he pointed to the whiskey bottle.

"Of course." Kat got another glass and poured a healthy shot.

Peter stared at her. "I just can't believe you're alive, Kat."

"Yeah, well I guess news of my death was greatly exaggerated, as they say." She offered him another smile.

Peter nodded. "So, what are you doing here?"

"Just waiting for Rush," she said. "Where's Daisy? Is she okay?"

"Oh, of course. A tropical storm has nothing on her."

"Glad to hear it." She turned to her brother. "Daisy is Peter's wife."

Danny just nodded and took another sip of his drink.

Peter downed his in one swallow. "Ahh, that's nice. Rush always has the good stuff. Too bad he's not here to join us."

Kat stared at Peter for a second as what he'd said dawned on her. *Oh shit!* The hair on the back of her neck went up. "How did you know Danny's name?"

"Oh, dear." Peter smiled coldly, then pulled out a gun and aimed at Danny. "Where is the treasure?"

"You've gotta be shittin' me," Danny said. "Seriously? Dude, it's been like the worst day. Worst month. Worst year. I am so done with this treasure shit."

"You're right, you're finished with it. It's mine, so tell me where it is, and I'll be on my way."

Kat's knees were weak. She gripped the edge of the counter. "You're Smith."

Peter swung to face her but still kept his gun on Danny. "Yes."

"But why? Why risk everything?"

"What everything? My life is over. I wanted money for Daisy. She deserves to have a life outside of this. A life where she can do what she wants when she wants. I don't want her to have to keep working."

"Does Archer pay so little?" she asked.

His face clouded over. "It doesn't matter what Archer pays! She deserves the best and now she'll have it." He jabbed the gun aggressively toward Danny's ribs. "Tell me where the gold is."

Danny snorted. "Dude, you're old and sick. No way you're gonna get it out of here." The whiskey had taken over Danny's mouth.

"You leave that to me. Where is it?" Peter demanded again. "I don't mind killing your sister if it will make you tell me faster." He swung the gun toward Kat.

Her heart slammed into her ribs. The dead look in Peter's eyes told the truth. He had nothing to lose. He was a dead man walking and he knew it.

"He has pancreatic cancer." Peter narrowed his eyes, but kept the gun aimed at her head. She nodded. "Tell him where it is, Danny."

Danny stared at her.

"Tell him," she said and glared at her brother. He still wouldn't speak. "The treasure is at the bottom of the lagoon."

Peter's eyebrows flew up. A smile spread across his face, and he started to laugh. "All these years and it was right there the whole time. I used to dive in the lagoon. That's how I found the tunnel out." He laughed some more. "One of life's little ironies."

Finally, he stood. "Let's go." He gestured to Danny with the gun, but Danny refused to move. "Now!" Peter said as he pressed the gun into Danny's side.

"No." Danny shook his head. "You killed Timmy. You got me down here and now I'm screwed. Archer Gray's gonna kill me anyway. Hell no, I'm not helping you."

Peter's eyes narrowed. "How do you know I killed Timmy. Maybe he's still my hostage. You have to give me the treasure and then I'll tell you where you can find your friend."

"Bullshit, old man. I'm an idiot for getting involved in this but I'm not stupid. Timmy is dead. You killed him. You're on your own."

"Danny," Kat pleaded but she knew that look. Her brother had set his jaw and it didn't matter what Peter did now, he wasn't going to help, even if it cost him his life.

"I'll kill Kat." The gun swung in her direction again.

Danny's shoulders slumped. "Go for it. She's dead anyway."

It was true. Chances were good she was a dead woman, but this wasn't helping. "I'll take you to the treasure and I'll dive for it. Leave Danny here."

Peter stared at her for a moment and shrugged. "Fine. Either one of you will do." He swung the gun back toward Danny.

"Wait!" Danny yelled as he tried to stand.

Peter pulled the trigger and Danny hit the floor in a crumpled heap.

"No!" she screamed but Peter turned the gun toward her.

She stood still and watched her brother. He was motionless on the floor. His face was pale and she was sure he was dead but then his eyelashes flickered. The pool of blood was growing which meant his heart was still beating. There was hope. A slim chance but only if she got help right away. "Can I call the hospital so they'll come get him? We'll be gone by the time they get here."

"No." Peter wasn't playing anymore. He pointed the gun at her face.

She started walking towards the door. Putting on her shoes, she opened the door and stepped outside onto the veranda. Her brother was lying on the floor in an ever-widening pool of blood. He was going to die if she didn't get help to him soon. She was going to be killed by Archer Gray. Did it really matter what happened now? She started down the stairs and then stopped when she got to the bottom. She turned. "Shoot me."

"What? What are you playing at?" Peter demanded.

"I told you where the treasure was. Shoot me. I won't help you."

His eyes narrowed. He was on the second step. "You will dive for that gold or I will—"

"No, I won't. Shoot me now." She wasn't giving this asshole anything. Not in a million years.

Peter raised the gun. The sound of the shot was loud, louder than she expected. She looked down at her chest, but there was no spreading bloodstain, no holes in the fabric. She looked up at Peter. His brows were raised, and his mouth gaped open. He fell forward down the stairs and she jumped out of his way, staring at him as he hit the path. She kicked the gun out of his reach as she'd seen Rush do. Then she looked around. Where had the shot come from?

Daisy came around the corner. "I'm sorry, dear. I didn't

mean to take so long but my eyesight isn't what it used to be. I wanted to make sure I killed him with my first shot."

"Daisy?" she said in astonishment. "What? I mean…I—"

"Call the hospital and tell them about your brother." She offered her cell phone.

Kat grabbed it and made the call. "They're on the way." She went back up the stairs and into the cabin. She grabbed some towels from the bathroom to use to put pressure on her brother's bullet wound. She fell to the floor beside him, and he opened one eye.

"Is it over?" he whispered.

"Yes."

"Good. He opened his eyes and tried to sit up. "My ass. He shot me in the ass."

A laugh burst forth from her, and she couldn't stop. Eventually, she handed him the towels and leaned against the cabinets trying to stop laughing and catch her breath at the same time.

"Is your brother alright, dear?" Daisy asked as she entered the cabin.

Kat nodded. "He'll be okay."

"Good." She turned to Danny. "I—"

Rush came in the door after her and almost ran Daisy over. "Kat! Are you okay?"

Archer was right behind him.

Kat nodded as he pulled her up from the floor and gathered her into his arms. She blinked back tears. Crying now wouldn't help.

"Daisy," Archer said, "what the hell happened?"

"It would seem Peter lost his mind. He dragged this poor boy and Kat into this mess from what I can determine." She suddenly looked all of her seventy-plus years. Archer must have thought the same thing. He offered her a chair and she sat down heavily. "I'm so sorry. I didn't know until the storm. Peter took me to an old cabin in the north end of the island to ride out the storm and while he slept, I discovered what he'd done. He had that poor young man tied to a chair."

"Timmy?" Danny asked. "Is he alive?"

Daisy shook her head. "I'm afraid not, dear. Peter left him tied to the chair after he killed him. Sloppy. Not like my Peter at all. Then I found the research on the treasure and the pictures of you and Kat. He'd done his research on you two, as well. I surmised what must have happened. I tried to talk him out of doing anything foolish but he wouldn't listen. He actually tied me to a chair to keep me there. But the old coot didn't have the strength to tighten the ropes properly. It took me a while, but I finally managed to escape."

"How did you know where to find him?" Kat asked. She was still clinging to Rush, a fact she was sure Archer noticed.

"I tracked his cell. The storm didn't knock out the service. I am just so sorry, Archer. I can only guess that the cancer went to his brain. I cannot fathom why he would do this otherwise."

"For you, Daisy. He wanted to give you the best of everything before he died," Kat supplied.

Daisy's eyes filled with tears. "Silly old goat."

The door burst open and the EMTs came in. They tended to her brother and then lifted him onto a stretcher.

"Kat," he said when they started to take him out.

She grabbed his hand. "Don't worry. I'll come to the hospital shortly. Promise."

He didn't let go. "Will you be okay?"

"Yes. I'll be fine. You go get seen to. I'll be there soon."

He nodded and closed his eyes, letting go of her hand.

Archer indicated to one of the EMTs, "Take Daisy with you. She has some nasty cuts on her wrists."

Daisy started to stand but stumbled. Archer helped her out of the cabin and down the stairs.

"Are you okay?" Rush whispered.

Kat nodded. She wasn't really, but there wasn't anything anyone could do about that now.

CHAPTER THIRTY-ONE

He stared down at her. Her hair was a mess and there were dark circles under her eyes, but she'd never looked more beautiful.

"I'm so sorry," he said. "When it came down to it, I just couldn't come get you and run. We'd have been on the run forever and eventually someone would have found us. I've lived a life like that. Always afraid someone would come through the door and kill me. It's no way to live. I just couldn't do that to you. You would've been miserable."

She nodded. "I know. Escaping was never a real plan. I dreamed about it too but thought the same thing. I would rather die here with you than spend all my life running. My brother would never make it and, in truth, as much as I love him, he'd get us caught in about two seconds. We wouldn't have made it."

Rush kissed her then. Showing her how much he loved her, how grateful he was that she understood and how much he fervently wished things were different.

She kissed him back saying all the same things.

Someone cleared their throat.

Rush reluctantly broke off the kiss. "Archer."

"There is the matter of the broken rules." Archer had returned to the cabin after seeing Daisy off and took the seat that Daisy had vacated.

Rush brought a stool over for Kat and then sat down next to her on another one. He took her hand and drew it to his thigh. Then refused to let go. Archer had to see they were in this together.

"The way I see it," Kat started, "is my brother is an innocent in all this. He didn't want to be involved but Peter was holding Timmy hostage."

Archer smiled slightly. "You're ignoring the fact that he was willing to hunt for the treasure in the first place. But let's say I agree with you; what would you have me do with him?"

"Nothing. Let him go back to his life in New York. He'll keep his mouth shut."

Archer shook his head. "No, he won't. But for shits and giggles, let's say I agree. What about you?" He turned his head to include Rush. "You were thinking of running."

Rush nodded. "Yes. I love Kat and I know what the rules say. I thought about making a run for it but decided it wasn't worth it. A life on the run isn't a life worth living."

"Rush didn't do anything wrong. He did everything you asked. Everyone is allowed to have thoughts about stuff. The important thing is he didn't act on them. He stayed within the rules the whole time."

Archer hesitated and then nodded. "Let's pretend I also agree with that summarization. What about you? You did break the rules. You lied to us. You joined the Society under false pretenses. You faked your own death. You also discussed the Society with your brother. All these violations are punishable by death."

Rush couldn't take it. He stood. "You can't kill her. There were extenuating circumstances and you know it." This just couldn't be happening. Archer couldn't kill Kat. He wouldn't stand for it.

"Rush," Kat said and touched his arm. "Sit."

He glanced at her and she nodded. Then she winked at him. What the hell? Her eyes were dancing. What exactly did she have up her sleeve? He sat back down.

"Archer, as you know I found the gold. I'm prepared to strike a bargain with you. The gold for my life and my brother's life."

Archer went still. "But the gold belongs to the Society."

She nodded. "It may, but only I know where it is. You do not. Your Society hasn't found it in hundreds of years. What makes you think you can find it now?"

"If you found it—"

"I also rigged it."

He frowned. "What?"

"I rigged it to blow. If something happens to me, or my brother, or Rush, then you don't get your treasure. Even if someone does find it, they'll blow it and themselves to kingdom come. That will not be great press for the island, or for the Society. You might be able to buy off some people, but news of treasure is not something that can be contained. Treasure that kills is a major news event. Even you can't control that."

Archer scowled at her.

The knots in Rush's stomach tightened unbearably. Jesus, even he hadn't come up with something like this.

"Where would you get the explosives?"

"Peter supplied everything that was needed to get the treasure. Explosives in case some blasting needed to be done. Just a bit. Nothing major that anyone would notice."

Archer's jaw worked. He stared at Kat and then he looked at Rush.

Rush did his best to keep his face neutral. He was so proud and impressed by Kat it was hard not to smile. It was a hell of a gamble but she had nothing left to lose. *Go big or go home.*

Archer must have realized the same thing. He shrugged nonchalantly, like it didn't piss him the hell off to be cornered this way. "What are you proposing exactly?"

She smiled. "You let my brother go back to New York and live his life. You let Rush continue exactly as he has been since he's done nothing wrong"—she held up a finger—"with no punishment or retribution whatsoever. And you let me live. Not only that, you hire me to work for you. I think you could use someone who can manage your organization better. One of your employees tried to kill members and rip you off. Doesn't exactly scream well-oiled machine."

Rush blinked. Her solution was way off the charts. He hadn't remotely expected her to demand a job.

"Why would you want to work for the Society after all that's happened?" Rush asked.

She turned to him. "Because I love you. Because I don't want to be away from you. I've lived a quiet life and I know what that's like. I don't want to go back to that without you. You can't go. You belong here so I want to be here with you. Be your support. Be your home." She smiled up at him.

Then she turned to face Archer. "And because Archer needs to keep me close to know that I'm not breaking any more rules. Also, I can give him cover. He can tell anyone that asks that he set the whole thing up from the get-go. He used me to lure Peter out because there was no proof against him. The only person that knows anything different is Daisy and I doubt she wants the truth spread around. As far as anyone knows, Peter died of cancer. Your people won't say anything different. Everyone loves Daisy."

Archer's eyes narrowed. "And if I agree to this…what's in it for me?"

"Treasure. And a lot of it. Plus, one kick-ass administrator. Also, you get to keep one amazing monster wrangler."

Rush's body tensed. *Please God, say yes.* "It's a way out for all of us, including Daisy. More importantly, it's what's best for the Society."

Archer stared at the two of them for a moment, drumming his fingers on the arm of his chair. He heaved a breath and Rush let his shoulders drop a fraction.

Archer offered his hand to Kat. "Fine. You have a deal." Kat shook it but kept her expression neutral. Archer frowned. "You are now my assistant. The first thing I need you to do is tell my people where to find the treasure and how to disarm the explosives."

"There are no explosives."

Archer cocked an eyebrow. "Remind me never to play poker with you, Kat Rollings."

She grinned. "The treasure was on the bottom of the lagoon."

"Was?"

"Danny moved it. Now it's behind the waterfall."

Archer nodded. "Fine. See to your brother and then tomorrow you can start work." He locked gazes with Rush. "You were tempted, but you stuck it out. I always reward loyalty. Today you proved your loyalty to me. Even though you had every reason in the world to break your oath, you did not. I will not forget that." He offered Rush his hand.

Rush's entire body relaxed. Not only did he get to keep his job, but Archer saw the truth of the matter. They shook hands and then Archer left. He swung around to Kat and let out a whoop as he lifted her off the stool. "Are you sure you want to do this? Dedicate your life to the Society?"

She smiled at him. "I want to be with you. This is how that happens."

"I love you, Kat Rollings."

"I love you too," she said and then kissed him hard on the mouth.

EPILOGUE

Six Weeks Later

"You'll be fine," Rush whispered as he dropped a kiss on her neck.

"Easy for you to say. You know these people. I don't." Kat stood in front of the mirror in her apartment and put her earrings on. Straightening, she checked the effect of the whole outfit. The deep green of the silk blouse brought out the green of her eyes and the gray pencil skirt added just the right touch of professionalism.

"You look amazing." He kissed her neck again.

"Meeting the board is completely freaking me out. I still don't know all the rules of the Society. What if someone asks me a question I can't answer?"

"No one will. You have been dealing with boards for years," he reminded her.

"Hospital boards, not secret society types."

Rush smiled. "They're all the same."

She made a face. "Oof, I hope not."

He ran a hand down over her hip and then gently started tugging the skirt up. "How much time do we have?"

"Not that much," she said as she playfully smacked his hand.

"You'd be surprised how fast I can make this happen."

She laughed. "Yeah, for you, but speed isn't all that great for me."

Rush met her gaze in the mirror. "Is that a challenge?"

Thirty minutes later she took her place on a chair against the wall across the room from Archer. He'd already introduced her to everyone over drinks and snacks. It was time to get down to business.

"Kat?" Archer lifted a brow in question.

She nodded once. She was ready to go when he was.

He called the meeting to order. They were sitting in the meeting room at the museum in New York. The board members took their seats.

Archer said, "As you are all aware, we lost Frank Humber. His seat is now vacant. His widow still has his token, however, she's declined to take his place. That leaves a seat on the board vacant. Today, we're here to determine who will have that seat."

The room was silent. Rush stood guard in the corner. He winked at Kat and she smiled back. She was still adjusting to life in the Society but it was turning out better than she'd hoped. It actually was rewarding work, and she didn't miss the hospital or her old life at all. At least not yet.

"Does anyone have any suggestions?"

Austin Davis stood. "I would like to nominate Eli Fisher. He's a smart man who's excelled in business and knows how to make wise decisions."

Archer's face remained impassive, but Kat knew how much he loathed Fisher.

"Anyone else?"

The room was silent. No one was particularly interested in going against Davis directly if they could help it. He had a lot of power and was as mean as a snake, or so she'd been told.

"Then it's settled," Davis said as he sat down again.

"Sorry. Austin, not so fast." Remy stood up. "I would like to propose Tatum Wellington. First, we don't have enough female representation on the board. There are only four of us to your eight men, nine if you count Archer. Second, she's a partner in one of the top law firms in the city. She can help keep the Society out of trouble and advise us on business matters." Remy ticked off another finger. "Third, her family have been members for a long time and her father got his membership on his own. I think she would be a wonderful addition to the board." Remy took her seat again.

Archer looked around the room. "Anyone else?"

The room was silent. Davis glared at Remy.

Kat was glad she wasn't on the other end of that stare.

"Okay then. A vote. Those in favor of Fisher?"

Six hands went up around the table, all men.

Archer nodded. "Those in favor of Tatum?"

The other six hands went up, four women and two men.

"I see. This is most unusual for us. Until this point we have been unanimous on voting in new board members and indeed on almost all things." He made eye contact with each member. "Does anyone wish to change their vote?"

The room remained silent.

Kat had the feeling of being in quicksand. As if everything was shifting beneath her. Unease settled on her shoulders.

"Well then, I have the tie-breaking vote. The new board member will be Tatum Wellington." He waited a beat and then said, "Meeting adjourned."

No one moved.

Kat would've sworn the temperature in the room dropped twenty degrees. The look on Davis's face said battle lines were now clearly drawn and the war would be bloody.

She shivered and said a small prayer that she wouldn't be pulled into the fray.

Keep turning the page to read a sneak peek of the next book in the Lock And Key series: Locked In

SNEAK PEEK: LOCKED IN

She wiped her sweaty palms on the skirt of her little black dress as she looked around the room. All her life she'd heard about the house, how it was haunted. But every year people came and stayed there. Grand parties were thrown with all kinds of famous people attending. Even some of the TikTok Influencers she followed had stayed there. Now she was one of them. On the inside. No longer just a townie but someone who had been invited.

The heavy brocade curtains muted the howling wind, but the rain lashed against the windows and there was puddle growing at the base of one. Old houses were like that. They often had leaks and quirks. That's what her father had said. He said they were lucky they didn't live in one of the old mansions on the beach. The upkeep would be astronomical.

But she wasn't glad. She'd always wanted to live in one. And now she was realizing her dream. A smile crept across her face, and she hugged herself. If only Audry could see her now. Her best friend wouldn't believe it. They were due to go off to college this fall, but Astrid was going to have the best summer of her life here in Everlasting Manor.

She just knew it.

Wandering over to the bookshelves, she started reading some of the titles. Books about the Salem witch trials. Not surprising since Salem was just down the road. The room, a library of sorts, was only lit by a single lamp in the far corner. Dark paneling on the wall made it hard to see, even for her teenaged eyes. She looked around for another light but there didn't seem to be one. Odd in a room this sized.

A leather sofa sat in front of a fireplace, flanked by two matching chairs. A rustic coffee table and matching end tables completed the seating area. In the corner, there was a desk with a small lamp on top. She went over to it but hesitated before turning it on. He'd said to make herself at home. Surely turning on a lamp would be okay. After all, he'd promised her she would feel at home here for the summer.

Her stomach fluttered. Suddenly she didn't feel so good. The howl of the wind escalated and the light in the corner flickered. Her heart thudded in tempo with the rain lasing the windows. *What if the power went out?* She didn't have her cell phone. He'd taken it, quoting some regulation about them being forbidden in the mansion, but hadn't the influencers posted pictures on TikTok?

Her palms were sweaty once again, only this time it wasn't nervous excitement. Her breath quickened. She wished Audry was with her. She was the brave one. *She* wouldn't be scared. A loud banging sound came from the window. She jumped. Must be a loose shutter. All of a sudden she wanted to go home. She didn't care what Audrey or anyone else would think. She wanted to be back safely in her bedroom.

She moved as quickly as she could in her dress and sky-high heels across the floor to the door and turned the knob. But it wouldn't turn. She tried again but it wouldn't give. Was it stuck? No. She'd been locked in. Her breath came in gasps. *What was going on?* He'd said he'd be right back and now she was, for lack of a better word, a prisoner in the room.

She rattled the door and pounded on the wood, yelling for someone to help her. She stopped hitting the barrier and listened. No approaching footsteps, or shouted reassurances that someone would be there soon. She tried again but still…nothing.

Tears rolled down her cheeks. What had she done? She went over to the first window. The one that had been leaking. She tried to pull it up, but she couldn't. *Unlock it.* She flicked the lock, but it still wouldn't go up. Frustrated with panic gnawing at her throat. She went to the next one and tried again but it wouldn't budge either. Her teeth started chattering and her hands shook. How was she going to get out?

Looking around, once again she noticed the lamp on the desk. Going over to it she bent down and unplugged it from the floor and then picked it up. She'd throw it through the window and then clear out the glass and jump. She was only on the second floor. Surely, she would survive that fall.

She lifted the lamp, and someone grabbed her from behind.

"Where do you think you're going?"

Before she could scream a hand clamped around her throat cutting off her oxygen. "No, honey. I promised you fun and you shall have it. You wanted to belong and now you do."

Astrid tried to fight but the world shrunk to two small pin holes and the darkness closed. *This was all one big mistake.*

BONUS CONTENT

Would you be interested in receiving a bonus scene from Locked Away?

You can sign up for my newsletter and get bonus content, sneak peeks, see my hot new covers, and learn more about what makes me tick.

Please visit my webpage at https://lorimatthewsbooks.com to keep up on my news.

A NOTE OF THANKS

YOU READ MY BOOK. You read the whole thing! I cannot thank you enough for sticking with me. If this is the first book of mine you've read, welcome aboard. I certainly hope it won't be the last. If you are already a fan then I can only say, thank you so much for your continued support. Either way, you have made my day, my week, my year. You have transported me from writer to *author*. I feel so special. You have made my dreams come true. Genuinely, truly, you are a fairy god-parent. So thank-you!

Now I'm hoping you love this new-found power of making dreams come true and, like a truly dedicated reader, you'll check out my other series, Callahan Security, Coast Guard Recon, Coast Guard Hawai'i, and the Brotherhood Protectors World. You can find links to these books on my website, www.lorimatthewsbooks.com

If you would like to try your hand at being a superhero, you can always help make me a bestselling author by leaving a review for **Locked Away** on Amazon, (My Book) or Review On Goodreads or Review On BookBub. Reviews sell books and they make authors super happy. Did I say thank you already? Just in case I forgot, thank you soooo much.

And now that you are reveling in your superhero status, I would love it if you would stay in touch with me. I love my readers and I love doing giveaways and offering previews and extra content of my upcoming books. Come join the fun. You can follow me here:

Newsletter: Signup Form (constantcontactpages.com)
Website: www.lorimatthewsbooks.com
Facebook: https://www.facebook.com/LoriMatthewsBooks
Facebook: Romantic Thriller Readers (Author Lori Matthews) https://www.facebook.com/groups/killerromancereaders
Amazon Author Page: https://www.amazon.com/author/lorimatthews
Goodreads: https://www.goodreads.com/author/show/7733959.Lori_Matthews
Bookbub: https://www.bookbub.com/profile/lori-matthews
Instagram: https://www.instagram.com/lorimatthewsbooks/
Twitter: https://twitter.com/_LoriMatthews_

ALSO BY LORI MATTHEWS

Lock And Key Society

Locked Away

Locked In (Coming Soon)

Callahan Security

Break and Enter

Smash And Grab

Hit And Run

Evade and Capture

Catch and Release

Cease and Desist

Coast Guard Recon

Diverted

Incinerated

Conflicted

Subverted

Terminated

Coast Guard Hawai'i

A Lethal Betrayal

Brotherhood Protectors World

Justified Misfortune

Justified Burden

Justified Vengeance

Free with Newsletter Sign Up

Falling For The Witness

Risk Assessment

Visit Https://www.lorimatthewsbooks.com for details on how to purchase these novels or sign up for my newsletter.

ABOUT LORI MATTHEWS

I grew up in a house filled with books and readers. Some of my fondest memories are of reading in the same room with my mother and sisters, arguing about whose turn it was to make tea. No one wanted to put their book down!

I was introduced to romance because of my mom's habit of leaving books all over the house. One day I picked one up. I still remember the cover. It was a Harlequin by Janet Daily. Little did I know at the time that it would set the stage for my future. I went on to discover mystery novels. Agatha Christie was my favorite. And then suspense with Wilber Smith and Ian Fleming.

I loved the thought of combining my favorite genres, and during high school, I attempted to write my first romantic suspense novel. I wrote the first four chapters and then exams happened and that was the end of that. I desperately hope that book died a quiet death somewhere in a computer recycling facility.

A few years later, (okay, quite a few) after two degrees, a husband and two kids, I attended a workshop in Tuscany that lit that spark for writing again. I have been pounding the keyboard ever since here in New Jersey, where I live with my children—who are thrilled with my writing as it means they get to eat more pizza—and my very supportive husband.

Please visit my webpage at https://lorimatthewsbooks.com to keep up on my news.